NASTY CUTTER

NASTY CUTTER

A Raymond Donne Mystery

Tim O'Mara

Severn House Large Print
London & New York

This first large print edition published 2017
in Great Britain and the USA by
SEVERN HOUSE PUBLISHERS LTD of
19 Cedar Road, Sutton, Surrey, England, SM2 5DA.
First world regular print edition published 2016 by
Severn House Publishers Ltd.

British Library Cataloguing in Publication Data
A CIP catalogue record for this title is available from the British Library.

ISBN-13: 9780727895981

Severn House Publishers support the Forest Stewardship Council™
[FSC™], the leading international forest certification organisation. All
our titles that are printed on FSC certified paper carry the FSC logo.

MIX
Paper from
responsible sources
FSC
www.fsc.org   FSC® C013056

Typeset by Palimpsest Book Production Ltd.,
Falkirk, Stirlingshire, Scotland.
Printed and bound in Great Britain by
T J International, Padstow, Cornwall.

One

The second cop out of the men's room mumbled something about never having seen so much blood at a crime scene before. The first cop was still hanging around by the exit, looking as if he were deciding between pulling a Houdini through the security door or vomiting right into the waste-basket. I hustled over to him, and as I ushered him through the door, into the much bigger hall-way, I could hear my uncle trying to whisper somewhere behind me. 'This,' NYPD Chief of Detectives Raymond Donne was saying, 'is one fuck of a way to end a party.'

I put my arm around the young cop – Officer Gray, according to the nameplate below his badge – and walked him over to the nearest garbage can, a large industrial one on wheels. If he were going to vomit, he didn't need anyone else to see it, and there was no reason to mess up the floor outside the men's room. It was, after all, perilously close to the crime scene. The area we were in now was huge, going off in three different directions leading to a whole bunch of doors that seemingly would allow entry to any of the other businesses here at – more precisely, *below* – Chelsea Market. I noticed at least three security cameras. I wondered if they were on this late in the afternoon on a Friday.

Whoever had murdered Marty Stover – my

1

late father's law partner and tonight's Williamsburg, Brooklyn's, *Man of the Year* – could have gone almost anywhere, and with some luck, there was a picture of a blood-soaked killer on one of these cameras. Before tending further to the young officer, I took a quick three-hundred-and-sixty-degree look at the floor. From where I stood, there were no signs of blood.

'Shit,' Officer Gray was saying into the garbage can. 'Shit, shit, shit.'

I walked over, patted him on the back, and said, 'You've got about a half-minute to pull yourself together, or you've got the next twenty years to be known as the rookie who puked his guts out at his first murder scene.' I accented that with a few sharper slaps on his back, more for shock value than any real comfort. 'What's your first name, Officer Gray?'

He slowly raised his head and took a deep breath. Some of the color was returning to his face. The slaps were working. 'CJ,' he said and then swallowed hard. 'Christopher Joseph, but everyone calls me CJ.'

'OK, CJ. My name's Raymond Donne.' Before he could ask the obvious, I added, 'I'm the chief's nephew. You're his new boy, right?'

Chief Donne's Boys. Every graduating class of the academy had one: hand-chosen by my uncle to be his driver, his Cop Friday, and anything else that popped into the chief's mind. As far as I knew, Officer CJ Gray was the only one of my uncle's boys to be the first responder on a murder scene. The worst these guys usually saw was their boss drunk, hungover, or chewing out some

2

underling. Sometimes, all three at the same time. It also helped if they had a strong tolerance for cigar smoke and learned just the right ratio of Diet Coke to Jack Daniel's. Tonight, Officer Christopher Joseph Gray was getting quite the schooling.

'Yeah,' he said. 'I gotta get back inside.'

He stood up straight, shook his head – I guessed in hopes of waving off the nausea – and made a move for the door we'd just come through. I put my hand on his shoulder. 'Give it few more minutes, Gray. You still don't look too good.'

'The chief's going to want to know where I am,' he said. 'If I'm not around, he's gonna take a bite outta my ass.'

Having been on the receiving end of my uncle's insatiable appetite for other people's asses, I couldn't help but smile. Then I remembered Marty Stover's dead body in The Tippler's men's room and my smile disappeared. I looked both ways down the corridors and, forming a mental picture of the layout behind the wall across from me, I focused on the left.

'Let's go for a quick walk,' I said.

'But your uncle—'

'Is going to think you took the initiative to check out one of the likely exit routes of the killer. My uncle loves initiative. The other officer out there, the big guy, what's his name?'

'Virdon,' he said. 'Bill Virdon. He's from the local precinct.'

'Officer Virdon's got the crime scene secured. You're back here looking for a blood trail, witnesses, shit like that.' I patted his upper arm a few times. 'Uncle Ray chose you for a reason, Officer Gray. Let's not let him forget that.' I spun him gently in the direction I thought we should go. 'The Tippler is behind these walls,' I said, slapping the wall on our left. 'Did you notice the other exit inside?'

He closed his eyes and thought about it. After about ten seconds, he said, 'Yeah, all the way at the end, past the bar and the food prep station. That's also the handicap-accessible entrance. The door's got a picture of a guy urinating with a red line going through it. The waitress told me they've had problems with customers using the area back there as a piss place.'

Officer Gray was coming back to the world and starting to show signs of why my uncle had chosen him from among a few hundred candidates. He started off in the direction of the other exit and I followed. Since I'm a civilian now he should have told me to stay where I was or to go back inside. But the adrenaline pumping through his veins – and quite likely some gratitude toward me – made him forget that particular procedural element.

We didn't pass another person on our brief walk. A few of the doors we walked by were open, and we got a glimpse of kitchen workers from other restaurants who surely would be questioned later; right now it was all about Gray and me getting to that other exit. We did so in less than a minute. The exit door was propped open by a small block of wood. *Shit.* We opened the door and were met by one of the waitresses; if news of the murder had made it to the bar area, she was doing a good job of hiding it. She also didn't seem too surprised to see a cop and another guy coming in through the exit less travelled. She calmly turned and went back to taking care of customers.

Officer Gray and I stepped into The Tippler, and it quickly became apparent that the other guests still had not heard about the guest of honor's body being found in the men's room. Uncle Ray had obviously delivered orders to keep the murder quiet until the responding detectives arrived. My uncle's presence would draw lots of cops. I hoped no one made a big deal out of not being able to use the restroom for fifteen minutes. Which reminded me: my mother was around here somewhere.

'I don't like this door being propped open,' Officer Gray said. 'Means the killer coulda taken the same route we did and come right back into the party.'

I looked around at the seventy-five or so party guests still milling about and tried to determine which one looked most like a murderer. I didn't see my mother, but chances were good she was checking out the leftovers at the buffet table to see what she could take home. Uncle Ray was at the other end of the room, speaking with Michael Barrett, the owner of The Tippler. Barrett was an ex-cop who'd come out of the academy in the same class as my uncle. As my uncle was making his way up the NYPD ranks, Barrett had left the cops to become a surprisingly successful restaurateur and club owner. Both had looks of calm concern on their faces as they scanned the bar/dining area.

'No blood, though,' Gray said.

'Huh?' I asked.

'No blood,' he repeated. 'From the exit by the men's room, down the hallway, to here. You'd think there'da been some blood, what with that mess in the bathroom.'

'Pretty bad in there?'

He closed his eyes. 'Looked like someone decided to repaint the floor red and stopped halfway through.' After a few seconds, he reopened his eyes and gave me a long squinty look. 'Raymond, right?'

'Yeah,' I said, and offered my hand.

He shook it and his head. 'Thanks for that, by the way. Kinda took me by surprise.'

'How long have you been out?' I asked. 'Of the academy. With my uncle.'

'About four weeks. Shit, this was supposed to be glorified chauffeur duty for six months, then a nice assignment to a Manhattan precinct, and after that my detective's shield. I wasn't supposed to see any DBs until I hit the streets, y'know?'

The dead body had a name, but Gray would find that out soon enough.

'That's one thing about being one of Chief Donne's Boys,' I said. 'It's never boring.'

I looked over at my uncle, who was now locking eyes with either Gray or me, and then waved one or both of us over. Gray and I exchanged looks and shrugs, and together made our way across the room to where Uncle Ray stood.

'Where the hell have you been?' Uncle Ray said.

Not sure whom he was talking to, I stayed

6

shut. Officer Gray took a breath and said, 'I went around the back of the restaurant, Chief. Performed a preliminary perimeter check and found the back exit propped open.'

'And you decided to take my nephew with you – why?'

That question took Gray by surprise, so I stepped in.

'I was back there anyway, Uncle Ray.' I reached into my pocket and pulled out my cell. 'I was calling Allison and wanted some privacy.'

'Fuck, Ray,' my uncle said. 'Let me guess. You hear there's a murder – shit, your dad's ex-partner for Christ's sake – and the first thing you do is call your reporter girlfriend? She's got you trained pretty good.'

'I didn't know exactly what had happened. Officer Gray came back and asked what I was doing. I never got to talk to Allison, but I left a message. I was about to try her office when Gray advised me not to make any more calls.'

Uncle Ray gave me a look like he was trying to figure out whether he believed me. I'm not sure what he decided because the next thing he said was directed at Officer Gray.

'What'd you see back there, Gray?'

Gray swallowed hard. 'No blood, sir. If the murderer did exit by the back door, he or she could have re-entered the party. I'd like your permission to canvas the area back there. See if any of the kitchen workers saw or heard anything.'

'We'll wait on the other uniforms and detectives to get here. You're with me for now.' He turned to Michael Barrett; who'd been quiet the

7

whole time. 'This is Michael Barrett. He owns the place. He'll set up a room for his employees and the guests to be interviewed.' He looked at me. 'Ray, do you remember meeting Michael?'

'Absolutely,' I said, shaking Barrett's hand. Barrett had the kind of eyes and face that told you he'd seen pretty much everything. And laughed at most of it. 'You were at my dad's funeral. My mom still speaks quite fondly of the food you sent.'

'Lovely woman, your mother,' Barrett said. 'Shame about your dad. The heart's a sneaky son of a bitch. One day it's ticking along just fine and the next . . .' He snapped his fingers to finish his point. He looked over to the men's room and added, 'And then there's something like this. Jesus Christ, huh? Shitty way to get your ticket punched. Me? I plan on getting shot in the ass by a jealous husband as I'm sneaking out his bedroom window at two in the morning.'

'This,' my uncle said, 'coming from the guy with the gorgeous wife who'd cut his dick off if she ever caught him looking at another woman.'

'I think I met her inside,' I said. 'Karen, right?'

'Kar*in*,' Barrett corrected me. 'Accent on the *in.*'

'Right.' I turned back to my uncle. 'Where're Mom and Rachel?'

'We're keeping everybody inside right now,' Uncle Ray said, referring to the bar area. 'No one knows shit yet and I wanna keep it that way until we get a bigger presence at the scene. Then we'll interview all the guests and send them home.'

'How long until they get here?'

My uncle shot me a look. '*I* called it in, Ray. How long do you think it'll take?'

That shut me up. For a few seconds. 'How about the coat check girl?' I asked. 'She's right off the hall to the men's room. Anyone talk to her yet?'

'That's my daughter,' Michael Barrett said. 'Maeve. And no offense, Ray.' He was referring to my uncle. 'I don't want her talking to your guys. Cops make her nervous. Ever since the break-in we had at the house. Too much testosterone.'

I could do it.

Uncle Ray laughed. 'Smart girl. But she's gonna have to be interviewed, Michael. You know the procedure better than most civilians.'

'I'm telling you, Ray. She's not going to talk to a cop. She gets nervous, and I know how you guys work. She'll end up saying stuff your detectives wanna hear.'

My uncle was clearly frustrated by his friend's reaction. I could guess what he was thinking. He could waste the next thirty minutes convincing Barrett to let the cops interview his kid, or he could pull rank on his old NYPD pal and make things more uncomfortable than they already were. I saw an opening and I took it.

'I could talk to her,' I said and then looked at my uncle. 'If it's OK with you.'

I watched my uncle's face as it went from annoyed incredulity to something else. Credulity? He put his hand on my shoulder. 'What if I had someone talk to her who was *not* a cop? Someone who's very good at talking with kids.'

'That might work,' Barrett said.

9

Uncle Ray grinned at me and squeezed my shoulder. 'I ever tell you what my nephew – formerly one of New York's Finest – does for a living these days?'

Two

'For real,' Maeve Barrett said, sitting on a metal chair similar to the one I was on, her hands between her knees to keep them from shaking. She had long light-brown hair and the same mischievous eyes as her dad. Right now those eyes were having problems maintaining contact with mine. She was nervous. Good thing I wasn't a cop anymore. 'I didn't see or hear anything. I was mostly reading.' She had a firm grip on her cell phone as she told me this. *Mostly reading.*

Behind her stood her mother, her hand resting on the girl's upper back. The two of them looked like an ad for a high-end clothing line catering to beautiful women of all ages. I glanced over at Michael Barrett, who stood off to the side with his arms folded across his chest. Some people just always seem to be right where they should be.

'It's OK, honey,' Karin told her daughter. 'Raymond's not a police officer. There's no reason to be nervous.'

'If you're not with the police,' Maeve asked. 'Why're you asking me questions?'

Smart kid. 'I used to be a cop,' I said. 'Now I'm a teacher.'

Maeve gave me a look as if she were deciding which was the worse career choice. Her mother

11

rubbed her back and said, 'Just tell him what you saw and then we can go home.' She looked at me like it was my decision to make.

'Absolutely,' I said. I looked around the room, which seemed to serve as a coat check room as much as a storage area for the bar. There were boxes of liquor and beer piled against one wall and some soda tanks along another. From where we were sitting, I could see how Maeve wouldn't have noticed much. The half-door over which people would give her their coats and bags was across the room and obstructed the view to the outside hallway. 'So this is where you were sitting?' I asked.

'Most of the time, yeah,' she said. 'I was reading and got up to stretch a couple of times. I left for maybe a minute to get a bottle of water from my dad's office.'

I nodded and looked at the book under her seat. *Of Mice and Men*. One of my personal favorites. I asked her where she went to school. She told me and I said I'd heard of it. It was on the Upper West Side, right by the Museum of Natural History, and had a pretty good rep. The building had a flea market in the playground on Sundays that I'd been to with Rachel a few times. It was a long way from the public school I worked at as a dean in Williamsburg, Brooklyn. Same city, completely different world.

'So,' I said. 'You're reading your book, maybe doing a little texting, there's not much to see from here and I guess you were pretty bored, but are you sure you don't remember *hearing* anything out of the ordinary?' I had already

12

asked this question in another form, but figured it was worth a shot repeating it. A lot of times witnesses – especially young and nervous ones – remembered something the second time around when the question was either rephrased or combined with some prompting. It was similar to the strategy I'd take with my students during a class discussion. 'Maybe a raised voice? Someone running?'

She shook her head and closed her eyes. She had committed to a 'no' answer but was now giving that some thought. That was all I could ask. When she reopened her eyes, I could tell something had come to her.

'What is it, Maeve?'

She shook her head again. 'Maybe nothing. I don't know, but . . .'

'Maybe something?'

'I may have heard some heavy breathing,' she said. 'I did. I mean *real* heavy breathing. Like someone was running or something. Someone breathing heavy's not that unusual around here, so I didn't think much of it.'

She glanced over at her dad, who could barely control the smile that was building on his face. His kid was doing great.

'That's good,' I said. 'Could you tell if it was a man or a woman?'

'A man, I think.' She tightened her facial muscles as she thought that over. 'Yeah, a man. Almost like he was trying to catch his breath. Now that I think of it, he sounded like a kid in my class who has asthma.' Another pause. 'Maybe?'

I had no idea whether Marty Stover had

suffered from asthma, but anyone who'd got cut like I'd heard he'd been would definitely be gasping for as much air as possible. Or it could have been the killer.

Maeve looked up at her mom, and it was clear she was finished answering questions. The realization that she'd been only feet away from a murder victim was finally dawning on her. She wanted this conversation to end, and she wanted to leave. I didn't blame her.

'You did great, Maeve,' I said, getting up from my chair. I looked at her mom and said, 'You two should head home.'

'My idea exactly,' Karin said. 'Let's get your stuff together, kiddo.'

As they did that, I walked over to where my uncle was standing with Michael Barrett. 'The detectives here yet?' I asked.

'Just arrived,' said my uncle. He nodded with his head over to Maeve and her mom. 'That was pretty good, Nephew.'

'I agree,' said Barrett as he reached out to shake my hand. 'Was that more Raymond Donne, cop, or Raymond Donne, schoolteacher?'

I smirked. 'The correct balance of both, I guess.'

'You're being modest,' Barrett said. 'I read the papers, you know. For a teacher, you've been involved in some funky shit the past few years, my man. And with what your uncle's been telling me about you, it's a shame you left the job.'

My uncle laughed. 'He may have left the job,' he said, 'but the job never left him. Ain't that right, Raymond?'

'Something like that,' I said, surprised by my

14

uncle's subtle compliment. 'Can I go get Rachel and Mom, now? I think we should get Mom out of here as soon as possible.'

Uncle Ray gave that some thought. 'I'll have the detectives interview them first.' Before I could respond, he said, 'You know we have to talk to everyone, Ray. If I let your mom and sister out of here without being interviewed . . .' He stopped himself. 'I was about to say someone would have my ass, but that someone would be me, right? But just to be on the safe side, I'll have my guys go through the motions and they'll be on their way. Where's your mom staying tonight, by the way?'

'She wasn't sure whether she was going to head back to the Island or spend the night at Rachel's,' I said. 'I think now it would be a good idea for her to stay in Queens with Rache.'

Uncle Ray nodded. 'Yeah,' he said. 'Your mom's not such a hot driver under the best of conditions, and now with this . . .'

'Speaking of which,' I said, 'where's Helaine? *Mrs* Marty Stover,' I added for Barrett's benefit. 'Does she know about her husband yet?'

'She left about a half hour ago,' Uncle Ray said. 'She hates these types of things. Marty Junior drove her back to the Island.'

'She left her husband's benefit early?' I asked. 'The guy's getting a big award, some much deserved press for his charity, and she books out early. With her son?'

'I got the feeling from Marty that they haven't been getting along too well lately,' Uncle Ray said. 'She thinks he should've been retired by

15

now, or at least working less hours, and here he is – was – working more and spending lots of time with the charity.'

'Makes ya wonder which came first,' Barrett chimed in. 'Are they not getting along because of the time he's spending away from her, or is he not spending time with her 'cause they're not getting along?'

I smirked at the cynical observation. Not because I found it amusing but because it reminded me of my own father, and how he had always thrown himself into his work. He'd spend all day at the office – the one he had shared with Marty for almost twenty years – and then come home after dinner was over, eat some leftovers, and head into his home office. This went on for most of my childhood until the night my mother, my sister Rachel, and I came home from another three-day weekend upstate without him and found him dead of a heart attack on his office floor.

I was thirteen at the time and still remember telling myself I'd never treat my family that way. Now, roughly two decades later, it was getting more and more doubtful I'd have kids. Not that my girlfriend hadn't brought it up on occasion, but we both had lives that didn't exactly lend themselves to being great parents.

Which reminded me, I did need to call Allison. Or as my uncle would say, my 'reporter girl-friend.' Tragedy or not, there was no reason she shouldn't be the first journalist on the scene. It was going to be a big story, and she might as well get the jump on all the other reporters who'd

16

be circling like vultures in an hour or so. And, yes, I'd score some big points with her. I needed those points. If she got here early enough, maybe she'd even get an exclusive with the other guest of honor.

I reached into my pocket and fingered my cell phone. 'Where's Bobby Taylor?' I asked my uncle and Barrett.

Bobby Taylor was not only the brother of a former client of Stover's, but also a former professional baseball player. We'd grown up in neighboring towns. He and his twin brother Billy were four years ahead of me, and star athletes. They always seemed to be beating my high school at one thing or another, usually baseball. As early as twelfth grade, Bobby Taylor had a fastball that clocked in the mid-nineties. Both brothers had been awarded baseball scholarships, but as life would have it, they got into some trouble over the summer before college. A high school classmate of theirs accused Billy of sexual assault, and that's when my dad and Stover got involved. The case never went to trial, but before the summer was over, Billy had pleaded out to ten years for aggravated sexual assault, and Bobby was off to college stardom and then the big leagues.

My uncle looked at my hand in my pocket. 'I thought you already called Allison.'

Not much gets by this man, I remembered. 'I told you, Officer Gray shut me down before I could talk to her,' I said. 'I was barely able to leave a voice message. I just wanna see if she's on her way.'

17

'Of course she's on her way, Raymond. She's a *journalist*.' He said that last word the way some folks say 'pedophile.' 'She's probably outside at this very moment trying to talk her way past Officer Virdon. I'd bet ten dollars she's asking him how to spell his name correctly.'

I pulled my cell out of my pocket and punched up Allison's number. 'I'll see if that's where she is, Uncle Ray. In the meantime, is our celebrity guest still around, or did he get special treatment from someone whose ass is . . . unbiteable?'

'Now,' my uncle said, turning to his buddy Barrett, 'you can see one of the reasons why Raymond's not a cop anymore. He's a wiseass who thinks he can go around making up his own words.' To me, he said, 'And you being a teacher, Ray.'

I ignored him as soon as Allison picked up. I stepped away so I could privately tell her what I knew up to that point.

'Fuck, fuck, fuck, fuck, fuck,' my reporter girl-friend said. 'I knew I should have gone with you to the benefit. I could have written a fluff piece for the paper.'

'You hate covering benefits,' I reminded her. 'And writing fluff pieces.'

'Yeah, but not as much as I hate missing a big story.'

'You couldn't possibly know there was going to be *a big story*. And I invited you as a guest, not a reporter. Besides, you're not missing it. Get your ass – your *self* – over here as soon as

18

you can and you'll probably beat the rest of the reporters.'

'Unless one of my colleagues has already heard from an unnamed police source that Marty Stover's been murdered.'

'Which is different from what I'm doing for you right now *how*?'

There was about five seconds of silence while she considered that. Five seconds of silence during a conversation with Allison Rogers is a lot of time.

'OK,' she said. 'I'm on my way. Do I ask for you when I get there?'

'Probably best if you ask for "Raymond Donne." By the time they figure out which one you want, you'll be inside.' I looked over at the owner of the place. 'If that doesn't work, tell whoever's got the door you're here for Michael Barrett.'

'Where will you be?'

Good question. 'I'm not sure. My mom's here with Rachel and I may have to go back to Queens with them, depending on my mom's reaction to the news.'

'She doesn't know yet?'

I switched the phone to my other hand and lowered my voice. 'I think all the guests are just now finding out. Stover's wife doesn't even know yet, unless someone called her or her son on their cell. They left before the murder.'

'You sure about that?' my reporter girlfriend asked without missing a beat.

And I had to admit, 'No. I'm not. It's just what I was told.'

'Keep that in mind, tough guy,' she said. 'I'm out the door.' She ended the call without saying goodbye. She'd been doing that a lot lately.

Three

'Ray. How the hell are ya, man?'

Bobby Taylor's hands were huge, and when he shook mine – trying to remember exactly who I was after my uncle introduced us – my hand practically disappeared. I looked up at his face. He had about six inches on me and maybe fifty pounds – most of it apparently still muscle by the way he filled out his expensive-looking suit. I've seen a lot of ex-athletes who look like ex-athletes, but Bobby Taylor looked like he could step back on the mound tomorrow and blow it past some young hotshot just up from Triple-A.

That is, if it weren't for the four surgeries he'd had on his pitching arm. Throughout his time in the minor and major leagues, Bobby had been the victim of too many managers and pitching coaches not knowing what to do with him in the rotation. Was he a starter? A middle reliever/set-up man? Or was he a closer? Three different teams tried all three, and none of them could get it right. The only thing they all agreed on was that Taylor's cut fastball was one of the best they'd ever seen. Not Mariano Rivera great, but up there. In the meantime, Bobby Taylor's once-guaranteed sterling arm had been opened and realigned by a gaggle of surgeons, and his promising career ended after only four seasons. That

21

still left him with a five million dollar signing bonus and a smile as powerful as his left arm.

Now he had his hand in a few different businesses – mostly automobile-related – and he was one of the biggest supporters of Marty Stover's Bridges to Success that hooked up kids in Williamsburg, Brooklyn, with business leaders around the city. Marty was born and raised in Williamsburg and always talked about giving back. That was why we were all gathered here this night to honor the man.

'I'm good, Bobby,' I said. 'I wasn't sure you'd remember me. My dad was kind of one of your lawyers back when . . .'

'Sure I remember,' he said. 'Good man, your dad. Good lawyer. Sorry to hear that he passed away.'

'Thanks,' I said. 'Heart attack. You were away at college.'

'Shit, man.' He shook his head. 'Those four years of college. I barely remember going to classes. You know what it was like, right? First time away from home. All that freedom. All that partying. All those girls.'

Maybe for you, I thought. Some of us had to work our way through those four years. Those of us who couldn't throw a baseball ninety-five miles per hour. And as far as Bobby Taylor actually attending classes, let's just say I'd heard a few things. Star athletes got treated a little differently than us mere mortals.

'Yeah,' I said anyway. 'Crazy times.'

'Too bad about your dad.'

'Thanks,' I said. Then, to be polite, but also

22

because I was damned nosy, I asked, 'How's your brother doing? I read in the papers he got out ten years ago and went into business with you.'

Bobby shrugged. 'He's OK, I guess. Never had much of a head for business, you know what I mean? Truth be told, he always seemed to be struggling. Academically, socially, that kind of thing. Most people don't know that.'

I nodded. I did know that about Billy, mostly because my father was their lawyer's partner. My dad would come home sometimes after sitting in on a meeting with Billy Taylor and, uncharacteristically, talk to me about his frustration with his partner's client. Maybe because I was just a few years younger than Billy, and my dad wanted to try getting inside his head a bit through me. Bobby was not only more skilled than his twin brother on the field, he was also sharper when it came to understanding the severity of the charges brought by the girl and the damage those charges could do to his family's name if his brother was found guilty after a long trial. The quick settlement and the admission of guilt by Billy took everybody by surprise. Including, I remembered, my father. Standing there in the coat check room of The Tippler, I couldn't remember what happened to the girl. Or her name.

'Billy's working for you now, though, right?' I said.

'Yeah,' Bobby Taylor said. 'He's always been good with his hands. He caught every game I pitched in high school, played second when I

23

was at short. And when he was . . . away, he took some automotive classes. It's not like it used to be, you know. It's all computerized and shit, but damn if he doesn't have the head for it, so I got him running the maintenance division of my dealerships. He started out working on the cars, now he's supervising the guys who are. He's doing a great job.'

I nodded. 'Sounds like he's put his life back together.'

'One day at a time,' Bobby said. 'One day at a time.' He looked at his watch. 'I'd love to talk more, Ray, but I got a long ride back to the Island, and I gotta give the detectives a quick statement. My boy's got a game tomorrow, if you can believe that.'

'What does he play?'

'Baseball. Just like his old man.'

'Really?' I said. 'March is kind of early for Little League, isn't it?'

'He's with a traveling team. I don't wanna brag' – *But here it goes anyway* – 'he's pretty good. I mean, he's only twelve, but he's got some of his old man's skills. I do a little coaching with the team – one of my dealerships sponsors them – and he's the starting pitcher. You know the drill.'

I did. When I played Little League I was a pretty good shortstop. I could go either way quickly and had a decent arm from deep in the hole. I also had the bad luck of having a coach who called his kid 'Scooter.' Guess where Scooter played. I spent my days between second base and right field, and by the time I hit high school, it was clear I couldn't quite get around on a high school-level fastball. Instead of spending three years riding the pine, I found other ways to fill my extra-curricular time.

'Well,' I said, allowing Bobby's hand to engulf mine again. 'Good to see you again. Sorry it had to be like this, but . . .'

'Yeah, I know. Later.'

He walked away and I was left standing on my own. This was as good a time as any to find my sister and my mom. Just as I was about to leave the coatroom, Rachel walked in without our mother.

'Jesus Christ, Ray,' Rachel said, rushing to give me a hug even though we'd just been drinking with each other less than half an hour ago. 'What the hell happened?'

'I have no idea, Rache. I came back here to hit the men's room and got stopped by a cop.' *That was mostly true.* 'Before I knew it, I found out about Marty, and Uncle Ray had me interviewing the owner's daughter.' I looked behind her. 'Where's Mom?'

'She's sitting down inside having a cup of tea. She's pretty shaken up. I guess we all are. I'm gonna have her stay at my place tonight.' I saw a lightbulb go off over my sister's head. 'Unless of course you wanna have her spend the night with you.'

Without missing a beat, I said, 'You know I'd love to. But you have more room than I do, and I don't think Mom will find my futon too comfortable. And besides, you're closer to the railroad. Mom can just jump on the train after

25

breakfast tomorrow and pick her car up at the station.'

Rachel grinned. 'I don't know whether you find that futon comfortable or if you just hang on to it as an excuse not to have Mom stay over.'

'When did you get so cynical?' I asked my little sister.

'I think it was the day I surpassed you in the grown-up department.' She held up her right hand and wiggled her ring finger at me. *Better than the other finger she could have flashed.* 'I'm engaged, big brother. There should be one of these on your girlfriend's finger by now.'

Dennis Murcer, my sister's fiancé, was NYPD through and through. I couldn't prove it, but my guess was he pissed blue. We had been in the same class at the academy. He started out as one of my uncle's boys, got his detective shield, and was now months away from becoming the Chief of D's nephew-in-law. Unless he screwed up big time – some in the know say you have to be caught with either a dead girl or a live boy – he had a golden career ahead of him. Of course, he'd have to put up with my sister as well. Whom I loved dearly.

'Oh god, Rachel. Is that what you and Mom were talking about in there? How I'm still single?'

'No, Ray,' she said. 'I hate to break the news to you, but not every conversation we have is about you and your love life.' She paused for a few seconds before adding, 'But it did come up.

26

I mean, what the hell are you waiting for? Allison's beautiful, smart. She's got a great job. Am I missing something?'

I shook my head. 'You know we had some problems last year.' I lowered my voice. 'After the whole Ricky Torres thing.'

Last summer, Ricky Torres, a good friend from my cop days, was shot and killed right in front of me. Three feet to my left, to be exact. It was pure luck I wasn't killed as well. I got caught up in the case and was privy to certain details I could not share with my girlfriend due to her job. Allison took that as me not trusting her. That wasn't exactly the case, but I'd be lying if I said her being a reporter had nothing to do with my relative silence about what I knew and what I had gone through. We'd spent so much time dancing around the thin line between girlfriend and reporter the whole mess had taken a pretty big toll on our relationship. We were just now getting back to something resembling normal. Whatever that meant.

'It's been over six months since the shooting, Ray,' Rachel said. 'You guys have been together for over two years now. That's the longest you've been with anyone by . . . a lot of months. And just because she hasn't mentioned it to you, her biological clock is ticking.'

'Does that mean she's mentioned it to you?'

That caught Little Sister off guard. She rebounded quickly, though. 'It's come up. She's not dwelling on it, but you can't be in your early- to mid-thirties, dating somebody for two years, and not be thinking about kids.'

27

I was about to say something when she added, *'If you're a woman.'*

I'm glad I stayed shut. Rachel had me, and we both knew it. This was a position I often found myself in when discussing life issues with her.

'Can we have this discussion another time, Rache?' I said. 'Like, not now, and not thirty feet from where Dad's old partner was murdered?'

'I don't want to have the discussion *at all,* Ray. You should be having it with your girlfriend. Of two years. Who's thirty-four.'

I pulled her into a hug and said, 'Thanks for understanding.'

'Whatever.' She broke the embrace. 'Hey, was that Bobby Taylor I saw walking out? The big guy in the blue suit?'

'One and the same.'

'What was he doing here?' she asked.

'He's a big supporter of Bridges to Success,' I said. 'Marty recruited Bobby to be a board member right after he left baseball and started his auto business. Smart guy. I think he's even one of the mentors. His name still carries a lot of juice in some circles.'

'Rich white people circles?'

'Rich white people who like to have their picture taken with former pro baseball players, yeah. It's amazing how much that helps some folks open up their checkbooks.'

Rachel shook her head. 'I've always hated these galas. They cost so much to put on, they might as well take that money and give it to the charity.'

'I hear ya,' I said. 'But a lot of folks won't

28

donate to a cause – no matter how worthy – unless there's something in it for them. Besides, I know Michael Barrett must have cut Marty and his group a deal for this shindig. Everybody comes out ahead.'

'Whatever.'

'Have you and Mom been interviewed by the detectives?'

'Yeah,' she said. 'We told them we didn't see or hear anything.'

'I'm gonna have to tell them pretty much the same thing.'

'Pretty much?'

'You know how cops are always asking witnesses to mention anything that comes to mind even if it seems like nothing?'

'I've seen it on TV, yeah. Why? Did you see something?'

'It's probably nothing,' I said. 'But Marty was kinda getting into it with his son, Marty Junior.'

'About what?'

'I wasn't close enough to hear, but it wasn't about baseball, I can tell you that. It's not like they were being loud, just a lot of speaking through their teeth, you know?'

Rachel shook her head. 'You're right. It was probably just family shit. Mom told me that Helaine wanted Marty to start cutting back on his time at the office and with the charity. He and Dad always had that in common, didn't they? Measured their success by how much time they weren't at home.'

'Yeah,' I said. 'I remember thinking as a kid that Dad didn't like us that much.'

'And now?'

'I don't know,' I said. 'I think he equated being a good father with working a lot. That's what his generation did. But kids need their fathers around.'

'You talking as a teacher?' Rachel asked. 'Or an ex-cop?'

I smiled. 'You're the second person to ask me that question in the past hour.'

'And what does that tell you?'

I smiled and shook my head. This was another typical conversation with my sister. After what had happened to Marty, I was not in the mood to have it, though.

'Put me on the couch some other time, Rache,' I said. 'I'm gonna head upstairs and see if Allison's here yet. She may need some help getting in.'

'I wasn't trying to put you on the couch, Ray, I just—'

I held up my right index finger. 'I'm going up. You got Mom?'

Rachel looked at me like she wanted to say more. She thought better of it.

'Yeah,' she said. 'I *got Mom*. Don't I always?'

Four

As I had expected, Allison was at the upstairs door showing her press credentials to Officer Virdon, explaining who she was, and why she should be allowed to enter the premises. I couldn't hear everything she was saying, but the words 'First Amendment' came through loud and clear. Virdon didn't seem too impressed or much interested in the civics lesson. She hadn't noticed me yet, so I waited a few moments to see if she'd use the magic words. I didn't have to wait long.

'Raymond Donne is expecting me,' she said. 'He just called me.'

That got Virdon's attention. 'Chief Donne called you?'

'*Raymond* Donne,' she repeated. 'Yes.' She pointed to the shoulder clip on the officer's walkie-talkie. 'Just call him, please. Tell him it's Allison Rogers.'

I took this as my cue to climb the stairs. Virdon touched the button on his clip and said, 'This is Virdon. Anyone got a twenty on Chief Donne?'

'He's still downstairs,' I said, as I approached Virdon from behind. I stuck out my hand and said, 'I'm his nephew. I think we met earlier.'

I knew we hadn't, but he wouldn't admit to it. He shook my hand.

31

'You'll vouch for her?' he asked. 'I let her in, I'm not gonna be buying new underwear tomorrow, am I?'

'You know my uncle well, I see.' I reached out and took Allison by the hand. 'I'll take full responsibility, Officer. But don't let any other reporters in unless you hear it directly from the chief.'

It took Officer Virdon a little while to decide which was the greater risk: letting in a reporter without hearing from my uncle or not listening to the chief's nephew when he said it was OK. He looked like he'd had a long day and just wanted to be on his way home. I felt for him but also knew I'd score major points with Allison if I could get her inside. Virdon shook his head, made his decision, and waved us along.

'Hey,' he said, as we were halfway down the stairs. We both turned back. 'I'm only doing this 'cause I saw what you did for that Gray kid. No one's gonna hear it from me. Good looking out.'

I smiled and waved good-bye as we made our way down the steps to The Tippler. When we got to the bottom, I gave Allison a kiss on the cheek.

'You're welcome,' I said.

'Thank you,' she said and gave me a hug. 'Who – or what – is a gray kid?'

'Someone who just needed a little diversion earlier. Anyway, Uncle Ray's not gonna be exactly thrilled that I got you in here. I think your best move is to talk to some of the guests and maybe get a quick quote from one of the detectives before he senses your presence. I can probably get you a quote from Officer Gray. He found Marty.'

'How about I just hand you my notepad and you do my job for me? I'll just hit the bar and drink some high-end vodka.'

Shit. 'You're right,' I said quickly, realizing I was going to have to say it anyway so I might as well get it over with. 'Sorry. I'll distract my uncle while you make your way around the place. And be careful.'

'I know how to handle cops at a crime scene, Ray.'

'I know,' I said. 'I was talking about my mother. She's around here somewhere.'

She laughed. 'Maybe she'll give me a quote I can use.'

'She'll definitely let your readers know how the food was.' I heard my uncle's voice behind us. 'Go,' I whispered, pointing to the bar area. 'I'll see you in a few.'

'Thanks.'

As soon as she was gone, I felt a hand on my shoulder. I turned to see my uncle.

'I'm glad to see your girlfriend made it here OK, Nephew.'

I looked into his eyes. He didn't seem nearly as annoyed as I thought he'd be. Maybe he was softening up a bit in his old age. Maybe it was all the Jack Daniel's and Diet Cokes he'd had that afternoon.

'She's just—'

'She can talk to the guests we've already interviewed, Ray. Those that are still around. She's not to talk to any of the detectives or the ME until I clear it. Understand?'

'You sound like you think I can tell her what to do.'

'You want me to escort her out now?'

'I'll talk to her.' I looked over to where she was speaking with the same waitress who Gray and I had run into earlier. Even from across the room, the server seemed quite upset now that she'd heard the news. She'd make for a good quote or two. I turned back to Uncle Ray. 'So what the hell happened? One minute we're celebrating Marty Stover and the next he's lying dead on the men's room floor.'

My uncle gave me something close to a shrug. 'We're still piecing that together. Right now it looks like he went to the head to take a leak and someone followed him inside and stuck him in the upper thigh. I'm guessing they got him in the femoral artery, based on the amount of blood on the floor.'

I grimaced. 'They check the security cameras yet?' *Shit.* That was the second time in less than five minutes I told someone how to do their job. Uncle Ray let it pass. 'I mean, were the cameras any help?'

'They woulda been,' he said, '*if* they had any outside the men's room. And the ones in the back – down the hallway where you and Gray were – were not on. Down for maintenance or upgrading or some shit. The only ones working are the ones inside behind the bar area. Crime Scene's checking them as we speak. And before you ask your next question, don't.' He paused to make sure I got his point. 'I'm not going to tell you what kind of weapon was used or even whether or not we recovered one. I'm not going to tell you if we found anything on Stover's phone of any importance. In short, I am not going to tell you anything I don't want showing up in your girlfriend's newspaper tomorrow morning that'll possibly screw with an ongoing investigation.'

'Can you tell me why there was no blood outside the men's room?'

I couldn't help it. The point was bugging me.

'Keep it up and there will be, Raymond.'

I was about to press the issue but then realized he'd just made my life easier. I couldn't tell Allison anything I didn't know, which meant I wouldn't have to withhold information from my reporter girlfriend. I could just blame Chief of Detectives Raymond Donne. At the moment, that worked a whole lot better for me than getting my own sense of curiosity satisfied.

'Have you reached Marty's family yet?' I figured that was a safe question.

'I called a friend in the Nassau County PD. He's going to meet Helaine and Marty Junior at the house. I don't think this is the kind of news you give someone over the phone while they're driving on the Long Island Expressway.'

'And then what?'

'I have one of my guys heading out there now. He'll bring Helaine and Junior back into the city, and they'll have to make a positive ID.'

'They have to do that tonight?'

'Better that than waiting around all night at

35

home, not getting any sleep, and not being any use to each other except as shoulders to cry on.'

My uncle looked like he needed another drink. I'd almost forgotten that Marty Stover was a friend of his as well. Not that they were close, but back when my dad was alive, all three were at many of the same social functions. My uncle had even offered to get Marty Junior into the academy before Junior decided to follow his dad's footsteps and become a lawyer. My father had similar hopes for me. *The road not taken and that shit.*

'I guess they're going to have to be interviewed anyway, huh?' I asked.

Now he gave me the look. 'Yes, Raymond. It's a new technique we've been working on when your spouse or parent has been murdered. We're finding it quite useful in ascertaining pertinent information.'

There are two times when my uncle uses ten-dollar words: when he's had a fair amount of drink or when he's being overly sarcastic. This moment fit both.

'Just thinking out loud,' I said and shook my head. 'Still can't get over this. I was literally talking to him minutes before it happened.'

'Not like this is the first time that's happened to you, Nephew.'

Now *I* needed another drink. The Ricky Torres thing stayed fresh in my mind to this day. I still woke up from the occasional nightmare, swearing that I heard gunfire, and I don't think I'll ever watch a movie shootout without cringing again.

'You're not officially on-duty are you?' I asked.

'Why?'

'I was thinking of hitting the bar again and don't want to drink alone.'

Uncle Ray grinned. 'And me being on-duty would affect that how?'

I waited for a wink that never came. Instead he said, 'Why don't you get yourself interviewed first? Then you can join me at the bar.' He looked around. 'Hell, by then maybe your girlfriend'll be done working and we can all have a drink together.'

'Sounds good,' I said. 'The detectives. They're in the coatroom?'

'Yeah. It shouldn't take long.' He put his hand on my shoulder. 'Make sure you leave out the part about your little stroll with Officer Gray, though. That might lead to more questions than you wanna answer.'

Damn. If my uncle didn't know everything, he had an amazing way of making it seem like he did.

Fifteen minutes later, I came out of the coatroom and saw Uncle Ray at the bar talking with Allison. She was holding a notepad in one hand and a drink I was pretty sure contained vodka in the other. I honestly couldn't tell if she was working or not. Maybe she was plying my uncle with more alcohol in hopes of getting a great quote from the great man. They were both very good at what they did.

Before approaching them, I looked around and didn't see my sister or my mother anywhere. As

37

I got closer, I could make out somewhat of what my uncle was saying. His words came out as clear as a politician on the stump even though I knew he'd been drinking since early afternoon.

'Marty Stover was a good man,' he was telling my girlfriend. 'Maybe not a *great* man. I'm not going to say he didn't have his bad side or any enemies. I mean, shit, the guy was a lawyer. The job description comes with a bad side and no shortage of people who don't like you. You win a case, you've made an enemy. You lose a case, you've made an enemy.'

Allison wrote something in her notebook and said, 'Damned if you do . . .'

'Something like that. But I will tell you, Marty won most of his cases or at least got the best deal for his clients. *That* you can quote me on: Marty Stover always had his clients' best interests at heart and knew how to use the law to achieve those interests.'

My uncle was on a roll now, so I stepped to the side in order not to interrupt, and I got the bartender's attention – we were the only customers left as the cops had ordered The Tippler closed for the night – ordered a Smuttynose Porter for myself and another round for my loved ones. With the amount we were all drinking, it occurred to me that this was starting to feel like a wake. Of the Irish sort.

'What can you tell me about his charity?' Allison asked.

'Bridges connects needy kids with mentors in the business world. Marty never forgot where he came from. He spent a lot of time and effort giving back. He was telling me earlier that he was in Williamsburg at least once or twice a week making sure Bridges was running the way he envisioned it. He was even thinking of expanding the program to the Island. Getting some of the local colleges involved.'

That must have pleased his wife, I thought. Helaine was already annoyed at all that time he was in Brooklyn, and now there he was thinking of bringing on more work with the charity? Marty Stover was not much for downtime. Just like my father. Maybe that's what he and his son had been arguing about.

The drinks arrived and that diverted my uncle's attention enough to realize that I had joined them at the bar.

'Thanks, Nephew,' he said as he picked up his new Jack and Diet Coke. 'Just having a nice chat with your lady friend here. You done already?'

'I didn't have much to say,' I reminded him. 'Where are Mom and Rachel?'

'Rachel took your mother home, Ray,' Allison said. 'She was exhausted and getting real anxious hanging around here. She did say that she wants you to call her tomorrow. At Rachel's.'

'Good,' I said. 'Should I leave you two alone or what?'

Before Allison could answer, Uncle Ray did. 'I think we're pretty much done.' He touched his glass to Allison's and added, 'We are now officially off the record.'

'I do have a few more questions,' Allison said.

39

'I'm sure you do. And many of them will be answered at the press conference.'

'And when will that be?'

He checked his watch. 'Based on the time now, I'm going to wager before the eleven o'clock news cycle. Not that it'll be a full conference.'

The look of disappointment on Allison's face was evident. She turned to me for help and then realized I had nothing to offer. When Chief Donne spoke, that was it. She wanted more, and she knew she was not going to get it from my uncle. I hoped she knew she'd gotten more than any other reporter would have, thanks to me, but mostly to my uncle's willingness to share what he knew with a journalist he respected. Allison had her reporter's bag with her, so I knew she had come with her tablet and would be able to file a story for her paper's website and beat all the other news outlets in town. The rest would have to wait for tomorrow's print edition.

'So what now?' I asked.

Uncle Ray grinned. 'Now, we drink.' To accent his point, he downed the rest of his cocktail, caught the bartender's eye, and signaled for another round. I guessed Allison and I were staying for another drink. 'To Marty, of course,' he said.

'Of course,' I agreed. 'To Marty.'

Five

I woke up at Allison's the next morning just after eight. My first thought was that the previous day's events were a dream; Marty Stover was still alive and well, and I'd just had a bit too much to drink. I'd experienced this feeling the morning after other tragic events in my life: my father's death, the World Trade Center attacks, and, more recently, the Ricky Torres incident. It took me a minute to get it through my sleepy and hungover brain that what had happened yesterday had truly happened.

Shit.

I turned over and looked into my girlfriend's face. As with any tragic event, it always helped to have someone close by whom you loved, even if that person was still asleep from one too many top-shelf vodka drinks. I tried shutting my eyes for another five minutes, until it became clear that sleep was not going to make a comeback. It rarely did once I was awake, even during the best of times. I rolled out of bed and went to the kitchen to make a pot of coffee.

I checked out the contents of Allison's fridge and was pleased to see there was enough in there to make some cheesy scrambled eggs with toast when she woke up. I took a cup of coffee and went into her living room to watch the morning news. Since it was a Saturday, the first story I came across involved a reporter's intrepid search across the country for the perfect late-winter bed-and-breakfast brunch. I flicked around some more, found a few more weekend fluff pieces, and finally settled on the local, twenty-four-hour news channel. They didn't have the time to do much fluff during their half-hour shows, but I had to wait until after the weather at eight thirty-one to see the story on Marty.

As Uncle Ray had predicted, it wasn't much of a press conference. The lead detective spoke for a sound bite or two, followed by someone representing the Medical Examiner's office. I didn't learn much I hadn't already known, except that the ME did confirm Marty had suffered a severe cut to the femoral artery from some sort of blade or other sharp instrument; the ME didn't specify. The blood was confined to the men's room because femoral wounds don't spurt. I knew this. Victims bleed out very quickly once the weapon has been removed. I wondered who had removed the blade. Was it Marty or his killer?

The screen cut back to the pretty reporter who informed me that attempts to reach the victim's family for comment were unsuccessful and there would be more on this developing story as it, well, developed. She gave it back to the very serious anchor who spoke briefly about Marty Stover's charity work and mentioned that former pitching phenom Bobby Taylor had been present at the benefit. Nothing like a little local star appeal to get the audience's attention. The anchor also mentioned that a small memorial service might be held tomorrow, followed by interment at a Long Island cemetery.

I'd forgotten that Marty was Jewish, and as such would be buried much quicker than if he'd been of another faith. Observant Jews wasted no time getting the body into the ground, sometimes in less than twenty-four hours. After that ritual was performed, the family would accept visitors for the mourning process. I'd been to a few shivas in the past and found them much more comforting than the Catholic wakes I'd been forced to attend since childhood. For one thing, there was no dead body in the room. And then there was the food. When Jews mourned, they ate. And ate well.

'How do you always get up so early?'

I turned and watched as Allison shuffled her way into her bathroom. She shut the door. The next noise I heard was the flushing of the toilet, so I stood to greet her as she opened the door with a toothbrush in her mouth. I'd have to wait for a good morning kiss.

I raised my cup and said, 'You want some coffee?'

She mumbled an affirmative and went back inside the bathroom. I heard her medicine chest close and knew from experience she was treating herself to some pre-breakfast ibuprofen. By the time she came out, I was back on the couch with her coffee.

As she sat down next to me, I turned down the volume on the TV and said, 'You didn't miss much by not going to the press conference. No surprises.'

She took a sip of coffee and closed her eyes as she swallowed. She leaned back into the couch and sighed. 'Late night pressers are bullshit anyway,' she said. 'Most of them are only so the cops can get on the eleven o'clock news and let the public know they're hard at work seeking truth and justice.'

'You know,' I said, giving her leg a squeeze. 'Vodka and lack of sleep make you attractively cynical.'

With her eyes still closed, she managed to give me a small smile. 'As long as it's not cynically attractive.'

'Never that.'

I massaged her thigh a bit and she let out a pleasurable moan. We'd been together long enough for me to know that it was not the keep-that-up-and-let's-see-where-it-goes moan. It was the moan of someone who just wants a little physical contact the morning after a long night. Before I could challenge that notion, I heard my cell phone ring from her bedroom.

'You might wanna get that,' she said. 'Could be your mother.'

It could be, I thought, but got up to check anyway. I found the phone in my front pants pocket and checked the caller ID. It was Edgar. Of course it was Edgar. He must have heard about last night's events and wanted to pick my brain about the whole thing. If I didn't pick up now and answer all his questions, he'd be obsessing about the details and particulars all day and calling me until I picked up.

'Good morning, Edgar.'

44

'What the heck happened last night, Ray?'

'Good morning, Edgar,' I repeated. These types of situations almost always made Edgar forget his social graces. I had taken it upon myself to work with him on that.

I heard him take a deep breath and finally say, 'Good morning, Ray.' This was followed immediately by, 'What the heck happened last night, Ray?'

I took the phone into the living room and mouthed 'Edgar' to Allison. She didn't seem surprised. As I went to get more coffee, I said, 'What have you heard?'

'I heard that Marty Stover was killed last night in the city at his own benefit, and the police have no motive or suspects at the present time.'

'Then you're pretty much up to date, Edgar.'

'But you were there, Ray,' he said. 'You must have seen or heard something that didn't make the news or the police scanner.'

Edgar Martinez O'Brien, cop junkie and technophile that he was, had his very own – and probably very illegal – police scanner. Top-of-the-line, to hear him tell it. And since he seemed to acquire a new one every two or three years, I had no doubt it was the best money could buy. All of Edgar's equipment was the best money could buy. He skimped in every other area of his life, but not on his equipment.

'There's really nothing more I can tell you, Edgar. The cops did interview me, but they interviewed all the guests. I'm not sure what anyone else was able to tell them.'

45

'Did you get to meet Bobby Taylor?' he asked, sounding – not for the first time – like one of my middle school students. As he spoke, I could hear him working the keys on his laptop.

'Yes, Edgar, I did. He was questioned also, and then he left.'

'What did he say to you?'

I gave him the condensed version of our conversation. When I was done, Edgar said, 'You never told me your dad was his lawyer.'

'It never came up, Edgar. Why would it? It was over twenty years ago. And he wasn't his lawyer. Marty was.'

'I know, but you're connected to Bobby Taylor. That's really cool. I love his commercials. "Sales pitches," that's funny. You have any idea what his high school ERA was?'

Of course I didn't, but Edgar did. I'm sure he'd spent the morning searching the Internet for any information he could find on any of the people who'd attended last night's gala. Poor social skills aside, Edgar was one hell of a researcher and he'd helped me out more than once over the years with my unofficial investigations. This was what he wanted to do when he retired – in less than a year and a half, I remembered – and the main reason I was working with him on improving his interpersonal skills. Most people had little patience for adults like Edgar. Not me. I owed him big time, and he'd become a good friend over the years. Especially when I'd gotten in over my head.

'I don't, Edgar. But I'm sure it was impressive.'

I refilled my cup and brought it back into the living room. 'Listen, Allison and I just woke up. Can I call you later?'

When Edgar pouted you could hear it, even over the phone.

'I guess, Ray,' he said. 'What time do you think that'll be?'

'I have no idea, Edgar. We haven't even eaten yet and I've got things to do.' That last part may or may not have been true.

'OK,' he said. 'In the meantime, I'm gonna keep working the computer and see what else I can come up with.'

'Pertaining to what?'

'I don't know yet. I'll let you know what I find out.'

He hung up without saying good-bye, another social skill I'd have to address with him. But he always got excited when I was somehow involved in a police matter. Even now, when I had made it as clear as I could that my involvement with Marty Stover's murder was minimal at best, he'd spend just about every minute until I called him back searching the web for anything he could 'come up with.'

'Let me guess,' Allison said. 'Edgar's going on an Internet hunt.'

'At least it keeps him off the streets.'

'It also keeps him pale, unhealthily thin, and practically friendless.'

'He's got me,' I said. 'And you. And who knows, maybe he'll turn up something interesting.'

Allison sat up. 'You told him you have things to do today. What are your plans?'

47

I took a sip of coffee. 'You're going in to work, right?'

'For a few hours, yeah. But I'll be back by three.'

The thought of lounging around for half the day seemed appealing. I knew I had laundry to do back at my apartment and the place needed a cleaning. The best idea was probably to head back home and knock that stuff off since there was a good chance tomorrow was going to be taken up mostly with Marty Stover's service and then heading to his family's house for shiva.

I wondered if the cops would release Marty's body to the family in order for them to conduct the services within the time frame of their religion. Man's law often superseded God's. Uncle Ray would know, but it was still too early to call him. Maybe Rachel? I'd be better off waiting until I got back to my apartment before calling her. In the meantime, 'You up for breakfast?' I asked Allison.

'If you're cooking, tough guy. Let me shower first.'

We got off the couch together and kissed. If I timed it right, the eggs and toast would be ready just as Allison came out of the shower. She might have to eat with a towel wrapped around her, but we all had sacrifices we needed to make.

Breakfast was over, Allison was doing the dishes – when I cook, she cleans, and vice versa – and I was sitting on the couch watching the highlights from last night's preseason baseball games. My cell phone rang. At first, I thought it was Edgar again, but I didn't recognize the number.

'Hello?'

'Mr Donne?' a female voice wanted to know.

'Yes. Who's this?'

'Maria,' she said. 'I'm sorry. Maria Robles.' When I didn't respond, she added, 'Hector's mother. From school?'

My mental bell went off. With all that'd happened over the past twelve hours . . .

'What's up, Mrs Robles? Is everything OK with Hector?'

'No,' she said. 'I don't know. He's in his room and won't come out.' She paused to catch her breath. 'He's very upset about the news of Mr Stover.'

Right. Hector Robles was not only one of my students from school, but I'd hooked him up with Bridges to Success, and Marty had taken a special interest in him. Hector lived on the same street Marty had grown up on. This meant a lot to Marty, and he watched Hector's success in the program with great pride.

'How did he hear?' I asked.

'It was on the news this morning,' Mrs Robles said. 'We were eating breakfast, and he was getting ready to go to Mr Stern's apartment. As soon as he heard what happened, he ran into his room and told us he's not coming out.'

'Well,' I said, knowing I was about to state the obvious, 'he was close with Marty – Mr Stover. He probably just needs some time to process what happened.'

There was silence on the other end for a while.

49

Then, 'That's what his father and I thought, but then . . .'

I waited for about ten seconds before speaking. 'And then what, Mrs Robles?'

'Then he asked to speak to you.'

'Really. Did he say why?'

'No. He just said that he wanted to talk to you and wouldn't come out of his room until he did.'

I stood up and muted the TV. 'Put him on the phone, then. Please.'

'Hold on.'

I waited for another minute. Allison came into the living room and gave me a quizzical look. I get them from her a lot.

'My student,' I said. 'Hector Robles. The one I hooked up with Marty. He's real upset and won't leave his room. For some reason, he wants to talk to me.'

'How do they have your number?' Allison asked.

'I gave it to them when Hector enrolled in Bridges. I figured Marty was doing me a solid and just in case—'

'He won't come out of his room,' Mrs Robles said. 'And he doesn't want to talk on the phone. He says he needs to *see* you. Is there any chance . . . I've never seen him like this before. I know I'm asking a lot, and it's Saturday and all that, but do you think you could come over, Mr Donne?'

It wouldn't be the first time I made a home visit, I thought. *And most of them had come in times of tragedy. Why should today be any different?*

50

'What's your address, Mrs Robles?'

She told me, and I figured if I left Allison's right away and the two subway trains I needed to catch were running a regular weekend schedule and not rerouted for some reason, I could be at the Robles apartment in a little over half an hour. I told her I'd be there as soon as I could.

'Thank you, Mr Donne.'

After I hung up, I turned to Allison.

'What's going on?' she asked.

'Well,' I said. 'Looks like you're not the only one who has to go to work today.'

Six

When I got off the M train at Hewes Street in Williamsburg, it felt like I was indeed on my way to work. Between the rumble of the subway as it made its way farther east, the Saturday morning traffic on Broadway, and the sound of the jets on their approach to LaGuardia Airport, I also felt like I lived in the busiest, noisiest city on Earth. Even the outer boroughs of New York City got very little time for sleep.

The Robles family lived in the middle of a block of row houses that had probably looked pretty much the same for many decades. Not far from my school, it was also around the block from the local library, two blocks from the subway I'd just taken, and close enough to the Brooklyn-Queens Expressway to hear the constant hum of traffic. This was a mixed block made up of Hispanic, black, white and a few Hassidic Jews. The wave of gentrification that had been sweeping through Williamsburg, Brooklyn, over the past twenty or so years had mostly skipped this block, but some of the buildings were under repair. I'm sure that meant part of the economy was getting better – at least for those people who could afford to buy brownstones and also had the cash to renovate them.

The building Hector lived in was a six-story brownstone that, according to the buzzer panel, housed twenty apartments and one super. I pressed the one for the Robles apartment and waited.

'Who is it?' came a scratchy voice through the intercom. Male or female, I couldn't say.

'Mr Donne.'

As I said that, the front door opened, and a large man in a blue work shirt and painter's pants came out. His hair was just turning gray, especially in his goatee.

'Mr Donne?' he asked.

'That was quick,' I said. Seeing the confusion on his face, I said, 'I just buzzed.'

'Oh. I was on my way down.' He offered me his hand. 'I'm Vincent Robles. Vinnie. Hector's father.'

I shook his hand. 'Raymond,' I said.

He nodded and held the door open for me. 'Thanks for what you did for Hector. Getting him into the program, I mean. He's learning a lot.' He paused and then added, 'Too bad about Mr Stover. It's got Hector all shook up.'

'That's why I'm here,' I said. If he was annoyed or embarrassed that his wife had called in another man to help out with his son, he did a good job hiding it. 'I guess he needs a little teacher time.'

'It's nice of you to come.' He looked at his watch. 'I gotta go. My ride's meeting me at the corner.'

I shook his hand again. 'Nice to have met you.'

'Same here. Thanks again.'

I watched as he made his way to the corner, then I went inside.

I had walked up two flights when a door

53

opened, and I saw Mrs Robles step halfway into the hallway. She was about forty, and this morning she looked every year of it. What I remembered of her parent-teacher-meeting smile was missing, replaced by a look of frustration. She also looked like she'd been crying and needed about four good nights of sleep. She held the apartment door open with her right foot.

'Thank you so much for coming,' she said, the exasperation in her voice dripping like a leaky faucet. 'I didn't know what else to do.'

'You did the right thing,' I said. *What else was I going to say?* 'I'm not sure exactly what I can do to help, but let's give it a shot.'

'Please come in.' She stepped aside to let me do so and then shut the door behind us. She slid the chain lock back into place and said, 'Can I get you something? Coffee?'

'I'm good,' I said. 'I've already had my two cups.'

I looked around the small apartment. We were standing in the kitchen, which had a four-person dining table in the corner. To my right, I could see through an arched doorway into the living room. A young girl was sitting on the floor watching – from the sounds of it – a Saturday morning cartoon. I did a one-eighty and saw two doors that must have led to the bedrooms. Unless someone slept in the living room, Hector shared a bedroom with his little sister.

'Is Hector in his room?'

She sighed, walked over to the door on the right, knocked, and waited. When she got no

54

response, she knocked again. I wasn't sure she had a third knock in her.

'Hector,' she said, her lips practically touching the door. 'Mr Donne is here. Please come out.'

She stepped back and waited. I'd been working with middle school kids for the better part of a decade. If there was one thing they could do, it was make the grown-ups in their lives wait. It was hard-wired into their brains.

I stepped over to Hector's door and got Mrs Robles's nod of approval to give it a shot. I wrapped on his door with my knuckle.

'Hector,' I said, half-schoolteacher/half-friendly. 'It's Mr Donne. Your mom called me. Just like you asked her to. I know you're upset about Mr Stover. I am, too. Come on out and let's talk about it.'

As Mrs Robles and I exchanged glances, I heard the door unlock. Five seconds later it opened, and Hector stood on the other side. It was clear he'd been crying, and it looked as if he was going to start up again. He just stood there with his shoulders slumped as if he were trying to make himself smaller. He was actually just about my height and had a slight eighth-grade teenage mustache thing going. I stepped back to let him come out. He took his time, but he eventually made his exit.

'Come, Hector,' his mother said. 'Sit at the table. I was just about to get Mr Donne a cup of coffee.' She turned to me and winked, the coffee an obvious ploy to get us to the table. 'How do you take it?'

'With a little milk,' I said. 'No sugar. Thanks.'

I went over to the table and took a seat. Hector did the same without making eye contact with me. I got the feeling he thought if he looked directly at me, he'd start crying again. And no kid wants to do that in front of a teacher. Actually, I was a dean again this year, but the same rule held true. *Never let a teacher see you cry.*

We sat there in silence until his mother came back with a cup of coffee for me, one for herself, and a glass of water for her son. She sat down across the table from me and wrapped her hands around her coffee cup.

'I told Mr Donne how upset you are, Hector. He came here to help.'

Hector remained quiet.

'I was there last night,' I said. 'At the benefit.'

That got Hector's attention. 'You were?' he said.

'Yeah. My family and Mr Stover's family go way back. I think I told you when we signed you up for the program, my father worked with him many years ago.'

'Oh, yeah. You did tell me that. You got an uncle works with him, too, right?'

I smiled. 'Not quite. My Uncle Ray is a sponsor of the program, and he gets a lot of his cop friends to help out.'

'Right,' Hector said. 'Your uncle's a big man with the five-oh. I forgot.'

'Chief of Detectives,' I said, trying to impress the kid.

'So.' Hector now looked me square in the eyes. 'Your uncle gonna catch the guy who did this to Mr Stover?'

'He's going to do everything he can to make that happen, yes. He's got a lot of good detectives working for him. They'll get whoever was responsible.'

'You promise?'

That's another thing middle schoolers were good at: putting grown-ups on the spot. I wasn't in a position to promise much of anything.

'I promise you they'll do their best, Hector. They're very good at their job.'

'When it comes to white people they are.'

Mrs Robles slammed her hand on the table. 'Hector!' she said. 'You don't talk like that, especially to Mr Donne. I know you're upset, but you show some respect.'

'I'm not trying to disrespect Mr Donne, Mom, but I know what happens when a rich, white guy gets killed compared to someone else.' He looked at me again. 'Tell me I'm wrong, Mr D. Tell me the cops ain't gonna work harder on Mr Stover's case.'

I hadn't come all the way over here to debate with a fourteen-year-old, especially one as sharp as Hector. I chose my next words very carefully.

'The cops I know work hard on every case,' I said. 'If you read the newspapers and watch TV, you mostly hear about the times when things go wrong. But that's why those stories make the news, Hector, because they make better stories. You don't hear about all the times the cops do exactly what they're supposed to. Those stories don't make good TV.'

As he thought about that, he took a sip of

water. I did the same with my coffee. At least he was talking now, I thought. As my sister was fond of saying – quoting her therapist – 'It's better than not talking.'

'Are the cops gonna talk to me?' he asked.

That question took me by surprise. 'Should they?' I said, keeping my voice calm. 'Do you know something the detectives should know?'

'I don't know. Maybe.'

His mother reached over and put her hand on top of his. 'Is that why you were so upset, baby? *Do* you know something?'

Hector took his hand back and dropped his head. I had a feeling he'd said more than he wanted and was about to shut down again. Then again, he did ask for me to come over, knowing full well I used to be a cop. And as for that part about forgetting who my uncle was, maybe that wasn't the complete truth. I decided to push it a little before he disappeared back to his room.

'What do you know, Hector?'

Still looking down at his lap, he said, 'I didn't say I knew anything, Mr D.'

'OK.' I paused and took a breath. 'What do you *think* you might know?' This was like last night's interview with Maeve, the coat check girl. 'When was the last time you saw Mr Stover?'

He thought about that. At least that's what I hoped he was thinking about. It was hard to tell by looking at the top of his head.

'Mr Donne asked you a question,' Mrs Robles said. 'He came all the way over here on a Saturday because—'

'Tuesday,' he blurted out and then looked up. 'I saw him Tuesday. He came by Mr Stern's shop when I was there.'

The details were coming back to me now. Hector was assigned, through Bridges, to work with a family twice a week – the Sterns – who owned an art supply warehouse or something like that in the neighborhood. Once a week, Tuesdays, he worked a few hours with Mr Stern learning to catalogue and process orders. On the Sabbath, he worked with Mr Stern's father, an elderly man who needed a Shabbos goy for a few hours on Saturdays. Like today.

Orthodox Jews, which Williamsburg had plenty of along with the slightly stricter Hassidim, are not supposed to use technology on Saturdays, their Sabbath. Many of them hired local non-Jews to perform simple tasks for them, mostly anything involving electricity. God forbids even turning on the lights. My understanding was that this was a fading practice, but the elder Mr Stern was old school. Literally. From what Hector had told me, the elder Mr Stern was quite the Torah scholar.

'Did Mr Stover do that often?' I asked. 'Come by the warehouse?'

'It's not a warehouse, Mr D. They do art supplies and photography equipment.'

'OK. So did he come by often?'

'No,' Hector said. 'This was only the second time I knew of. The first was when he introduced me to Mr Stern a few months ago, and then on Thursday.'

'Do you have any idea why he dropped by?'

Hector didn't answer right away. I got the feeling he was trying to choose his words as carefully as I had before. Why would a fourteen-year-old have to do that?

'He spoke to me for a bit,' he finally said. 'He wanted to know how I was doing. Said he was proud of me. Then he and Mr Stern went into the office. I don't know what they were talking about, but they were loud. They both sounded pissed. I mean mad.'

'And you have no idea why?'

'I couldn't hear them. Just, you know, their voices.'

'So this is why you were so upset this morning,' I said. 'You heard about Mr Stover being killed and remembered the argument he had with Mr Stern on Thursday?'

He gave a weak nod. 'Is that important?' he asked.

'It's important enough to tell the police, Hector.'

Mrs Robles said, 'Do you really think so, Mr Donne?' She touched her son's hand again. 'I mean, it was just an argument. He didn't even hear what it was about.'

Her boy was not the only one in the family who didn't quite trust the police. With all the stuff in the news lately about police interactions with minority groups, who could blame them?

'It may be nothing,' I said. 'It probably is. But I think Hector needs to tell the detectives what he knows and let them decide what to do with that information.'

'And how do we do that? We just call up the cops and . . . what?'

60

I nodded. 'I can call my Uncle Ray. He'll put the detective in charge of the case in touch with you and set up a time to talk. And don't worry,' I said, knowing that's exactly what she was doing. 'You can be there when they talk to Hector. Or his father can. I met him on the way out, by the way. I guess he was running off to work?'

I realized I had no idea what the guy did for a living or what hours he kept.

'No, no,' Mrs Robles said. 'He had to go run some errands. We're trying to give the kids a little more privacy in their room, so a friend with a car is taking him into Queens to one of the big stores to get some supplies.' She shook her head. 'Plywood, sheetrock. I don't know. I let him handle the man stuff.'

I nodded as if I knew all about 'man stuff.' As far as my home improvement skills went, I could swing a hammer and turn a screwdriver. I've even been known to use a paintbrush from time to time. Anything else, I called the super or landlord.

'Well, listen,' I said to both Hector and his mother. 'Today's Saturday and you're expected to show up at Mr Stern's house, right?'

'Yeah,' Hector said. 'But with what happened last night . . . .'

'That doesn't involve Mr Stern, Hector. He still needs you. It's Saturday, and it's your responsibility to show up. That's part of what the program teaches.'

It also, I wanted to say, will help keep your mind off of Marty Stover's murder. I caught Mrs Robles's eye and she read my thoughts.

61

'Mr Donne is right, Hector,' she said. 'You have an obligation to show up even when you don't feel like it. Especially with someone as elderly as Mr Stern.'

'He's got his family in the building.'

'And the whole family observes the Sabbath, just like Mr Stern. They need you there whether you like it or not.'

'You gotta go over there,' I said.

I could tell that thought didn't sit well with Hector. *Too bad. That's how you learn. By doing things you don't want to do, following through on your commitments.* If I shut my mouth and listened more closely, I could probably hear my father's voice trapped in the back of my head. I decided to keep talking instead.

'If you want,' I said, 'I'll walk you over. It's pretty close, right?'

'A few blocks,' he said. 'You'd do that? Walk me over there?'

'Sure. I wouldn't mind meeting the old guy anyway. It must be pretty cool working with someone so . . . learned.'

Hector shrugged. 'I guess. He talks a lot about the Torah and the Old Testament. He even talks about the Holocaust sometimes, but that's mostly when he gets tired or has a little too much wine.'

'Sounds like you're getting a free history lesson every time you go there. Maybe we can get him to come by school and talk to your class.'

'I don't know, Mr D. He's really old.'

I laughed. According to most middle school kids, I was pretty old. 'I guess I'll see for myself. Go get dressed.'

He got up and headed into his room. Mrs Robles gave me a big smile.

'Thank you so much, Mr Donne,' she said. 'I didn't mean for you to go through all this trouble. I just wanted you to talk to him.'

'It's fine,' I said. 'It'll be interesting to see where Hector's been working and to meet Mr Stern.'

'You're very kind.'

I stood up. 'That's what I keep telling people. Maybe you can call my sister and vouch for me.'

'Anything,' she said, her smile turning into a small laugh. 'But I bet she knows.'

'Deep down, yeah. You're probably right. What time does Hector usually get to Mr Stern's apartment?'

'Ten o'clock. He's going to be a little late.'

'We'll get there,' I said.

Hector came out of his room, dressed in a T-shirt and jeans, and with a book bag slung over his shoulder. He still looked upset, but at least he had something else to focus on besides Marty.

'Let's go,' he said, as if I were the one keeping him waiting.

'You have your phone?' his mother asked.

'Yes, Mom. I have my phone.'

'Excuse me for asking.'

'You *always* ask.'

She went over and kissed him on the cheek. 'Because I *always* care,' she said.

'Bye, Mom,' he said and headed for the door.

'Goodbye, Mrs Robles,' I said.

'Thank you again, Mr Donne. Maybe one day we can have you over for dinner.'

'That would be nice,' I said as I followed Hector out of his apartment. It occurred to me how often Hispanic women wanted to thank me with food.

Seven

The walk from Hector's building to Mr Stern's was quick, less than ten minutes. It was one of the things that continued to fascinate me about Williamsburg. Where Hector's block was completely residential and racially mixed, Mr Stern lived on the part of Harrison Avenue that was mostly commercial and Jewish. The Orthodox and Hassidim didn't mix much with the other communities in their neighborhood. They sent their kids to different schools, shopped mostly at different stores, and didn't allow their kids to play or hang out on the streets. Many of their apartment buildings had immense window guards that served not only as protection but as makeshift backyards. They put fake grass up there, a few chairs, and presto! – instant mini-suburbia. Some of these window guards went up six or seven flights, as if the residents had a fear of flying home invaders.

When you saw a new building go up in this part of the Willy B, with its bright exteriors and manufacturers' stickers on the windows, it more than likely was not going to house people who looked like my students. In fact, many of my kids referred to these new buildings by a not-very-politically-correct nickname.

The Jew Houses.

In a way, this was very much in line with the

65

history of the neighborhood. When the Williams-burg Bridge was built in the early part of the last century, it was called 'The Jew Bridge' because it allowed the Jews who lived and worked on the Lower East Side – the other side of the East River – to find homes in Williamsburg, Brooklyn, while continuing to work in Manhattan. To this day, many of the local Jews walk to and from their jobs across the bridge.

As we stood in front of Mr Stern's building, I thought that it wouldn't surprise me to find out that the building had been in his family for many years, going back before the Holocaust. Probably even World War One.

The signs in the window of the 'shop' Hector spoke about announced they sold photo equipment, small appliances, and also provided local artists with everything from brushes to frames. The store was closed today, of course, for the Jewish Sabbath.

As I was reading the signs, I heard the jangle of keys. I watched as Hector reached into his bag and pulled out a key ring. He fumbled a bit, but after finding the one he was looking for, he slid it into the lock and turned.

'They gave you keys to the building?' I asked.

'They had to, Mr D,' he said. 'Mr Stern's not allowed to use the buzzer to let me in. That's kinda why I'm here?'

Duh. 'Right,' I said. 'I guess he can't take the elevator either, huh?'

'Look around, Mr D. This building's old. It ain't got elevators. Mr Stern lives on the third floor. Sometimes he gets out – I take him for walks – and sometimes he don't.' He shook his head as he opened the second door. 'Must be hard getting old, huh?'

I gave him a sneer and said, 'I'll let you know when it happens, Hector.'

The smile on his face – the first one I'd seen since getting to his apartment – made him look like he'd gotten one over on the teacher. He needed that this morning, so I let it slide as he motioned me toward the stairs. If he had any comments about my ability to climb them, he was smart enough to keep them to himself.

When we got to the third floor, I followed Hector to Mr Stern's apartment. We were both surprised to see the door open a crack. Either Mr Stern went out on his own – and from what Hector had told me, that was highly unlikely – or he'd let someone in and had forgotten to completely close the front door.

The raised voice we heard from the other side answered that question.

'You just cannot go around doing things like this!' the voice yelled. There was a pause for a few seconds, then, 'She called me, that is how I found out. We have had this talk, Father. I do not want to have to explain – again – what will happen if we cannot trust you to live on your own.'

'That's Mr Stern's son,' Hector whispered to me. 'He runs the store.'

Hector and I listened and waited for a response. When none came after about ten seconds, Hector knocked on the door and pushed it open a few inches. 'Hello?' he said.

I heard footsteps coming our way. The door opened revealing a man of about fifty dressed in black pants and a white shirt. He wore a black vest, a yarmulke, and black curls hung from both sides of his head. Under his arm, he carried a framed painting. Judging from the shadow on his face, he had not shaved that morning. The rest of his face did not look happy. He looked to Hector and then to me.

'Hector,' he said. 'My father was expecting you fifteen minutes ago. Why are you late? You know how he gets without his morning tea.' He had a slight accent I would have pegged as German, and his words were enunciated quite clearly.

Hector stood there speechless. This was the second time this morning he'd been admonished for shirking his responsibilities. And it wasn't even noon.

'That's my fault,' I said, sticking out my hand.

'And who are you?' To his credit, he took my hand.

'Raymond Donne. I'm one of Hector's teachers. He asked me to come by his apartment this morning to discuss last night's events.'

'Joshua Stern,' the man said as he released my hand. 'I am not sure what you are referring to. What about last night's events?'

It hit me then that he hadn't heard. How could he have? Being an Orthodox Jew, he was not allowed to use technology on the Sabbath and that pretty much ruled out the news of Marty Stover's murder reaching him. Where was the town crier when you needed one?

So why was he holding a painting on the Sabbath? Wasn't that work?

I put my hand on Hector's shoulder. 'You want to explain?' I asked.

Hector looked up at me, his eyes filling up, and shook his head.

'Why don't you go make Mr Stern's tea, then,' I said. 'I'll talk to . . . Mr Stern.'

Hector made his way inside the apartment, and the younger Mr Stern said, 'Talk to me about what? What happened last night?'

'May I come in?' I asked.

It took him a few seconds, but then he shook his head as if realizing he'd forgotten his manners. He stepped aside. 'Yes, of course.'

I walked into the foyer, and Mr Stern shut and locked the door behind us. 'Please go in,' he said. 'The living room is straight ahead.'

I did as instructed and ended up in an unnaturally dark living room, which I estimated to be about half the size of my entire apartment. The room appeared larger due to the sparseness of the furniture. There was a small couch and two chairs, all of the same brown – maybe dark green? – and white design, and one decent-sized coffee table. The two floor-to-ceiling windows were covered by dark red curtains. It was clear this room did not see many parties.

The walls were another story. As my eyes adjusted to the lack of light, I could make out various pieces of carefully displayed artwork. There were a few oil paintings and some stained glass. It was like stepping into an impressive, yet minuscule, museum. There was an obvious

69

gap between two pieces that made me think one was missing.

'Please,' Mr Stern said behind me. 'Have a seat.'

I sat in the one closest to the window. He took the other, placed the painting he carried against the chair, and leaned forward, his hands clasped.

'I see you have noticed our collection of paintings,' he said.

'It's hard not to. Even in this light. Impressive.'

'It is not as impressive as one might think, Mr Donne. Most of them are from customers who wanted their own work framed and never returned to pick them up.'

'Really?'

He nodded. 'Our store has a ninety-day policy. If one does not pick up the work we have done for them, we do everything we can to contact the artist. You would be surprised how many people move without leaving a forwarding address or contact information.'

'Artists,' I said, trying to sound like I knew what I was talking about.

'I suppose,' he said. 'After waiting a sufficient amount of time, we donate most of the art to a local thrift store. Some' – he looked up at the walls – 'I have decided are good enough to hold on to. Each piece you see on the wall has been documented and catalogued in the event that the artist does eventually return to claim their work.'

'Sounds more than fair to me.'

Stern leaned forward in his seat. 'What happened last night?' he asked.

70

There was no other way to say it than to just come out with it. 'Marty Stover was murdered late yesterday afternoon,' I explained. 'Hector was pretty shaken up when he heard the news this morning, and that's why he's late.'

It seemed to take Joshua Stern a few moments to let that information sink in. When it did, he said what most people ask when hearing such news for the first time.

'Murdered? How? Why?' He took a few seconds before adding, 'Was he mugged? Carjacked?'

'It was at his benefit, actually,' I said. 'You do know he was being honored last night, I assume?'

'Of course. I could not attend due to the timing of the event. Friday evening we have Sabbath services at the temple.' He took a deep breath. 'How horrible. Have the police caught the killer?'

That's the second thing a lot of people ask.

'Not yet. They're still piecing things together.' I remembered the yelling when Hector and I reached the door. 'They'll want to talk to anyone associated with the charity and Marty's legal work.'

Stern nodded. 'That will include me and my father then. Do you know when I can expect them? I do not wish for my father to be interviewed alone. He is an old man and his mind is not so keen anymore. Perhaps they can interview us together?'

'I'm not sure about that,' I said. 'But you can ask.'

He sounded a bit like Hector's mom: protective

71

and defensive at the same time. He must have read the look on my face.

'So, now,' he said, 'you are maybe thinking, why the yelling?'

'We couldn't help but hear. Sorry.'

'No, no. It is quite all right.' He tapped the painting. 'My father has a habit of giving things away. This, he gave to his housekeeper.'

The missing painting I thought I had detected. I allowed myself an internal smile. The one I get when I actually detect something.

'Is it valuable?' I asked.

He gave that some serious thought. 'It is worth maybe two hundred dollars,' he said. 'And that includes the frame. The money is not what worries me. It is his painting; he can do with it what he wants. He just does not remember when he gives things away and then he accuses people of being thieves. We have lost a few housekeepers because of this. A home health aide, as well.'

'I can see where that would get frustrating.'

'Thank you.'

'Can't you just tell people to refuse his . . . gifts?'

'That, a few have tried. He becomes quite offended. It is easier to accept and then return the item to me. Most of the time, they bring it to my store downstairs. If it happens when I am not around, they leave it, call me, or I go to their place. I'm sure there are things missing I do not yet know about. You can imagine.'

We sat there in silence for a few moments and, with nothing more to talk about, I was beginning to think it was time for me to leave. I had fulfilled my promise of getting Hector here. I stood.

'I think I'll be heading home, Mr Stern,' I said.

He got up, too. 'I apologize for the . . . yelling. And thank you for getting Hector here. My father does depend on him on Saturdays.'

'Is your father able to attend services on the Sabbath?'

'Most of the time, no. He wants to, of course. For the High Holy Days, we can get him downstairs and to the temple. Many times, the rabbi is kind enough to come by here and we pray.' He let out a deep breath. 'On occasion, we have found my father at the downstairs door trying to get out. Thanks to God, he cannot work the locks so well.'

'How many people live in this building?' I asked. 'I assume you own it?'

'For many years now, yes. My grandfather bought it right before the war. He moved his whole family here before it was too late to leave Germany.' He was silent for a few seconds as he thought about that history. 'Now we have the store and storage on the floor below this apartment. My father has this floor to himself, and the top two floors we have for my family.'

I was right. There was a lot of family history in this building.

'Between the housekeeper, the home health aides, my wife, and my children,' he said, 'my father has someone with him part of every day. Of course, I see him when I come to work, and Hector has proven quite reliable for the Sabbath.'

'I'm glad,' I said. 'He's a good kid. Bridges has been good for him. I know Marty took a personal interest in his involvement.' I was real curious about Marty Stover's visit the other day that Hector had mentioned. Maybe if I kept the conversation going, we'd get to it. 'So,' I said, 'how many children do you have?'

'Five. Three boys and two girls.'

'That's a group.'

'They keep us busy. Not so bad when you consider the benefits.'

'Excuse the question, but do you ever think of moving your father into an assisted living facility? I imagine it would be easier to have someone else take care of him.'

'It is not something we tend to do in our community,' he said, a small smile crossing his face. 'And even if we did, he is stubborn and wishes to remain here. It was he who started the photography business downstairs. Before that, we – the family – were involved in framing and restoring works of art only.' He looked at the walls. 'We have a modest collection of our own.'

'Was Marty Stover into art?' I asked.

'If he was,' Mr Stern said, 'we never spoke of it. Our conversations mostly revolved around my father and the charity.'

'When did you speak to him last?'

Now I got the look. The look that's says: *What are you? A cop?* I'd like to say I couldn't help myself, but that wouldn't be completely true. I could help myself. I chose not to. The desire to ask these questions had gotten me into more than my share of trouble over the years – just ask my uncle – but I kept going right ahead and asking them. Not so long ago, a big-shot public relations guy referred to me as a 'curious motherfucker.' I couldn't argue with him, and since my curiosity had helped get his missing daughter home safely, I'm sure he didn't mind all that much.

Joshua Stern considered my question and also whether he should answer. It didn't take him long to make his decision.

'We spoke on Tuesday,' he said. 'He visited my shop downstairs.'

'Was he checking up on Hector?'

Stern nodded slowly. 'Something like that, yes.'

I was bursting to ask about the argument, but even I knew that was crossing the line and could possibly get Hector into some hot water. Showing up fifteen minutes late is one thing, gossiping about your boss was another.

'He was happy with Hector's progress?' I asked instead.

'Very much. Mr Stover was quite pleased to be able to give back to the neighborhood in which he was raised. We need more people like him.' He paused as he bowed his head. 'His loss diminishes us all.'

That was followed by more silence. Stern looked toward the front door as if wishing I would leave through it now. I figured it best not to push my luck.

'Well,' I said and offered my hand again. 'Thanks again for everything you're doing for Hector.'

'You are welcome,' he said. 'When do you suppose I can expect the police?'

'I'm sure they'll get your name from the charity. After that, they'll prioritize their interviews, and you'll probably hear from them in a few days.'

'Excuse me for saying this,' he said. 'But you sound as if you have done this before. You speak as the police do.'

I smiled. 'I used to be a cop, Mr Stern. It's a hard thing to shake, I guess.'

'Yes. I would imagine. I was once an artist, now I sell to them.'

'Why did you give it up?'

'There is more to be gained by selling to artists than by being one. Especially when one wishes to have a family.' He looked me over again. 'Do you have children of your own, Mr Donne?'

'No,' I said. 'Not yet.'

'Do not wait too long. They are truly a blessing.'

I knew enough not to get into a conversation with an Orthodox Jew about blessings. I gave the artwork in the living room one more look and said, 'Can I say goodbye to Hector?'

'Let me get him.'

When he left the room, my curiosity got the better of me and I picked up the framed painting Stern had rested against the chair. I held it in both hands and inspected it. To my untrained eye, it was your basic landscape painting and reminded me a little of the Hudson Valley area, which started about an hour north of the city. I couldn't tell for sure, but the signature, in this low light, appeared to read '*J Stern.*' So not only had the elder Stern given away a painting – worth 'maybe two hundred dollars' – it looked to have been one painted by his own son: a frustrated artist who ran the family business.

'Mr Stern said you're leaving.' Hector had returned.

'Yeah,' I said. 'I've got some errands to take care of.'

'Thanks for coming, Mr D. And for making me come here. I'm glad I did. He was sitting in the dark till I turned on the lights for him.'

'What else do you do for Mr Stern?'

'The father?'

'Yes.'

'I make his morning tea. I have lunch with him. It's mostly stuff one of his aides made during the week. I warm it up. Sometimes we play checkers or chess. A lot of times, I just listen. Old people like to talk, you know.'

'So I've heard.' I thought about the conversation I'd just had with Joshua Stern. 'Has he ever given you anything? Anything maybe he shouldn't have?'

'You mean like a painting?'

'That's exactly what I mean. So he has?'

'Once,' Hector said. 'About a month ago. I told my dad and we brought it back to Mr Stern. The son, I mean. He was a little pissed, but I think it happens a lot.'

'That's what he told me.' With nothing else I could think of to say, I said, 'OK, Hector. See ya at work, Monday.'

It took him a few seconds to get my joke. He obliged with a small laugh. 'Yeah.'

He saw me out of the apartment, and I could hear him lock the door behind me. You can never be too safe, I guess.

Eight

Since the weather was cooperating and I really had no major commitments, I decided to walk home from the Sterns' building. It took about twenty-five minutes and made me feel a lot better about how little time I'd been spending in the gym lately. I made a deal with myself that I'd go to Muscles' twice this upcoming week. He'd be glad to see me and gladder still to bust my balls about coming more consistently. Then he'd assign me penance, usually something to do with my abdominal section and lower back.

'The core,' he'd say. 'Even if you have time for nothing else, work the core.'

When I got back to my place, I shoved a load of whites into the washer and took a shower. After I was clean, shaved, and dressed, I moved the laundry into the dryer where it would magically convert back to clothes. The stackable washer/dryer in my kitchen was one of those luxuries I never took for granted. And, although she'd never admit to it, it was probably one of the reasons Allison stayed over as much as she did. We were at the point where she had a few changes of clothes at my place, and being able to wash them on a Sunday night allowed her to head right to work on Monday morning. As much as my sister claimed my bachelorhood was a sign of immaturity, the washer/dryer screamed grownup.

I was about to turn on the TV and computer to see if there were any new details about Marty, when my cell phone rang. It was Rachel.

'Hey,' I said. 'You get Mom on the train?'

'Change of plans,' she said.

'What's up?'

'The way I figure it, there's gonna be a service tomorrow for Marty. I might as well drive Mom home and spend the night at her place.'

'That's a pretty smart idea, Rachel.'

'I have them occasionally,' she said. 'You wanna take the subway to my place and we can all go out together?'

Another smart idea, I thought, but I had Allison to consider.

'Allison's working until at least three,' I said. 'Can you wait until then? I'm not sure what she wants to do.'

Five seconds of silence. 'No,' she said. 'I need to get Mom home so she can pick out what to wear and make some calls to change plans she had for tomorrow.'

'Can't she do that from her cell phone?'

'She could if she brought it, Ray. But, at the moment, it's sitting in its charger next to the coffee machine in her kitchen.' Pause. 'I need to get her home.'

My mother was likely driving my little sister a bit crazy in her one-bedroom apartment. Lately, she'd been bugging Rachel about all the little changes she'd have to make once she was married. Everything from new dishes to bed linens. It was always better to be in motion with my mother, and the bigger the space the better. I did not envy Rachel the half-hour drive to my mom's house.

'Maybe we'll come out tonight then,' I said. 'We'll have more details by then anyway. Are we even sure there's a service and that we're invited?'

'*We're* not sure of anything yet, Ray. But if there's a service, I'm guessing we will be invited. Marty and Helaine didn't have that many friends, according to Mom.'

And my mother would know. 'OK,' I said. 'Let's do this: I'll call you later this afternoon and we'll come up with a plan. Allison and I will either come out tonight or early tomorrow morning. You can get us at the station, right?'

'Instead of you taking a car service, of course.'

Rachel couldn't help but take those little shots at me. Apparently not having a car was yet another sign of my immaturity. In truth, not owning a car was one of the major reasons I loved living in Brooklyn. My sister insisted on owning one, even though she lived in Queens. This meant she had to move it from one side of the street to the other a few times a week – the famous 'alternate side parking' hell of the five boroughs – and also pay a good chunk for insurance money just for the privilege of driving around the New York City area a few times a month.

'I'll call you later then. Give my love to Mom.'

'I'll be sure to do that, Ray.'

We ended the call just as the buzzer told me

my clothes were dry: one more accomplishment for the day. The socks and underwear were in their respective places in my bureau when the phone rang again. This time, I did not recognize the number. I thought of letting it go to voice-mail, but after the events of last night, opted instead to pick up.

'Hello?'

'Raymond?' A male voice.

'Yeah.' I waited for a response. None seemed to be coming. 'I'm sorry,' I said. 'Who's this?'

I heard some coughing and then the caller cleared his throat. 'Oh, sorry, man,' he said. 'It's Martin. Martin Stover.'

The name sent a tingle up my arms. It took me a few seconds: Marty's kid. I guess he was going by Martin now. *What the hell is he calling me for?*

'Hey, Martin,' I said. 'Listen, I'm so sorry about what happened to your dad. How are you and your mom holding up?'

'Honestly, Ray,' he said. 'It's hard to tell. We got home last night, heard the news, and then had to head back into the city. Your uncle had one of his people drive us back in, though. Good thing, too. I don't know if I'd have made it.'

'Yeah, he told me he was going to arrange that. Are you back home now?'

'No. The cops kept us until after midnight. Mom and I decided to stay overnight. Not that either one of us was able to sleep. We got a room downtown. Not the Village. Chelsea, I guess? I don't know the city like my dad did.'

'Were they able to tell you anything new?'

'Who?'

'The cops. Were they able to tell you and your mother anything about . . . you know, what happened to your dad?'

He was silent for a few beats. 'No,' he said. 'That's not why I'm calling.'

Why are you calling?

'We just got a call from the cops.'

'They need to talk to you again?'

'No,' he said. He was coming across like this was all too much for him. I heard him take a deep breath. 'Not those cops. The Nassau County cops.'

'Nassau? What do they want?'

He cleared his throat again. When he spoke again, he sounded like a two-pack a day smoker. 'Dad's office was broken into.'

Shit. 'When?'

'Late last night, early this morning. They're not quite sure.'

I was about to ask if the police thought the break-in was connected to the murder, but that's the kind of question I was working on not asking. But still: why was he calling me? What could I do for him now?

As if reading my mind, Martin Stover said, 'They want a family member out there. To sign off on some paperwork or something. You know better than I do how this stuff works, right?'

'I guess,' I said. 'But I'm not family.'

'Actually, Ray. You are.'

It took me a while, but then I got it. Marty Stover had never dissolved the partnership after my dad's death. He had arranged it – the way

83

only lawyers can understand – that my family would be a limited partner and be eligible for what amounted to profit sharing from the practice. From what I understood, it worked better for my mother in the long run than Marty just buying her out. Marty was good that way.

'So you want me to . . .'

'Yeah, Ray, if you would. Mom finally passed out a few hours ago after I gave her some of my sleeping pills.' *Which you just happened to have on you?* 'Anxiety meds, actually,' he explained. 'They knocked her out, and I don't wanna wake her up until I have to. I'm sitting here in the room making arrangements with the temple for tomorrow and trying to get the word out. I could head back to the Island, but I don't wanna leave Mom alone, you know?'

'Yeah,' I said. 'I gotcha.' I wasn't quite sure what I could do at the law office, but if that's what the cops wanted, I'd do it. 'I'll be there as soon as I can.'

'Thanks, Ray. I guess I'll either see you later or tomorrow.'

I ended the call and looked at the time. I'd have to call Allison and my sister. It looked like I'd be on Long Island before Rachel and my mother. I also needed to call Edgar. He had a car and was always willing to let me borrow it.

And he was going to love the reason why. A murder victim's office had been broken into the day after his murder and I was going to the scene of the crime.

My second one in two days.

84

Nine

'I really appreciate this, Edgar,' I said as he got out of his car, illegally parked in front of my apartment. 'I owe you one.'

He joined me on the sidewalk and said, 'I know a way you can pay me back, Raymond.' He paused for some dramatic effect that he couldn't quite pull off. 'Immediately.' He adjusted his eyeglasses, tilted back his baseball cap, and stuck his hands in his pockets. Even behind those thick lenses, I could see his eyes grow three sizes. 'I mean, like, right now.'

Oh, really? I thought. Then I asked the question I already knew the answer to.

'And how's that, Edgar?'

'You can take me with you, Raymond. I mean, how cool would that be? You're going to check on your dad's old office that was broken into right after – or during or before – your dad's old partner was murdered. That is real cop stuff, man. Talk about cool beans.'

Edgar talked a lot about cool beans, usually in relation to something to do with 'cop stuff.' This clearly fit the bill in his mind.

'Edgar,' I began, 'I'm only going out there as a formality. They need someone to sign off on the crime scene. Legally, my family – my mother – still owns part of the firm, so . . . Besides, there's not going to be much to see. It was a

85

break-in, at a law firm, when no one was around. It'll be boring.'

'Not to me,' he said. 'And don't try telling me it'll be dangerous, either. You just said it was going to be boring. Boring is not dangerous.'

He had me there. For better or worse, he was learning to think like me.

'How am I going to explain your presence at the scene to a bunch of cops I've never met, Edgar? I just brought a friend?'

'You can introduce me as your security specialist,' he said, almost imperceptibly puffing out his chest. 'I can check the alarms, the access points, see if anyone tried to get into the computers.' He smiled before his next sentence. 'Isn't this the kinda stuff you tell me I have to practice? Getting out into the real world, talking to real investigators at real scenes and not just at bars?'

Edgar was a regular at The LineUp, the cop bar where I worked every Tuesday night. It was owned by Mrs McVernon, whose deceased husband came out of the police academy with my uncle and had worked the same streets with him. Edgar did a lot of talking at the bar, and we'd been working on his listening skills. And, again, he got me. This was exactly the sort of situation I'd been helping him become more at ease with.

I held out my hand. 'Give me the keys, Edgar.'

'Oh, come on, Raymond. I promise, I won't say a—'

'Give me the keys so I can drive, Edgar. I

don't want you all excited behind the wheel on the Long Island Expressway.'

It took him a few seconds to realize I had just said yes. He put the keys in my open palm, opened the passenger-side door, and got inside the car before I could change my mind. Anybody watching might think I was taking a kid out to see his first Yankees game.

Traffic on the Long Island Expressway – also known as the LIE or 'The World's Longest Parking Lot' – was not too bad this particular Saturday afternoon. On the ride in from Brooklyn, Edgar suggested it would be a good idea to get any computer passwords we'd need from Marty's son. I made a quick call, told him what we needed, and he obliged.

We pulled into a parking spot behind the law firm about fifty minutes after leaving Brooklyn and parked between a Nassau County cop car and a dark-blue town car that probably belonged to a detective. The break-in at Marty's office was getting the royal treatment. My uncle's friend on the Nassau PD must have received another call.

I always liked going to my dad's office. He and Marty had purchased an old two-story house, one of the oldest in this town. They had turned the bedrooms into offices, the living room into a waiting and reception area, and the kitchen into a break room. Since my father's death, Marty had finished the upstairs and rented out those 'offices' to a variety of lawyers throughout the years. I think that's where Marty

Junior got his start. Now he was downstairs with his dad.

'Now remember,' I said to Edgar as I pulled the key out of the ignition, 'you are not to speak unless you're spoken to.'

'Or if I notice something they clearly overlooked,' he said as if that made all the sense in the world. Edgar, like a lot of techie folks, likes to point out others' oversights.

'Uh-uh. Then you speak to me. *I'll* bring it to their attention.'

'You sound like you don't trust me, Raymond.'

I opened my door and he followed suit, bringing his laptop bag with him. 'It's not that I don't trust you,' I said across the roof of the car. 'Think of this as your first class. You're more of an observer than a participant.'

'But what if I—'

'Then you talk directly to me.' Before he could argue again, I added, 'You're *my* security specialist, remember? Not theirs.'

That cheered him up. We walked to the front of the house – around an attached garage that Marty had put in after my father's death – and were met by a uniformed Nassau County officer. She was about forty, made the uniform look good, and seemed to be thinking of better ways to spend her Saturday than babysitting an office robbery. She slipped her cell phone into her pocket and stood a little straighter as we approached.

Behind me, I heard Edgar mumble, 'Wow.' He was never easy around women, and now he was about to meet an attractive one in a cop's uniform? It was every cop nerd's dream. I just hoped he could keep his cool.

'Can I help you gentlemen?' she asked. Her badge read 'Mueller.'

'I'm Raymond Donne, Officer Mueller,' I said. It was weird saying that to a cop and getting absolutely no reaction. We were not in New York City anymore. 'I'm here about the robbery, representing the Stover and Donne families.'

'You a lawyer?'

'No,' I said. 'Schoolteacher.' Again, no reaction. 'Is there a detective inside we can talk to?'

'Wait here, please.' She disappeared through the front door. Edgar let out a deep sigh he'd been holding in. A minute later, Mueller re-emerged and said, 'Go on in.'

'Thanks,' I said and motioned Edgar to follow me. He did, careful not to get too close to the woman he'd be thinking about for the next few days.

It had been a lot of years since I last stepped foot into my father's offices. It still smelled the same – like old law books – and I was hit by a jolt of nostalgia. This was where my dad spent most of my youth, away from his family. I would go here sometimes on weekends when my mother had things to do. Rachel and I would set up in the living room and either do homework or watch TV. It was almost like our parents were divorced and this was my father's new house. The living room we were standing in was familiar. The TV was gone and the furniture had been updated, but it still looked the same.

A large man in a dark suit came out of one

89

of the offices. In honor of this being a Saturday morning, he apparently had chosen not to shave or completely tie his purple necktie. As he tapped his notebook against his thigh, he stepped over to me and Edgar, gave us both a look, and asked the two of us, 'Which one of you is Mr Donne?'

'That would be me,' I said, sticking out my hand. As he shook it, I said, 'And this is Edgar O'Brien.'

'Detective Carney.' He shook an obviously pleased Edgar's hand as well. 'So this is your father's place, huh?'

'It was,' I said. 'He's been dead for a while now.'

He scrunched up his eyes. 'Then why are you here?'

I explained about the deal between Marty and my family the best I could. The detective pretended to understand my non-legal and confusing explanation. He looked around the place. 'Well, the good news is it was a pretty clean break-in, as far as these things go. A neighbor was walking his dog this morning and noticed the front door was open. He knew Mr Stover and had never seen the door like that. When he called inside and got no answer, he called nine-one-one.' He scratched the inside of his ear and then examined his finger. Finding nothing of interest there, he said, 'If you see something, say something, I guess.'

'Was anything stolen?' I asked.

'I thought that's what you're here to tell us, Mr Donne.'

How the hell was I supposed to know if

90

anything had been taken from the office? The living room looked fine to me after twenty-something years, and I wasn't sure what I'd be able to tell the detective about the offices. I thought I had been summoned just to sign some papers and make sure the place was locked up again.

Edgar cleared his throat. I looked over at him and watched as his face closed in on itself. He was clearly dying to say something. 'Excuse me,' I said to the detective and pulled Edgar off to the side. 'What is it, Edgar?'

'Access point?' he whispered, sounding like an impatient teenager. 'How'd the burglar get in without setting off an alarm?'

I thought about that and nodded. I turned back to Detective Carney. 'Mr O'Brien is a security specialist,' I explained. 'He'd like to know how the burglar got in without setting off any alarms.'

Carney looked at Edgar as if he were a rare specimen. Edgar got that look a lot.

'You brought a security specialist? For this?'

'He happened to be with me when I got the call from Martin Stover. Junior. He also offered to drive me out, so . . .'

'Doesn't your security specialist talk to anyone but you?'

'He does, of course. It's just that when he's taking in a scene, he prefers to speak only to his client.' I stepped closer to the detective and added, 'It's a bit of a quirk, I know, but he's real good at his job, so I live with it.'

I let Carney soak that in. 'Well,' he said after a while, 'for a lawyer, Mr Stover didn't have the best security system. He did have the front and back doors alarmed, along with all the first-floor windows. Apparently, our burglar accessed the house through an unalarmed *upstairs* window, and when it was time to leave, he was able to walk out the front door without setting off the alarm. It's one of those old-school systems you can shut off from inside without a password.'

I nodded like I knew anything about home alarms and security systems. 'Any idea when the break-in occurred?'

Carney checked his notebook. 'Neighbor called it in at eighty-thirty-five, so any time before eighty-thirty-four would be my guess.' He followed that with a sly smirk.

You gotta love a detective with a sense of humor. I could just imagine my uncle chewing on this guy's ass after a comment like that.

'Obviously,' I said. 'I guess we should have a look around.' I felt myself getting into this now. If not for my curiosity then for the sheer joy of extending the funny detective's Saturday afternoon. 'Edgar.' I turned to my security specialist. 'Why don't you check the computers in the offices down here? See if anyone tried to access them.'

That got Carney's attention. 'I don't think he should be touching anything, Mr Donne. This is a crime scene.'

'Do you want to call in your tech people?' I asked. 'I have complete faith in my man here. We have the passwords for the computers and he is here. How long would it take your people to arrive? On a Saturday?'

Carney mulled that over and it didn't take him long to see the plus side of having Edgar check out the computers. The quicker the computers were checked out, the quicker we could all get out of here.

'OK,' he said. 'But I'm gonna have Officer Mueller come in and watch him.'

Edgar let out a sound I'd never heard from him before. It was somewhere between ecstasy and fear. The detective stepped over to the door and said something I couldn't quite hear. A few seconds later, Mueller came inside.

'If you find anything, I wanna be the first to know,' Carney said. 'The offices are behind those doors.' He pointed to the one he'd come out of. 'That is Senior's. And the other one is where Junior works. You probably know all this, right?' He pointed over to our left. 'You wanna check the upstairs first? Mr Stover rented out the office space up there on a month-to-month basis.'

'Absolutely,' I said, and Carney and I headed up the stairs as Edgar and Mueller stepped into Marty's office. It was all he could do, I thought, not to trip over his own feet.

The upper floor of the law firm was laid out quite simply: two former bedrooms had been turned into offices and were separated by a short hallway and a bathroom. I followed Carney into the office to the left.

'This is where the burglar came in,' he said as he walked me over to the window. 'Just slipped something – crowbar or big screwdriver – between the window and the wood and slipped

93

inside. I guess when he didn't hear an alarm, he knew it was safe to go in.'

I stepped over to the window and noticed a few scratch marks on the wood. I also noticed that it would be an easy climb from the ground up to the top of the attached garage, an easy reach to the window. Marty had added the attached garage to the old house, apparently not considering the security aspects.

'That's interesting,' I heard myself say out loud.

'What's interesting?' Detective Carney asked.

'Why would you break into a house from the second floor and then leave the front door open when you left?'

'Huh. Hadn't thought of that.' But now he did, and a light bulb went off over his head. 'Maybe the burglar wanted to make sure Mr Stover knew his place had been burglarized for some reason.'

That was an interesting thought. But then that would mean . . .

'Then that would mean the burglar didn't know that Marty had been murdered.'

'Which,' Carney said without missing a beat, 'would mean that the murder and the burglary are not related. What are the odds of that, I wonder?'

Having taught math for a few years, I knew this was one of those situations where you couldn't apply actual odds and percentages, but the detective's point was well taken. Any reasonable person would connect the murder to the break-in. Of course, reasonable people didn't go around killing other people at their own benefits. And the idea that the burglar wanted Marty to know the place had been broken into was just that – an idea.

I looked around the office and, to my eye, everything looked fine. There was a desk, two chairs, a couch, and a small fridge. No computer on the desk told me the tenant-lawyer probably did all his work on a laptop. I guessed the other office on this floor would look pretty much the same, and I was right. People who rented by the month didn't need a lot of stuff.

'Ready to check in downstairs with your guy?' Carney asked.

'Yeah. Everything looks . . . I don't know, fine up here.'

We found Edgar in front of Marty's computer, tapping away, unaware of us entering the office. He even seemed oblivious to the female officer standing behind him. Between his job, his love of baseball, and his 'security/research' work, I thought about how many hours a day Edgar spent in front of some sort of screen. No wonder he kept getting his eyeglasses updated.

'Anything, Edgar?' I asked from across the room.

He startled a bit at our presence, like we'd interrupted a meditation session. He took his glasses off and said, 'If anyone breached the system, he's better than I am. Mr Stover's computer is password-protected, of course, and there's no log-in info since yesterday morning.'

'So the burglar didn't – or couldn't – access the computer,' I said. 'Maybe he was looking for something else.' I felt that tingly feeling I still got sometimes when faced with a puzzle. Probably

95

similar to the feeling a poker player gets after drawing a straight.

There was silence in the room for a moment. Officer Mueller used this silence as an opportunity to head back outside. Carney said, 'Unless we're overlooking the complete obvious and this was just a couple of knucklehead kids out for a joy ride, you know, "Let's see if we can get in/get out without setting off the alarm." Something like that.'

That was another thought.

'Edgar,' I said. 'The alarm system to the house. You wouldn't need the code to deactivate it? Shouldn't Marty have updated that?'

'Years ago,' he said. 'I don't like to judge, but I'm guessing Marty was maybe a bit on the cheap side? The system's old, Ray. I don't know why people skimp on such things. A good alarm system is worth every penny you pay for it.'

Edgar managed to sound both judgmental and offended at the same time. He could not understand why everyone didn't treat technology with the same respect he did.

'What about the computers?' I asked.

'They're pretty up-to-date. At least enough to satisfy the needs of a law firm.'

Carney stepped forward. 'Are all his records stored on there?' he asked. 'I mean, how long has the firm been around?'

'Almost thirty years,' I said and then saw the detective's point. 'Are there three decades of files on that computer, Edgar?'

'Nope. You know I'm not one to assume, Raymond, but I would say he's got hard copies

96

of the years before his latest upgrade. Probably on CDs and, older than that, floppy disks. Where are they stored? This house has no basement, so that's a good question.'

'We can find that out from his wife or son,' I said. 'But right now you're telling us nothing on that computer's been compromised?'

'That is what I'm telling you,' Edgar said.

'I assume you checked the desks for any signs of a break-in, Detective?'

'All the drawers – upstairs and downstairs – are locked, and there's no evidence of anyone trying to force them open,' Carney said.

I stood there in the middle of the office trying to think of something else to ask or add to the conversation. After thirty seconds, I had to admit I was done.

'If that's all, Detective Carney,' I said, 'I'll sign whatever you need me to sign, and we can get out of your hair.'

'You're signing for the Donne family, right?'

'Yes.'

Happy not to ask any questions as that task was completed, the detective locked up the house and stood on the front lawn. Officer Mueller had made her way to the street and was talking on her phone. Carney said to me, 'You don't by any chance have a key to the place, do you? Or the password to the alarm system?'

I smiled. He was interrogating me, which made sense. Of course he should ask a family member about a key and the alarm code.

'No,' I said. 'My mother might, but I doubt it. And just to offer her an alibi, she was in the city most of yesterday and definitely when the house was broken into.'

Carney gave me a smile of his own and said, 'Had to ask, you know?'

'I'd be disappointed if you hadn't.' We shook hands. 'If there's anything else I can do, you can reach me through the Stover family.'

'I don't think that'll be necessary,' he said. 'But I do have one more question.'

'Go ahead.'

'How long were you a cop?'

I looked down at the grass and laughed. 'It's that obvious, huh?'

'Let's just say it's not unobvious.'

Edgar and I were sitting in his car behind the house: I was in the driver's seat, and he was in the passenger's, the picture of two guys with nowhere to go. Maybe we should have grabbed a six-pack and turned to the classic rock station. If the trip out to the Island had gained us anything, I wasn't sure what it was beyond doing a favor for the Stovers. That would have to be enough.

One thing was bugging me, though. How did the burglar know about Marty's crappy security system? Before I could give that much thought, Edgar spoke.

'Didn't you grow up around here, Ray?'

I put my hands at ten and two on the steering wheel. 'Five minutes away,' I said.

'You wanna go by the house?'

'For what?' I said, maybe a little too harshly. 'No one's home.'

'I just figured since we were so close . . .'

'You want to see where I grew up, Edgar? Is that it? If that's what you want, just come out and ask, OK?'

Even I could tell I sounded like an asshole.

'That's not it, Ray,' Edgar said, his voice letting me know his feelings had been hurt. 'Let's go back to Williamsburg then, OK? Maybe watch some preseason at The LineUp. Yanks are playing the Cards. And I'm hungry.'

I turned to my friend. 'I'm sorry, Edgar. I'm tired and still shaken up by what happened to Marty. Going into my dad's old office didn't help much, either. It feels like we wasted a few hours just so I could take a trip down memory lane.'

'It wasn't a complete waste.' He reached into his pocket.

'What do you mean by that?' I asked.

He pulled out a flash drive. 'I downloaded some of the contents of Marty's computer. I thought we might find something useful.'

'Holy fuck, Edgar! I invite you out to a crime scene for a little experience and you not only contaminate the scene but you walk away with evidence? What the hell were you thinking?'

He adjusted his glasses. 'I was thinking,' he said, 'that you might wanna know what was on the murder victim's computer. And it's not technically evidence, Ray.'

'Don't do that, Edgar.' I took a breath. 'I'm not going to sit here and play legal semantics with you. *Everything* is evidence until the cops say otherwise. You of all people should know that. Just because I referred to you as my security guy doesn't mean you get to play the role of hacker. Jesus.'

He turned away to look out his window. 'I'm sorry, Ray,' he said. 'I got a little carried away. I was sitting there at Stover's computer and the urge just came over me. You and the detective were upstairs. The cop was back on her cell phone, so I figured there was no harm in it.'

'You figured wrong,' I said to the back of his head.

He reached down by his feet and grabbed his laptop bag. For a moment, I thought he was going to hug it like a security blanket. Instead, he unzipped it, pulled out his computer, inserted the flash drive into a USB port, and said, 'You want me to delete what I downloaded? It'll take five minutes, and no one'll know anything.'

That was *exactly* what I wanted him to do. It was *exactly* what I should have told him to do. Instead, I turned the ignition key and shifted the car into reverse.

'You got until we get back to Brooklyn,' I said. 'If you find anything by the time we get to my place, let me know. If not, *then* you will delete whatever you got off the computer. Understand?'

'Yeah, Ray. I understand.'

'Good.'

I pulled out of the parking lot and pointed Edgar's car toward Brooklyn.

We had just arrived at the entrance ramp to the Meadowbrook Parkway when I heard Edgar go, 'Huh.'

'What?' I said.

100

'You know anything about a company called HMS Realty?'

'No.' I looked over my left shoulder and merged on to the parkway. 'Should I?'

'I'm not sure. But it says here that your friend Marty Stover owns two properties in Williamsburg, Brooklyn. One residential, one mixed-use.'

'Where are they?'

He read me the addresses and it took me five seconds to realize why one sounded very familiar.

The mixed-used property – part residential, part commercial – was on the Northside of Williamsburg. The residential address was on the Southside. It was the building where Hector Robles and his family resided. You would think that would have come up in our conversation this morning.

'Can you find out who lives in those apartments, Edgar?'

'Yeah,' he said. 'Give me a few minutes.'

A few minutes later as we got back on the LIE, Edgar said, 'You want the residents of both buildings, right?'

'That'd be great. Give me the ones on the Southside first.'

He read off a bunch of names; Robles was one of them. Then he read off the names of the residents of the Northside property, starting with the two businesses. After reading off five or six names of the other tenants, he abruptly stopped.

'Cheese and crackers,' he said. 'That's weird.'

'What's weird?'

He looked at the screen and punched a few more buttons. I gave a quick glance over at him and thought he was about to pick up the laptop and shake it.

'Your dad's name was Robert, right?'

'Yeah,' I said. 'Why?'

'Middle initial J?'

'Robert James Donne,' I said, and again asked, 'Why?'

'It says here,' Edgar said, 'that Robert J. Donne lives in one of the apartments.'

It was all I could do to stay in my lane.

Ten

I'm not sure how he did it – how he always seemed to do it – but Edgar found a spot right down the block from the building on the Northside. If parking were an Olympic sport, Edgar's face would be on a Wheaties box. We could see the edge of McCarren Park from where we were. I was sure that on a decent early spring day like this, the place would be packed with soccer players, skateboarders, handballers, and anybody else who needed some sunshine and a little exercise. I was also sure there'd be more than a few young couples getting a head start on a warm-weather romance. Some of them were probably my students.

Edgar and I got out of the car and met up on the sidewalk.

'Whatta you gonna do?' he asked.

'I'm going to find out who this Robert J. Donne is and see how he's connected to Marty Stover.' I rubbed my eyes. It had been a long twenty-four hours. Now this. 'I gotta tell ya, this feels weird, Edgar.'

'Yeah,' he said, hardly containing his enthusiasm. 'But it's a good kinda weird. I have that feeling cops get when they're about to find out some important key to a case.' He saw the look I was giving him and added, 'At least that's what I've heard.'

'Right. OK, we're a couple of friends looking for Robert J. Donne. We'll say we're worried about him because he hasn't been answering his cell phone in the last week and his family asked us to check his place out.'

He grabbed his laptop bag, ready for action. 'Sounds like a plan, Ray.'

Like Edgar would say anything else. 'OK,' I said. 'Let's go.'

As promised, the first floor was commercial: an independent real estate company that seemed closed for the day. Or maybe they were out showing places. We headed over to the door and checked out the buzzer panel. Along with the apartment numbers, it was all first initials and last names. This was a small security measure so some knucklehead looking for trouble couldn't tell if the resident was male or female. Some of the nametags looked so old, I was sure they were from three or four tenants ago. But we found the one we were looking for.

It seemed strange seeing *R Donne* listed as the resident of Apartment 4S. That was my father. *Me, too.*

I pressed the buzzer and waited. After thirty seconds, I did it again. No answer. So I started with 1N and after waiting thirty seconds, kept pressing the other buzzers until 3S finally answered.

'Who is it?' a garbled voice wanted to know.

I leaned into the speaker. 'My name's James Hunter,' I said. 'I'm trying to reach my friend Robert Donne.'

'Ya got the wrong buzzer.'

'I know,' I said. 'He's in the apartment above

104

you.' I said that because it wasn't that uncommon for residents of the same building not to know each other's names. 'I'm a friend of his and kind of worried. He's not answering his phone or his buzzer.'

There was a pause for about ten seconds. 'If you think something's wrong or something, why don't you call the cops?'

The hardened New Yorker's answer to everything. 'That's my next step,' I said. 'But I'd like to knock on his door. See if something's wrong with his buzzer or if maybe he's passed out. You know Robert.'

I thought the light touch would make this guy more likely to buzz me in. Instead, I got, 'You check the girlfriend?'

Girlfriend? 'No,' I said. 'And I wouldn't wanna get him in any trouble anyway.'

More silence, followed by laughter. 'I getcha. Hold on a sec.'

The buzzer sounded, unlocking the door, and Edgar and I entered the building.

We walked up to the third floor and the guy in 3S who had buzzed us in was standing in his doorway. He was wearing a blue T-shirt and gray sweatpants. I couldn't tell if he was getting ready for the gym or for bed.

'Thanks,' I said. 'When's the last time you saw Robert?'

'I don't remember, man,' he said. 'I work nights bartending. You're lucky I even heard the buzzer. Sometimes I don't see any of my neighbors for weeks. Him, I see less than that.' He looked up. 'You think he's OK?'

105

I decided I liked this guy. As little as he knew about his upstairs neighbor, he was still worried about him. Maybe it was the kind of worry that came with thinking, if something bad had happened to the guy who lived upstairs, it could happen to me. Either way, the guy decided he cared.

'That's what we're gonna find out,' I said. 'You want us to let you know on our way down?'

'Yeah,' the guy said. 'I might be in the shower, but I'd appreciate that. Thanks.'

'No problem,' I said, and Edgar and I headed up to the next floor. We stopped when the guy yelled out to us.

'You guys said you're his friends?'

'Yeah,' I said. 'Why?'

'Well, nothing, I guess. It's just that you're like twenty years younger than he is.' He gave us a closer look. 'Unless you guys are older than you look.'

'Work friends,' I said, and motioned for Edgar to keep moving before this guy had any more questions for us.

When we got to Robert Donne's apartment, I placed my ear against the door to see if I could hear anything. When I didn't, I knocked. We waited half a minute and I knocked again, louder this time. No answer. I knocked again, and followed that with a loud, 'Robby! You in there, buddy? It's James and Edgar.'

I half-expected the other two doors on the floor to open up, the tenants wondering who the hell was screaming after their floor mate on a late

Saturday afternoon. Neither door opened. I did it again. Louder this time.

'Hey, Robby. Buddy. You OK?'

Nothing.

'Shit,' I said. I turned to Edgar, looked at his laptop bag, and said, 'Could you get his phone number off that list?'

Edgar shook his head. 'I already checked when we were in the car,' he said. 'He was the only one without a number. I thought that was kinda weird.'

'Right. Well, looks like we may have wasted a trip.'

Edgar gave me a sly look. Or as close to sly as Edgar can get. 'Maybe not, Ray.'

'What does that mean, Edgar?'

He paused before whispering, 'You promise you won't get mad?'

I looked him square in the eyes. 'I'm going to get mad if you don't tell me what you mean.'

He closed his eyes and reached into his front jeans pocket. I thought he was going to pull out his cell phone. What he did pull out surprised me.

'What's that for, Edgar?' I asked.

He grinned. 'Come on, Ray. You know what it's for.'

'I know what it's for,' I said, looking at the lock pick set in his hand. 'What I mean is why do you have that with you?'

He shrugged. 'I brought it with me to Marty Stover's office. Just in case we needed to get into something that was locked. A closet. A drawer.'

'Knowing that there'd be cops there?'

'*Just in case*, I said. Hey, you had the one guy

upstairs and the lady cop was outside half the time on her phone. I coulda used it if I needed to.'

I shook my head. 'You didn't *need* to do anything, Edgar.' I was starting to rethink the idea of bringing him along today, and I told him so.

'So,' he said. 'You *don't* want the lock pick?'

Jesus. 'Give it to me, Edgar.'

He did. I rolled it over in my fingers as I mulled over the idea of opening Robert J. Donne's door. Before I decided, I knocked again and yelled out his name one more time. If there was anyone on the fourth floor in their apartment, they did not make their presence known. Or maybe they'd already called the cops.

I decided it would be a wise choice to hedge my bets. I went over to both of the other apartments and knocked on the doors. If no one answered: great. If someone did answer, I'd just repeat the same story I told the guy who had buzzed us in. We were friends of Robert's and were worried about his wellbeing. No one answered and I walked back to Robert's apartment.

I looked down at the set of lock pick tools in my hand. I'd used one before. They were pretty handy, truth be told. And pretty much the same size as a small screwdriver, about the same weight. The big difference was that the person using a screwdriver wasn't usually breaking the law.

There was that tingling sensation again. The buzz I got when doing something I knew was crossing the line just to satisfy my curiosity. Maybe it would be a better idea to squash the buzz now before I found myself in trouble. Maybe not.

'OK.' I could hardly believe what I was about to say next. 'I am just going to open the door. We will look inside – *from the doorway* – and see what we see.' I took a deep breath. 'Unless there's someone on the other side who needs help, we are not going in.' Therein lies the difference between 'breaking and entering' and just 'breaking.' I could just picture myself explaining that one to Uncle Ray. 'The last thing we need is Buzzer Guy hearing us traipsing around his upstairs neighbor's apartment without permission. Are we clear on this, Edgar? We *are not* going inside.'

Edgar looked like a six-year-old being teased with a wrapped present. 'I get it, Ray,' he said. 'I get it.' He inched toward the door and motioned with his head. If I listened closer, I was sure I could hear his heartbeat. 'I'm ready when you are.'

'Maybe even more so,' I said.

I inserted the pick into the lock, and with a few twists and turns of the tension wrench, and a slight upwards motion, the door unlocked. *How many schoolteachers could do that?* I pocketed the tools and waited a few seconds before turning the knob, briefly reconsidering the legality of what I was about to do. *Briefly.* I turned the knob and held on as I opened the door slowly. It was about a foot open when I yelled, 'Robby! You home, man?' Again, no answer.

I opened the door wide enough to see inside

the apartment. To describe the living room as sparsely furnished would not do it justice. There was one couch, a matching chair, and a coffee table. It looked like the place had been robbed of all valuables, but it didn't have that feel. The wood floor looked as if it had recently been polished, and there was a small pile of books on the coffee table. There was no TV, nothing on the walls. Whoever this Robert J. Donne was, he was not into possessions.

I could feel Edgar breathing down my neck. Literally.

'What is it, Ray?' he asked. 'Whatta ya see?'

I stepped over and let him get a look inside.

'Man,' he said. 'This guy's got no stuff.' He turned to me with hopeful eyes and said, 'Can we check the other rooms?'

'I told you we're only opening the door, and I meant it. That's already more than I should have done. He's not here, and I'm not going to risk our friend downstairs getting suspicious about what's taking us so long to figure that out.'

I shut the door to make sure Edgar knew I was serious about this. I never should have opened it to begin with, but no harm was done. I also didn't learn anything about the guy who happened to have the same name as my father.

'Let's go,' I said.

We walked down a flight, and knocked on Buzzer Guy's door. As we waited for him to answer, I heard the front door downstairs open.

'What'd you find out?' Buzzer Guy asked as he came to the door. 'He OK?'

'Not home,' I said. 'We're thinking maybe he just headed out of town without telling anyone, and he's not answering his phone.'

Buzzer Guy shook his head. 'People do all sorts of weird shit, man.' Spoken like a true New York bartender. 'Ain't no crime to disappear for a bit. Fall off the grid, y'know? I feel like doing it myself sometimes.'

Someone was coming up the stairs. I couldn't help but hope it was Robert Donne.

'Thanks again for letting us in,' I said, distracted by the footsteps.

'You want me to tell him to call you if he shows up?'

I hadn't thought of that. 'Yeah,' I said. 'Edgar, you got a card and a pen?'

Edgar reached into his laptop bag and pulled out one of each. I almost wrote my real name on the back of Edgar's business card, but remembered my earlier lie. I wrote the name James Hunter and my cell phone number. Maybe he'd call, maybe he wouldn't. Maybe I'd have to figure out another way to find out who he was. I handed Buzzer Guy the card. The footsteps kept coming.

'Thanks again.'

'No problem, man,' he said. 'I hope everything's cool.'

'Me, too.'

With my back to the stairs, Buzzer Guy looked over my shoulder and said, 'Hey, you're in luck. It's the girlfriend.'

111

I turned and looked into the face of Robert Donne's girlfriend.

She did not look nearly as happy to see me as she had that morning.

Eleven

The three of us now stood outside the building where 'Robert Donne' lived. The clouds had opened up a bit, letting some more sun hit the streets. It was noticeably warmer than when we had arrived less than thirty minutes ago. Edgar and I were by his car, while Mrs Robles paced nervously by the steps of the building.

'Edgar,' I said. 'Why don't you head home? I'll call you later.'

'Shouldn't I wait around to drive you back to your place? I got nothing going on today, Raymond. Really. Nothing.'

I looked over at Maria Robles. Her look of surprise a few minutes ago had transformed into one of confusion mixed with fear. We needed to talk, and I could tell she didn't want to do so in front of Edgar.

'I'll call you later,' I repeated, lowering my voice so Mrs Robles couldn't hear. 'And I can walk home from here.'

Edgar wanted to argue more, but he was learning to read the tone of my voice. He knew I was not going to budge from this position.

'OK,' he said. 'But call me. You promised.'

'I will.' I shook his hand. 'Thanks for all your help today.' I gave a quick glance over at Maria Robles. 'I wouldn't have made these connections – Robert Donne, and now Hector's mother – without you. You did good.'

'Thanks.' The rejection was still in his voice. 'I'll talk to you later.'

As he headed off to his car, I walked over to Mrs Robles.

'There's a pretty decent diner a few blocks from here,' I said. 'Let's go get some coffee and talk.'

She nodded silently and followed me. It was starting to get dark.

'I know it sounds like a cliché,' Maria Robles said. 'But we didn't mean for it to happen. It just kind of did.'

'How did you and Marty meet?' I asked.

'I was doing some temp work at a law firm in Manhattan that he did a lot of business with. I was half reception, half clerical. We'd talk a lot while he waited for my bosses. He could have waited in the other rooms, but he liked to talk. It turned out we were both from Williamsburg. When he found out that I was studying for my real estate license, he paid for the rest of my studies. He called it "an investment."'

I took a sip of coffee. The thought had occurred to me that I was sitting across the table from someone the cops would consider a suspect in a murder investigation. But after considering my talk with her that morning, seeing the obvious distress on her and her son, that didn't seem very likely. But I'd been wrong before.

'How long had he been your landlord?' I asked.

'About five years,' she said. 'That building was my first sale, actually. My family'd been living there for a while when the owner decided he wanted to sell. Marty grew up on that block. When I told him about it, he told the landlord he'd buy the building for the asking price, but only if I brokered the deal. He gave me my start.'

'How long had Marty had the apartment?'

'I'm not sure. Before I met him.'

'And he'd been "Robert J. Donne" for how long?'

'I don't know,' she said. 'It was something he didn't tell his family about obviously. He told me a lot that he sometimes needed to be alone. That apartment was where he'd go.'

'When did the affair begin?' Speaking of things he didn't tell his family about.

She waited before answering that question. That question is one you should wait a bit before answering. It basically comes down to admitting at what time did you decide your marriage – and your family – was worth risking.

'A few years ago,' she began. 'My husband and I had been having problems for a while. He's been out of work for years now. He gets the occasional part-time construction job, but mostly it's me who brings the money into the house.' She wiped her mouth with her napkin. 'That hurt him. He's a proud man. He was a good provider before the economy took a turn.'

'Does he have any idea about you and Marty?'

'No,' she said. 'We've been very . . . discreet. Between temp jobs and the two kids, I have to

115

show apartments at night, mostly. He doesn't like it, but he knows we need the money, so there was not much he could do. Some nights, I would come see Marty.'

'Why were you there today?' I asked.

'I wanted to make sure I'd left nothing behind in the apartment. I thought that someone would find out about his properties and check them out.' She gave me a weird look. 'I thought it would be the police and obviously didn't want them to connect me to him in this way. If my husband ever found out, it would kill him.'

She cringed a little when those words came out of her mouth. Maybe the possibility had just occurred to her that it was not her husband the affair had killed.

I leaned back into the booth to process all of this. Marty Stover was having an affair with the mother of one of my kids. The kid I got involved with Marty's charity. That couldn't have been a coincidence. I thought back to the time when Marty had asked me if I knew of any kids who'd benefit from the work Bridges to Success did. 'Only about a few hundred,' I had told him. It was his idea to pick one from the area he'd grown up in. When I'd told him Hector lived on the same block he'd grown up on, he seemed genuinely surprised and thrilled. Now, if I had to guess, it seemed like he'd known it all along and made me think it was my idea to get Hector involved.

'Marty even helped out with our rent,' Maria Robles said. 'During those months when things were especially tough for us, he let me pay less

116

than what we owed. I do the family bills, so my husband wouldn't know the difference. Some months Marty even told me not to pay anything.' She stopped as her eyes filled with tears. 'My God,' she said. 'I was sleeping with a man who paid my family's rent. I sound like a whore.'

She started crying full out now. Because she thought she sounded like a whore? Because Marty's death was going to affect her family financially? Or maybe, the nicer side of me thought, she actually felt something deeper for Marty. He was a charming guy. He was old enough to be her father, but charming nonetheless. And with him helping out her family, maybe she *had* fallen for him.

I pulled another napkin from the dispenser and handed it to her. I followed that gesture with, 'You don't sound like a whore, Maria. You sound like a mother looking out for her family. Unless you're going to tell me you only had the affair with him because of what he could do for your family?'

'No,' she said with a sharpness I hadn't expected, wiping her eyes with the napkin. 'He was a good man. Maybe I loved him, maybe not. But he was a good man. He helped people. He helped us.'

'Then stop being so hard on yourself,' I said.

She took a couple of deep breaths. 'But what will the police say when they find out? Don't they always look for stuff like this when someone's murdered?'

'Maybe they *won't* find out.'

That seemed to surprise her. 'Aren't you going

to tell them?' she asked. 'Your uncle being who he is, don't you—?'

'I don't have to do – *or say* – anything to my uncle. They're going to find out he owned those buildings, but as far as me telling them about your relationship with Marty, I don't see how that's going to help them solve his murder.' A thought occurred to me. 'You're sure your husband knew nothing about the affair? Jealous husbands make great murder suspects.'

That shook her up a bit. *Good. It was meant to.*

'I don't see how he could know. Like I said, we were very discreet, and I always had a good reason to be out of the house.'

'Then say nothing unless you're asked. The cops may come around and talk to some of Marty's tenants, but they're not going to be looking for a secret lover.'

'So what do I do?'

'Do what you were going to do.' I couldn't quite believe I was saying this. But if the cops did find out about her affair with Marty, they'd be all over the family. I've seen what that can do to families, to husbands and wives. And to their kids. There's no returning to normal after something like that. 'Go back to the apartment. Make sure there's nothing at the place connecting you to Marty.'

'What about the neighbors? The guy you were talking to?'

'Does he know your name?'

She gave that some thought. 'I think he just knows me as the woman who comes by Robert Donne's apartment.'

'Then he doesn't know much and just assumed you were his girlfriend. Hell, he thought Marty's name was Robert Donne. He's not going to be much help besides the fact that he can prove Marty had an apartment his wife and son didn't know about.'

She took a sip of coffee and held the warm cup between her hands.

'I feel like such a bad person,' she said. 'Now that I've admitted it out loud.'

'Murder has a way of making people feel like that,' I said. 'We want to make it go away somehow. We question our involvement and ask ourselves what we could have done differently to change things.'

She put her cup down. 'You sound like you've been there.'

I didn't answer that. I just nodded knowingly. Truth was, I didn't know shit. It just looked like I did sometimes. I knew what almost getting killed felt like. I knew what losing someone close to me felt like. Right now it probably looked like I completely believed that Maria Robles's husband knew nothing about her affair with Marty. Who knew what he knew? What he was capable of?

I finished up my coffee and put five dollars down on the table. As I stood up, I said, 'Go do what you have to do back at the apartment, Maria. Then go home. Be with your family.'

She stood. 'You're not mad at me?'

'It's not my place to be *mad* at you. You and Marty were adults. You did what you did. It could get a lot worse if his wife found out about

119

you. That would be more than she could handle.'
Before I let her off the hook completely, I added,
'This doesn't mean I think it's OK. You've got
two kids at home to think about.'

'I think about them all the time,' she said.
'Believe me.'

'They're your priority right now,' I said.

'They always have been, Mr Donne.'

'I just meant that right now is a real good time
to focus on them. And your husband.'

She thought about that and nodded. 'Thank you.'

'You're welcome,' I said and walked out of the
diner, probably looking for all anyone else knew,
like a guy who thought he knew what he was
talking about.

Twelve

'She was sleeping with the murder victim?'

'Having an affair,' I said. 'Yes.'

'And you're not going to tell the police?'

'Tell them what, exactly? That once again Chief Donne's nephew – who used to be a cop but is now a schoolteacher – was sticking his civilian nose into places it doesn't belong and illegally obtained information their own detectives may or may not have uncovered because a friend of mine accessed the murder victim's computer and I broke into an apartment?'

A pause. 'I can see your point.'

'I thought about not telling *you*.'

'Why did you?'

'Because you're my girlfriend, and I tell you things.'

'But not before you make sure we're talking off the record?'

'About some things, yes. This is one of those things, Allison.'

'This is a *big thing*, Ray. Marty Stover's murder is big news. Him sleeping with – having an affair with – the parent of one of his charity's recipients—'

'Would do serious damage to some innocent people if it came out in the papers.'

'You mean *my* paper?'

'At this point,' I said, 'since you are the only

121

reporter who has knowledge of the affair, yes, I am talking about your paper.'

Allison paused long enough this time for me to think she was going to hang up on me. Part of me wouldn't have blamed her if she had. The other part would've been real pissed, because we'd been over this before. During the past couple of years, due to my getting involved in situations I probably shouldn't have – *probably* – I had become privy to certain sensitive information that Allison could have used to advance her career as a journalist. We almost broke up over it not so long ago, so we had *the talk* and agreed that if we ever found ourselves in a similar situation – which I honestly didn't think would happen again – I'd preface anything I didn't want public by telling her we were 'off the record.' I wondered how many other couples had similar arrangements.

'You still there?' I asked.

'Yes, I'm still here. You think I'm gonna get all pissy and hang up because you're not giving me what I want? Please, Ray. Give me more credit than that.'

I took a breath. 'Sorry, you're right. It's been a long twenty-four hours.'

'Yes,' she said. 'It has. Do you know anything more about a memorial service? I know he was Jewish and they usually like to bury the deceased as soon as possible, right? Like within twenty-four hours?'

'That's how I understand the tradition, but with Marty being a homicide victim, I'm not sure about that time frame. He's going to have to be autopsied. The Office of the Medical Examiner takes precedence over the Old Testament.'

Allison thought about that for a few seconds and said, 'Gee, if only Marty's family knew someone who could expedite the whole process.'

Ha! 'You're right,' I said. 'I should call Uncle Ray.'

'I didn't say you should call your Uncle Ray.'

'No, but I should. I don't know Helaine all that well, but I would think she'd want this done as quickly as possible. Can I call you back after I talk to him?'

'I'm not going anywhere. Either way, we are seeing each other later, right?'

'Absolutely. I'll call you back as soon as I know something.'

I ended the call with Allison and gave myself a mental pat on the back for avoiding another argument with her. Then I called my uncle. He picked up after two rings.

'Nephew,' he said. 'I hope today was less eventful for you than yesterday.'

I told him how I had gone out to the Island to sign some papers for the police.

'Right,' he said. 'I forgot Marty kept your family on as limited partners or some shit. Anything interesting?'

'The exact opposite,' I said, sounding pretty convincing. 'I hadn't been there in years, so I couldn't tell them much and whoever broke in was real neat about it. Came in through an un-alarmed second-floor window and left through the front door.'

Uncle Ray laughed. 'Marty always was a cheap

son of a bitch. What the hell, who breaks into a lawyer's office, right?'

'Somebody was looking for something. I'm just not sure if they found it.'

'Good thing it's not your job to know that stuff, right, Nephew?'

'Right, Uncle Ray.'

He was silent for a bit, and I could make out the sound of traffic. Maybe he was heading back home.

'So why the call?' he asked.

'I wanted to know if you heard anything about a memorial service for Marty. I'm not sure how religious he and Helaine were, so . . . .'

'Religious enough where Helaine called me this morning to ask if I could request a rush job on the autopsy.'

'What good is having the Chief of Detectives as a friend if you can't call in the occasional favor?' He didn't respond, so I went on. 'Were you able to do what she wanted?'

He laughed again. 'Whatta you think, Ray? Of course I was. I even called in one of the best medical examiners we got down there. Not that we needed him, but I figured Marty deserved the best I could get, right? No big mystery. Guy sustained a serious wound to the upper thigh, severing the femoral artery, and he bled to death on a men's room floor. There were no other wounds and – we haven't released this yet – the murderer left the weapon behind.' Another pause as he said something to someone, probably Officer Gray, his driver. 'Actually, he left the weapon in Marty. That's how Marty was able to

124

make it to the men's room without bleeding all over the place. The ME said as soon as he pulled out the blade, that was it. Bled out in less than five minutes.'

'Shit,' I said.

'Big-time. So, anyway, Marty Junior's gonna get back to me about the shiva. It starts sometime tomorrow.'

'What about the burial?'

'Family only,' he said. 'Helaine's a fairly private person, and she doesn't want a big show. Junior said she also didn't want to wait for relatives to travel in from all over the place. They'll do the burial tomorrow morning and then have people back at the house. You ever go to a shiva?'

'Yeah. It's like a wake without the body. I've been to a few.'

'And there's food,' he said. He said something else to the person in the car. 'Anyway, I should know more later. You'll make sure your mom gets there, right?'

'She's with Rachel right now, so I guess so. Allison and I will take the train in the morning.'

'Oh, good. You're bringing a date.'

'She's my girlfriend, Uncle Ray.'

'Just make sure it's your girlfriend you bring and not the reporter.'

If you only knew, Uncle Ray.

'We've already had the talk,' I said. 'It wasn't easy.'

'Like all the other conversations we have with women are? Just wait 'til you get married, Ray. It don't get any better.'

'Mom put you up to that?' I asked.

125

'To what?'

I shook my head. 'Never mind. Call me later, OK?'

'As soon as I know something.'

'Thanks.' I decided to ask one more question. 'What kind of blade was it?'

'Excuse me?'

'What kind of blade did the murderer use?'

Uncle Ray laughed. 'I heard the question, Raymond. I just couldn't believe you were asking it. What the fuck difference does it make to you what kind of blade the murderer used? It was a blade. Sharp enough to penetrate Marty Stover's upper thigh, sever his femoral artery, and cause his death.'

'I was just curious, Uncle Ray.'

'You're never just curious, Nephew.' He laughed again. 'But since it's probably going to bug you – and since the information is going to hit the papers and TV tomorrow anyway – it was a box cutter. Happy now?'

'A box cutter?' I said.

'Yep.'

'Damn. Marty Stover was killed with a box cutter?'

'Why does that surprise you?'

'It doesn't. It's just that they're so easy to come by. Shit, I take a dozen of them away from students every year.' I gave that some thought. The cop part of me was hoping Marty had been killed by a rare, easily traceable knife. 'Did they say what kind of box cutter?'

'There're different kinds?'

'Yeah,' I said. 'Some are the cheapies you can

126

pick up for about two bucks anywhere in the city. Then there're the professional-grade ones the pros use.'

'Professional-grade box cutters? I didn't know that. I got a couple of 'em at home and keep one in the glove compartment of the car.'

'You probably have the cheap ones. No offense.'

He laughed. 'I'm a little more thick-skinned than that, Raymond.' He was silent for a bit and then said, 'Hey, didn't you have a kid involved in Marty's charity?'

'Hector, yeah,' I said. 'I was over there this morning. He was upset about Marty, and his mother called me. I ended up walking Hector over to the Sterns' building – that's where he works – because—'

'Because you just can't stand not getting involved. Do I have to stick your teaching degree in your face again, Raymond?'

'I was there because I *am* a teacher, Uncle Ray. He's my kid. I got him involved with Marty.' *Who, by the way, was sleeping with my student's mother.* 'All I did was get Hector to his job. I met Joshua Stern and then left. The whole thing was uneventful.'

'Make sure it stays that way.'

'I will.'

I heard cars beeping on the other end of the phone. Through my cell, they sounded like my uncle was riding with a bad orchestra.

'I gotta go, Raymond,' he said. 'I'll call you later when I hear from Junior or Helaine about tomorrow.'

127

'Thanks, Uncle Ray.'

He hung up without saying good-bye. Maybe he was thinking that some of the people involved in Marty's charity worked at or owned an art supply store where box cutters – cheap ones and professional ones – were sold and used. Maybe he was thinking about one of the cardinal rules of being a detective: *There are very few coincidences.*

I know I was.

Thirteen

'I will never get tired of this view.'

I stepped over to my girlfriend, wrapped my arms around her waist, kissed the back of her neck and said, 'Neither will I.'

Both my thighs got slapped. 'I was talking about the skyline, Ray.'

'What did you think *I* was talking about?'

She turned and pulled me into a deep kiss. Until she had, I was unaware of how much I needed it. We kissed like that for about a minute before we stopped.

'But if you wanna go any further,' she said, 'you're going to have to buy me dinner. I may be many things, but a cheap date is not one of them.'

'That's why I asked you over, Ally,' I said. 'We can order in Italian, Chinese . . . .'

'Or you can take me to the new Polish place that just opened.'

'*Or*,' I said, 'I can take you to the new Polish place that just opened.'

She looked at me and grinned, and then she kissed me again. When she was done, she said, 'See what happens when you listen to your girlfriend?'

'I think there was a little something in there for you, too. Girlfriend.'

She held her index finger an inch away from her thumb. 'Maybe a little.'

'I told you about that gesture, Ally. No man with any Irish in him likes it.'

This time, she slapped me in the middle of my chest. 'That's the least of your worries, tough guy. Put your coat on. I need me some pork roast, pickled beets, and pierogies. And some good Polish beer.'

As I opened the closet to get my jacket, my cell phone rang. I was about to let it go to voice mail when I saw it was my uncle.

'That was quick,' I said.

'I hope your girlfriend never says that.'

Deep down, under the gold badge, stripes and blue uniform he wore with great pride, my uncle was sometimes just an immature frat boy at heart.

'You call to make fun of my sexual skills, or was there another reason?'

'Oh, excuse me, Nephew. No time for banter? I assume that means the girlfriend in question is in the room?'

'You are good, Uncle Ray.'

'You don't even know the half of it, son. The Stovers are having people over tomorrow at two. Like I said: the burial's going to be quick, Jewish, and private.' He paused for a few seconds. 'Are we supposed to bring anything to this . . . shiva?'

'I don't know,' I said. 'I'll ask Mom. She may be Catholic, but she knows all the etiquette stuff.'

'How you getting out there?'

'Ally and I are going to take the train. Rachel'll pick us up at the station.'

'Don't be stupid,' he said. I'd heard those words from him many times. 'I'll have Officer Gray pick you up.'

'You don't have to do that, we can—'

'Of course I don't *have to,* Raymond. I want to. He's gotta come out and drive me around anyway. He might as well swing by your place and get you and Allison.' He thought about that for a second. 'You are at your place, right?'

'Yeah,' I said, 'but really . . .'

'He'll swing by and get you around one. It'll give you guys time to reminisce about your little walk around the crime scene, maybe talk about me a little.'

'You sure you want that?'

'I'll see you tomorrow, Nephew.'

When I put my phone back in my pocket, Allison asked, 'What was that about?'

'Looks like we got a ride out to the Island tomorrow.'

'On the taxpayers' dime, I suppose?'

I stepped over and kissed her. 'You know what it's like when dealing with my uncle, Allison. Don't ask too many questions.'

She put her hands on my lower back, pulled me closer and whispered in my ear. 'I've got a question for you.'

I kissed her neck. 'The answer's yes.'

With our entrees finished, Allison and I split something she ordered that looked and tasted like Polish baklava. It was crunchy and sweet and went very well with the beer we were both drinking. This new place was going to be a nice addition to the neighborhood for a long time. At least until the tourists found it.

131

'So,' Allison said, 'you've had a busier day than expected.'

'That's one way of putting it I guess.'

She raised her thumb. 'Someone breaks into Marty Stover's law office hours after he's murdered and nothing seems to have been taken.' Index finger. 'You find out Marty's been keeping a secret apartment using your father's name.' Middle finger. 'And to top it off, he's been carrying on an affair with the mother of one of your students. What kind of day would you call that, Ray?' She closed her hand.

'I suppose busy is the right word.'

'I'm a reporter. I only use the right words.' She took a sip of beer. 'It all makes me quite curious about what tomorrow's going to bring.'

'A nice boring shiva, I hope. We'll eat some deli, drink some Manischewitz, extend our condolences to Marty's family, and be back in the city for dinner.'

'You don't want to take Monday off? Visit with your mom a bit?'

I smiled. 'As nice as that sounds,' I said, 'I do have a suspension hearing to be at Monday morning and there's a school safety meeting after lunch.'

She shook her head. 'Your uncle's right about one thing, Ray.'

'What's that?'

'You never could fully give it up. Listen to you. You sound like a cop more and more these days. Suspension hearings. Safety meetings.'

'I'm a dean now, Ally. Those things come with the job.'

132

'And you love it, don't you?'

'For the most part, yeah,' I said. 'I miss the classroom every once in a while, but I'm working with the kids who need it. I'm getting to them before the cops do.'

She leaned back with her beer. 'You're the cop of the building, Ray. Admit it. You turned your gun and blues in for a walkie-talkie and blue jeans.'

'I took the job because the old guy retired and my boss asked me.'

'You took the job because it was so much like your old one,' she said. 'There's nothing wrong with that.' She took a sip. 'There *might* be something wrong with doing what you did this afternoon and checking out Marty's secret love nest.'

'I didn't know that's what it was.'

'But you couldn't resist the trip.'

'Hey. There was someone living in that apartment with my father's name. Tell me you wouldn't have done the same thing.'

'I wouldn't have had my friend access a murder victim's computer in order to get that information.'

'I never asked Edgar to do that. He did it on his own, and I told him how much trouble he could have caused for the both of us.'

'Before or after you used the illegally obtained information? Before or after you used a lock pick to open the apartment door?'

As gorgeous as I think my girlfriend is, she gets considerably less attractive when she puts that smug look on her face. It was there now. The look that said, *'I gotcha, tough guy.'*

133

And she did. We both knew it. I stayed shut for a while, trying to think of some clever thing to say. Nothing good was coming to mind, so after about fifteen seconds, I said, 'You're paying for dinner.'

'That's not fair,' she said. 'I'm right *and* I have to foot the bill?'

'Think about that the next time you want to be right.'

She laughed. 'You're lucky you're cute.'

'Yeah,' I said. 'It helps me in all situations. And I want another beer.'

The smirk turned back to a smile, and she was gorgeous again.

'Here,' she said, 'or do you wanna head back to your place?'

The thought of going back to my place with a six-pack and Allison sounded real good at that moment. I told her that just as my cell phone rang. I looked at the Caller ID; it was Edgar. His sense of timing would have to be put on his list of things to work on. I knew I'd better pick up, though, because if I didn't, he'd be calling all night.

'Hold that thought,' I said to Allison. Then into the phone, I said, 'This better be good, Edgar. It's been a long day.'

There was a brief pause on the other end, then, 'Raymond Donne?'

It was not Edgar's voice. 'Yes?'

'This is Doctor Gerena.' He told me where he was calling from, but it didn't quite register. 'Mr Donne?'

'Yes,' I said, obviously with enough concern

in my voice that it got Allison's attention. 'Yes. Is everything OK? Where's Edgar?'

'He's with my assistant at the moment. He said you were his emergency contact. Is that correct?'

'Yes, yes it is. Where are you calling from again?'

'City Doctor,' he said. 'We're on North Seventh.'

That was one of the new walk-in clinics that had been popping up all over the city the past few years. I stood up as I spoke. 'I know where that is.' I motioned to Allison to take care of the bill as I stepped over to the door. 'What happened to Edgar?'

'In layman's terms,' Dr Gerena said, 'he was . . . knocked out. I'm not comfortable giving out too many details over the phone. I recommended that he take an ambulance to Woodhull Hospital, but he refused. He insisted that I call you.'

Then he couldn't be too badly hurt, I thought. Woodhull is where you went when the choice wasn't yours. I've heard some of the locals refer to it as 'Wood Hell.'

'I'll be right there,' I said. 'Thank you.'

I hung up just as Ally came to the door. 'What happened?'

'I don't know. Edgar's been in some kind of accident.' I led her through the doors out on to Manhattan Avenue. It was still busy just after dinnertime on a Saturday night. 'That was the clinic on the Northside. I have to go get him.'

'I'm going with you.'

'I don't know if that's a good idea, Ally. He's still getting used to us as a couple.'

'Well, he's my friend, too,' she said.

135

She sounded just like I did when Uncle Ray teased me a few hours ago. I grabbed her by the hand and we headed off to the car service around the corner.

We pulled up in front of the clinic a little more than five minutes later. Normally, we would have walked such a short distance, but this was not a normal situation. I gave the driver a ten as I opened the passenger door and raced to the clinic door where I was met on the other side by a Hispanic doctor about my age. He was wearing the usual doctor's white coat, a stethoscope around his neck, and the look of a man who'd put in a few more hours that day than he'd planned on.

'Mr Donne?' he said.

'Yes. Where's Edgar?'

'He'll be right out.' He looked over my shoulder as Allison entered the clinic. 'I'm sorry, ma'am,' he said. 'We need to—'

'I'm with him,' she said. 'The hours on your door say you close at six on Saturdays. How long has Edgar been here?'

Dr Gerena laughed. 'The hours on the door don't quite represent the hours we keep. Especially on a Saturday. Your friend – Mr O'Brien – was brought in about thirty minutes ago by a good Samaritan. A livery driver, I believe. He was found sitting outside McCarren Park on the sidewalk. His speech was impaired and his vision was blurry. He's lucky the driver didn't think he was just drunk.'

'What did Edgar say happened?' I asked.

'He didn't say much. The most I got out of him was that he was knocked down and may have lost consciousness for a short period of time. He was quite disoriented.'

'Was he mugged?'

'He didn't come right out and say it,' the doctor said, 'but the nature of the wounds would lead me to believe he was, except . . .'

'Except what?'

'He had one pocket with about fifty dollars cash and his driver's license – no wallet – and another with his cell phone. No credit cards.'

'Edgar doesn't believe in them. Too much risk of identity theft.'

If the doctor thought that was odd, he kept it to himself. 'Well, then, if it was a mugging, it was a pretty bad one.'

'Did he have his laptop?' I asked.

'Not on him, no. Why?'

'That means he was mugged. He never goes anywhere without his laptop.'

'Well, you can ask him about that when you see him.'

'When *can* I see him?'

'My assistant is attending to his wounds now,' Dr Gerena said. 'We checked for all the usual symptoms of a concussion and broken bones, but we think he was pretty lucky in that regard. About as lucky as you can get when you've been mugged, I guess. He's sustained a few minor bruises, but other than that, he seems OK. To be on the safe side, though, if you can convince him to go to the hospital, a series of x-rays would put my mind at ease about the concussion.'

'He won't go for that if he's conscious,' I said. 'He hates the attention and all the bells and whistles. If it's your professional opinion that he's OK to go home, that's the best place for him.'

The doctor gave that some thought. 'I'm not OK with that,' he said. 'Legally, I can't force him to go. I will need your help filling out some forms and . . .'

Something stopped him. It took me a little while to figure out what it was.

'You need to get paid,' I said.

'It's the clinic, really. I'm not used to this end of the business.'

I reached into my own wallet-less pocket and pulled out the credit card I had planned to buy dinner with. I handed it to the doctor, who genuinely seemed to be uncomfortable taking it.

'We let the receptionist go at six,' he explained. 'The company frowns on overtime, at least for the per-hour employees. We all wear a lot of hats around this place.' He turned around, grabbed a clipboard off the counter and handed it to me with instructions to fill it out the best I could. 'I'll just run the card,' he said, stepping around the counter. 'If Mr O'Brien has insurance, they'll reimburse you for this, Mr Donne.'

'He works for the MTA. I'll worry about getting reimbursed some other time.'

He smiled and pointed the card at me. 'You're a good friend.'

'So's Edgar,' I said.

'Hey, that's my name.'

138

I looked over as Edgar came through a set of doors escorted by a woman in blue scrubs. He had a bandage above his left eye and walked over to me with a slight limp. Allison joined us. She put her arm on his shoulder. He surprised me by accepting it for the kind gesture it was and not as unwanted physical contact.

'How're you doing, buddy?' I said. 'The doc here says you took quite a fall.'

'With some help, yeah,' Edgar said. 'Guy ran up from behind me, grabbed my laptop bag, spun me around like a top right into the metal fence outside the park. Next thing I knew, some guy was shaking me. I thought it was a bad dream.' He closed his eyes and added, 'You gonna take me home, Ray?'

I looked over at the doctor. 'He thinks I should take you for some x-rays. Would you be willing to do that?'

His eyes popped open, frightened. 'No.' He said that clearly enough. 'You know I hate that kinda stuff.'

'I had to ask.'

'Edgar,' Allison said. 'Are you sure you don't—'

'I'm sure, Allison. I just wanna go home.'

Allison looked as if she wanted to push the point but decided against it. She'd had enough conversations with Edgar to know where this one would end up and the energy it would take to get there.

'OK,' she said. 'Home it is.'

The doctor touched me on the arm and handed me back my credit card and a copy of the paperwork without Edgar noticing. I slipped it all into my back jeans pocket and said, 'Then if we're done here . . .'

'We are,' Edgar said. He turned to the doctor and said, 'Thank you,' and then said the same to the doctor's assistant. 'You are both very good at what you do.'

The assistant gave us a tired smile, raised her hand to wave good-bye, and then disappeared through the same doors she'd come in through. Dr Gerena stuck his hand out to our small group. We all shook it.

'We're open tomorrow at nine,' he said, 'if anything bothers you more than it should, Mr O'Brien.'

'You'll be the first to know,' Edgar said and then added, 'Actually, *I'll* be the *first* to know, I guess. Then I'll call you.'

Not sure if that was a joke, the doctor just smiled and said, 'Take some ibuprofen if you start to feel achy tonight.'

We said our good-byes, got ourselves another car service, and were at Edgar's apartment ten minutes later. Safe, and a little sounder.

Fourteen

'My god,' Allison said standing in the middle of Edgar's basement apartment living room for the first time. 'It's like living in a mini Best Buy.'

'He's a man who likes his stuff,' I said.

The 'stuff' in his living room consisted of two big-screen, high-definition TVs, a Blu-ray *and* a DVD player, a desktop computer with something he called 'The Tower' next to it, a pair of top-of-the-line, three-foot-high speakers – and some smaller speakers built into the wall – that could be used with all the devices in the room.

'I like stuff, too,' she said, 'but *two* TVs?'

'One's just for sports,' I said, as if that made perfect sense.

She shook her head, again unwilling to put in the energy. The doorbell rang and Edgar shouted from the bathroom, where he was changing into sweats. 'Pizza's here!'

I climbed the stairs, paid the delivery guy, and brought the pizza to the coffee table in front of the couch.

'Does he have plates?' Allison asked, her sarcasm duly noted.

'Of course he has plates,' I said, pretty sure I was right. The last time I was here, we also had pizza and ate off of paper plates. I went into the kitchen, and after opening three cabinets I came across Edgar's plates. None of them matched, but that was OK, because we only needed one at the moment, even though after that big meal I'd just had, the pizza smelled pretty good. I grabbed three glasses – they did match – and brought everything into the living room. What Edgar saved on dishware, he spent on his technology.

'Should I leave you two alone?' Allison asked. 'He seemed a little uncomfortable next to me in the car over here.'

'I don't know. Let's see how he feels after eating. After what the doctor said, I can stay the night if he wants, and you can head back to my place. I know it's not what we planned, but . . . .'

'I'm not that high-maintenance, Ray. Your friend needs you, you do what you have to do.' She kissed me on the cheek. 'That's one of the things I love about you.'

I was about to give her a kiss back – not on the cheek – when Edgar entered the room not-so-subtly clearing his throat. He looked down at the pizza and said, 'Great! I'm starving.' After sitting on the couch, he seemed to be very aware of his leg. 'I heard getting injured makes you hungry.'

'You've never been injured before?' Allison asked.

'I'm a nerd,' he said as if that explained all. 'And I'm very careful at work. I've got enough sick days in my bank to take a year off if I want. But I don't want to because I'm gonna get paid for those days when I put in my papers.'

'You sure picked a hell of a way to pop your cherry, Edgar.'

142

Edgar looked up from the couch, confused by Allison's comment.

'She means,' I said, 'your first injury was a real doozy.'

He waited a few moments, processed that, and said, 'Yeah. I guess I did.' He looked at the box of pizza. 'You guys sure you don't wanna eat?'

'We're stuffed,' I said. I picked up one of the glasses. 'What do you want to drink? Some water?'

He opened the box of pizza, disconnected a slice from its brothers, and slid it on to his plate. 'There's a six pack of Bass in the fridge,' he said. 'You know how I like it.'

I did, because I'd been serving him Bass and tomato juice at The LineUp for quite a few years now. I picked up all the glasses, went into the kitchen and put his drink together. I also took the liberty of opening a second bottle and splitting it between the two other glasses. When I got back to the living room, Allison was sitting on the opposite end of the couch and Edgar was almost through with his first slice of pizza. I handed them both their drinks and sat down midway between them. Allison said, 'You sure alcohol's a good idea right now, Edgar?'

He either didn't understand the question or chose to ignore it. My guess was the former. As for me, I both understood it and ignored it. Edgar took a long sip and then grabbed another slice. The aroma of the pizza was tempting me to do the same.

'You know,' Edgar said between bites. 'One thing I didn't tell the doctor.'

143

'What's that?' I asked.

'When I went out for my walk before, as soon as I left the house, I had the weird feeling I was being followed.'

I leaned forward. 'What do you mean "followed"?'

He shrugged. 'I don't know, really. I'm not sure I've ever been followed before.' He turned to Allison. 'Ray and I have followed people before, you know.'

Allison gave Edgar a half-smile/half-grimace. She didn't find the stories of my previous exploits with Edgar quite as exciting as Edgar did. 'I know,' she said. 'But tell us about this feeling you had.' She was using her reporter voice now.

'When I left the apartment,' he said, 'the street was empty, but when I got to the corner, I thought I heard someone behind me. So I turned around but didn't see anyone, so I kept going.' He took another bite and another sip. 'When I got about a block from the park, I had to stop and tie my shoe. Then I was sure I heard someone behind me. I looked back and no one was there, just a couple going the other way. There were a lot of cars parked on the street so I figured maybe whoever it was ducked behind one of them. Then I just figured my imagination was getting the best of me.' He looked at me. 'Ray and I had quite an eventful day.'

'So I've heard,' Allison said. 'Did you go back and look?'

He shook his head. 'Nope. I was too jumpy at that point and felt kinda dumb getting all worked up like that. I guess now maybe I should have, huh?'

'No,' I said. 'Because if someone was following you and you got face-to-face with that person, you might have been hurt worse than you were.'

He squinted. Thinking hard. 'So you think someone *was* following me?'

'If you had that feeling, Edgar, and then you end up getting mugged? Yeah, I think it's a good bet someone was following you.'

'But why?' he asked. 'Why would – oh, for my laptop.'

'That's the logical answer,' I said.

'That's a long way to go for a lousy laptop.'

'*Lousy?*' I asked. 'When did you ever refer to computer equipment as "lousy"?'

'That's because I was carrying my old one, Ray. I just upgraded – again – and this one was from before my *last* upgrade. It's the one I bring to the bar and work. I don't really care – too much – if something happens to it 'cause I just use it now for getting on the Internet and taking notes.'

'So,' Allison said, 'a few hours ago, you had three laptops?'

'Yeah,' he said, like, *Doesn't everyone?*

'So,' I said, 'if you're right and you were being followed, it could have been someone who knew where you lived and that you usually carried a laptop.'

We all thought about that for a bit. Edgar said, 'Like a neighbor or something?'

That didn't sound right. Maybe he was just imagining he was being followed and the

145

mugging was a coincidence. That didn't sound right either. Then what? I thought back to our day together: going out to Marty Stover's office and then to the apartment he lived in under my father's name. I closed my eyes and pictured Edgar at both places.

'You had your laptop with you all day today, right?' I asked.

'Yeah,' he said. 'But not the one that was stolen. I had my second one.'

'Not the newest?' Allison asked.

'No,' he said, using the tone he puts on when another – non-technophile – adult doesn't get what he's saying. 'My *second* one.'

'So the one you put the flash drive on today – the one you uploaded Marty's files on to – that's still here?' I asked.

'In the other room. Why?'

We were all silent again until Allison slapped me on the thigh. Hard.

'You think whoever attacked Edgar tonight was after the computer Edgar used today,' she said.

'I'm thinking that's a possibility, yeah,' I said, rubbing my thigh.

'If that's true,' Edgar said, 'then that someone thinks I have something important on my laptop. Something I picked up from Marty's.'

'It's possible,' I repeated.

Edgar stood up, way too fast. He swayed a bit before speaking. 'Then we need to go through all the files I downloaded and see what's on them.'

I got up and eased him back down. 'You're not doing anything yet except eating and resting,'

146

said the overprotective mother in me. 'If that's true, that the person who mugged you did so to see if you got anything from Marty's, they're not going to find anything, right?'

'Right,' he said.

'So, we're good.' *For now,* I almost added. 'Besides, you said Marty had a few decades' worth of stuff on his computer. You're in no shape to spend however many hours it'll take to come close to figuring out what's on there that may or may not be important.'

He looked hurt. Not injured. *Hurt.*

'I'm pretty good at this, Ray.'

'You're the best, Edgar. Just not right now, OK?'

He answered me by stuffing the rest of his pizza slice in his mouth and chewing. It was his way of ignoring me. After he swallowed it, he finished his beer in two gulps and sat back.

'Maybe I should go,' Allison said as she stood. 'You guys can hang out.' She looked at the wall. 'Watch a game or movie or something, and we can hook up in the morning.'

As much as I wanted to spend the night with her, Allison had hit on a pretty good idea. For his safety – both medical and security-wise – I knew Edgar could use a roommate at the moment. I stood, reached into my pocket, and pulled out my cell.

'I'll call a car,' I said. 'And you stay at my place tonight. That way Uncle Ray's guy doesn't have to make two stops.'

'Sounds like a plan,' she said. She turned to Edgar. 'You make sure you get plenty of rest.

And don't go playing PI on your computer tonight.'

I touched her on the elbow. 'I got him, Allison.'

She looked me in the eyes and said, 'That doesn't necessarily reassure me, Ray.'

I looked into hers and said, 'Let's get that car, huh?'

'I hope I didn't get you into any trouble with Allison, Ray.'

'It's OK, Edgar. Just a little leftover tension from a previous conversation.' I saw the confusion in his face and added, 'She's pissed that I asked her not to tell anyone at her paper about Marty's affair with Maria Robles.'

He nodded. 'Yeah, that wouldn't be good. Gossip's not gonna help the case.'

'I hope that's all it is – gossip.' When I heard those words come out of my mouth, I knew I was second-guessing myself about keeping that information from the cops.

Edgar was about to say something, but thought better about it. Another skill he'd been working on with some success. Instead, he said, 'Whatta you wanna watch?'

I smiled. 'Something loud with lots of explosions and crappy dialogue. Something that doesn't require me to think too much.'

He grabbed the remote off the coffee table and pressed a series of buttons.

'I know just the movie,' he said.

It turned out he did, but we were both asleep on his couch before the ending.

Fifteen

In the morning – the late morning – I ran out to the bagel place and came back with breakfast for Edgar and me. This included two very large coffees. We ate in the living room with the TV on mute playing the local sports channel. We ate and watched last night's silent highlights of the Mets' and Yankees' pre-season games.

'Hard to believe the season starts in a few weeks, huh?' Edgar said.

'First sign of spring,' I agreed. You can keep your robins. Just tell me when pitchers and catchers report, and I can smell the vernal equinox in the air.

'You going to the memorial today?'

'To the house,' I said. 'There's no memorial, and the burial's private.'

'Can I come?'

'Why would you want to do that, Edgar? You didn't know Marty Stover.'

'Just thought it would be interesting,' he said. 'I've never been to a shiva.'

What he really wanted was to be around what he considered 'the case.' Maybe he felt that last night's attack earned him a place at the table. Maybe he was right. But that didn't mean I was going to take him to a stranger's shiva.

'You need to rest,' I said. Before he could protest, I said, 'And maybe you can go over

149

some of Marty's files you downloaded. See if you can find anything someone might consider worth stealing.'

He thought about that. 'You sure you're not just giving me busy work, Ray? Like I'm one of your students who needs to be kept out of trouble.'

He *was* learning.

'I know it's kind of like looking for a needle in a virtual haystack, Edgar, but if anyone can do it, it's you.'

'And now you do that thing where you flatter me. If you don't want me to go, Ray, just say so.'

'I don't want you to go. But I also want you to rest and take care of yourself, and there's no better way for you to do that than to pore over files looking for evidence.'

That made him smile. He took a bit of his cinnamon raisin bagel and a sip of coffee. 'I guess I'll work backwards. Chronologically, I mean. Most recent cases first, then the ones before that.'

'Sounds like a plan. But don't do too much.' Another thought occurred to me. 'And don't answer the door for anyone. If you were followed last night, the guy's still out there. If your vision starts to get blurry or you get a headache, give yourself a break.'

He'd spend the whole day going through those files no matter what. The only thing that would stop him would be a dead battery coupled with a blackout. Even then I couldn't be sure he didn't have a back-up generator

150

somewhere around the apartment. Before he could argue with me, my cell rang. I didn't recognize the number.

'Hello?'

'Mr Donne,' a young man's voice said.

'Yes?'

'This is CJ. Officer Gray. From the other day at The Tippler.'

I almost laughed. 'I remember you, CJ. How're you?'

'I'm good, sir. I'm supposed to pick you and Ms Rogers up at your place at one o'clock.' He recited my address. 'Do I have that right, sir?'

'Lose the "sir," CJ,' I said. 'It's Ray. And yes, you've got that right. You sure you don't mind picking us up? We can take the train. I feel kinda funny having you—'

'Chief's orders, sir. I mean Ray. And I'd feel even funnier *not* picking you up after the Chief's orders, if you catch my drift.'

'I gotcha, CJ. We'll be ready at one. Just call when you're downstairs.'

'That's a four, Ray.' That's a yes in cop-talk. He hung up without saying good-bye. I wondered if he learned that technique from my uncle.

I put the phone in my pocket but not before checking the time. 'If you're sure you're OK,' I said, 'I should probably get back to my place.'

'I'm good. What time are you getting back tonight?'

'Probably after dinner. Why?'

'In case I find something, I wanna call you.'

Whatever else I could say about Edgar, the guy was nothing if not optimistic.

151

'How about I call you?' I said. 'As soon as I get back.'

He nodded. 'That'll work.'

I grabbed my jacket and looked at the remains of my breakfast on Edgar's coffee table. I was leaving him with a small mess, but it would give him something physical to do before planting himself in front of his computer screen for the rest of the day.

'Later,' I said.

'Don't forget to call me.'

This was the second day in a row I was in a car headed east to the suburbs of Nassau County. Again, the traffic was light, but this time the ride was much more comfortable, as we were in my uncle's department-issued town car and someone else was doing the driving. I felt a little guilty enjoying the perks of Uncle Ray's position, but as Allison snuggled up next to me, the guilt seemed very far away.

'And you felt OK leaving him there by himself?' she asked. 'I mean not just his health, but what if he *was* followed?'

I answered her in a low voice, reminding her that what Edgar was spending the day in the safety of his apartment doing was the result of an illegal download and that the car we were riding in was being driven by one of New York's Finest.

'He'll be fine,' I said. 'He has enough food in the fridge for a few days and he's got his computers.' Before she could ask, I added, 'And he's got the number to the clinic, and there's a few car services minutes away. He also knows how to dial nine-one-one.' I patted her thigh. 'He's good.'

'I hope so,' she said. 'He seemed so . . . fragile last night.'

'He's always fragile. This time it's physical. It's like a kid getting into his first fight. Whatever doesn't kill you . . .'

'Jesus,' she said. 'Sometimes you sound so, I don't know, *male*. Do all guys think like you do?'

'Most of them, I guess.' I motioned with my head to our driver. 'I know most cops do. Every day is another opportunity to test yourself. You never know what's coming, so you never know how that test will present itself. *If* it will present itself.'

She shook her head. 'Doesn't sound like a healthy way to live.'

'It's not,' I agreed. 'But you learn how to live with it, or you don't last too long.'

'The same can be said about a lot of cops' marriages.'

'That's true.' I turned my head and raised my voice. 'Hey, CJ?'

'Sir?'

Again with the sir. I'd correct him later. 'You have a girlfriend?'

He waited before answering. 'Not at the moment.'

'But you had one recently?' Allison asked.

Gray turned his head just enough to give a look that said *How did you know that*? Then he said, 'We broke up just before I entered the academy, ma'am. Last year.'

153

'It's Allison,' she said. 'You mind me asking what happened?'

Again, a pause before he answered. 'She didn't like the idea of me being a cop. We were in our senior year of college together. I was less than a year away from graduating with an accounting degree when the NYPD called me up. It's not like I could ask the police academy to wait a year, you know?'

'So,' Allison said, 'she thought she was getting an accountant and ended up getting a cop? I can see how that would be hard for her to wrap her mind around.'

'Hard for both of us,' he said. 'If the cops had waited another year, I'm not sure what my choice would've been.'

'What do you think about your choice now?'

Damn, she was pushing it. I almost said something, but Gray beat me to it.

'I like the camaraderie, I guess. The feeling of being part of something bigger than myself.' He paused for a few seconds. 'I obviously never saw myself in this position, though. You know, driving the Chief around. Being his' – he didn't want to say *boy* – 'his assistant. But it's a step in the right direction.'

'And your ex?'

'That's enough,' I said. 'Leave the guy alone, Allison.'

'It's OK,' Gray said. He changed lanes and said, 'I miss her. We still keep in touch with emails and texts. I'm hoping she comes around to my way of thinking.'

154

'And she's hoping you'll come around to hers,' Allison said.

'You're probably right about that, ma'am. Allison.' Gray signaled again and took the exit ramp. 'Chief Donne said to drop you two off first. Then, I'm to pick up him and his wife. They're not too far from here.'

To Allison's credit, she took the cue from Gray that the conversation was over.

There were a lot of cars parked on Marty's street when Officer Gray dropped us in front of the Stover house. As he pulled away, I noticed a couple of men standing in the driveway, smoking. They each had a cigarette in one hand and a longneck beer in the other. Both of them looked as if they couldn't wait to get out of there and out of those suits. The shorter of the two made a swinging motion with his beer hand that made me think their current discussion revolved around golf.

Across the street, there was another guy standing outside a car; he was also smoking, but without a beer. He looked to be about my age, maybe a little older. He was wearing a white shirt and dress pants, no tie or jacket, but appeared untouched by the late-March chill. He didn't strike me as a driver waiting for his client, and the car he leaned against wasn't nearly as classy as the one we'd just been in. After looking at him for a bit, my curiosity got the better of me. I knew it was going to bug me if I let it go, so I headed over to him.

Allison grabbed me by the hand and said, 'What are you doing?'

'Introducing myself. You can go on inside if you want.'

'Not without you, I'm not.'

As we approached the guy, he gave me a quizzical look. He dropped his smoke to the street, stepped on it, and put his hands in his pants pockets. I offered him mine.

'Raymond Donne,' I said. He kept his hands where they were. 'Do we know each other? You look familiar.' He didn't, but it was always a good way to get someone to talk, or at least consider talking.

He stayed quiet for a five-count and said, 'You're the lawyer's kid, right?'

'Robert Donne was my father, yes. This is my girlfriend, Allison.'

They nodded at each other.

'You knew my dad?' I asked.

'Kinda,' he said. 'I'm Chris Miller.' When I didn't respond, he added, '*Melissa* Miller's brother?'

Why did that name— *Oh, shit*. The girl Billy Taylor was convicted of assaulting. The general public didn't know her name – back then the papers still did a good job of keeping the names of victims out of their stories – but my father had let it slip once at the dinner table, and after that he mentioned her a few times following the conviction. Again, it was primarily Marty's case, but my dad was there throughout and helped out when Marty needed an extra hand. What was her brother doing outside the house of the lawyer who defended his sister's attacker?

'You're wondering why I'm here, right?' he asked.

'I was wondering exactly that. Yes.' I turned to Allison. 'Chris's sister was the girl Billy Taylor was convicted of assaulting.'

He looked over at the house and took a few deep breaths. I could feel Allison do the same as she tightened her grip on my hand. Was there about to be trouble?

'Mr Stover treated my sister with respect,' Chris said. 'I was there when they took her deposition. She was real nervous and she wanted me there. We were – we *are* – close, and she wanted someone from the family with her, even if it was hcr younger brother. She knew our mother and father couldn't stand to hear the details, so I went. He never once asked a question that made it sound like what had happened was her fault.'

'Marty was a good man,' I said, feeling Allison's hand relax.

'He was. And then when he was able to get a confession out of . . .' He swallowed hard. This was still pretty raw for him even all these years later. How could it not be? If someone had sexually assaulted my sister, the anger would never fade. 'When he got Billy Taylor to admit to what he'd done, it meant my sister didn't have to take the stand and testify to what had happened to her. He saved my family a lot of . . . I don't know. Grief?'

He took out another cigarette and lit it. I looked at his feet. According to the crushed ones on the street, this would be his fourth.

'How long have you been standing out here?'
I asked.

'Half an hour, I guess. Maybe more.' He slipped
his lighter back into his pocket. 'I was about to go
in when I saw the Taylor brothers show up. They
got dropped off by a fancy town car, too. I wanted
to pay my respects to Mrs Stover, but there's no
way I can be in the same room as those guys.'

'I don't blame you,' Allison said. 'How is your
sister doing?'

Chris shook his head and took a long drag from
his cigarette. He let the smoke out about as slow
as humanly possible.

'She never went to college like she'd planned,'
he said. 'After the confession and the case was
over, we kind of felt that maybe things would
get back to normal, you know? That we'd all
get a new start.' He stared down at the cigarette
burning in his hand. 'People talk about closure
in these kinds of things, but there isn't any. Not
really. Not for the victim.'

Allison stepped forward. 'And not for the
family of the victim, either.'

Chris gave her a look and said, 'You a therapist
or something?'

'Worse,' I said. 'She's a reporter.'

That got a small grin from Chris. 'Really?
For who?'

Allison told him. She also reached into her
pocket and pulled out a business card. You got
to hand it to the girl: she was always prepared.
Chris looked at the card as if Allison had just
offered him a sharp knife. Before I could stop
her, she spoke again.

158

'What's your sister doing now?' she asked.

'Why?' His tone was more wary, now that he knew what she did for a living. I didn't blame him.

Allison couldn't help but put on her professional voice. 'I've always been very interested in what happens to survivors of sexual assault. And their loved ones.'

He squinted. 'For a story or something?'

'Possibly,' she said.

Chris considered that as he took another drag from his cigarette. The idea didn't seem to be sitting too well with him. He had just told us how much it meant that the Millers hadn't had to go through a trial. Why would he, or his sister, want to talk to a reporter two decades later? I was about to say something, when he beat me to it.

'I don't know, Ms Rogers, was it? Melissa's done a lot of work putting her life back together. I know it was over twenty years ago, but it doesn't seem like that to us. To her. She still has nightmares about that night.'

Allison nodded. 'That's part of why I'd like her to consider telling her story. A lot of people think after twenty years these victims should be over it. I've got an old friend from college who was date raped, and it took her years to recover to the point where she was able to go back and get her degree.'

She had never told me about that old friend from college.

Chris nodded. 'It's like that with Melissa. She never went to college.' He paused for a second.

159

'Well, she never made it out of her first semester. It was too much for her. All those guys, all the parties she couldn't bring herself to go to.'

'What's her life like now?' I asked.

'She took an online program in proofreading and copy editing,' he said. 'She works out of the house. *Our* house. We inherited it when our folks passed away. We live there together. We never got out of the house we grew up in.' He gave that some thought. 'She puts in about ten hours a day, six days a week. The work just keeps coming. It's all on the computer, and she rarely meets her clients face to face.'

'Does she get out at all?' Allison asked.

'Yeah. We go out to dinner once in a while, catch a movie. She has her therapy. She still loves the beach,' he said, 'but not during the summer. We go during the fall and winter when there's hardly anybody there.'

From the back region of my brain came the memory that Melissa Miller had been attacked after a high school beach party. A bunch of jocks with matching cheerleaders and some of their hanger-on friends went to Jones Beach just before graduation. Melissa was part of the latter group. The party eventually ended up back at the Taylor boys' home and that's where the assault took place. Most of the guests were too drunk to know anything had happened until Melissa went to the police later that week. It was like a bad TV movie come to life.

'Allison,' I said. 'Let's leave Chris alone and head inside.' It wasn't a request.

'I'm sorry,' Allison said. 'Occupational hazard,

I guess. Too many years doing what I do. I hear an idea for a story and I can't help but pursue it.'

'It's OK,' Chris said. 'It's not like you're the first. The first in about fifteen years maybe, but when the story was still fresh, lots of reporters came around looking for Missy's side of the story.' He took one last drag of his smoke and added it to the collection on the street. 'That's what we used to call her: Missy.' His eyes were on the cigarette butts; his mind was in the past. 'Since the attack, she goes by Melissa. "Missy" takes her too much back to high school.'

The three of us stood there in silence on the quiet suburban street. After a while, I said, 'We need to go inside, Chris. It was nice meeting you.'

'You, too,' he said. This time he did shake our hands. To Allison, he said, 'I'll talk to Melissa about your idea. Maybe it is time for her to talk about what happened.'

'It's completely up to her,' Allison said.

'Yeah,' he said. 'Not too many things fall into that category these days.' He looked over our shoulders at Marty's house. 'Give my regards to Mrs Stover, will you? Tell her what I said about Marty being a good man. I meant it.'

'I will,' I said. 'Take it easy.'

'Thanks.'

As we walked across the street to Marty's, Allison said, 'I probably shouldn't have done that, right?'

Now she asks? 'If you had used the word "cathartic," I would have yanked you away,' I said. 'Sometimes you just can't help yourself.'

161

'Oh,' she said. 'Like you can? How many times have you been told *not* to get involved in other people's business and you just ignored it?'

'That's different,' I said. 'Just as many people ask me *to* get involved. You just pulled out your business card and put that guy on the spot.'

'He's an adult, Raymond. He could've just said no.'

I stopped her before we got to the front steps. 'I think he just did, Allison.'

She thought about that and said, 'I thought I heard a maybe in there.'

I gave her a half-grin. 'Now you know how I feel.' I squeezed her hand tighter and kissed her on the cheek. 'You ready to go in?'

She kissed me back. An argument for another day, perhaps. 'I'm following you, tough guy.'

The front door was open, and there was the hum of muffled chatter from inside. We went into the house without knocking. The first room we came to was the living room, packed with mourners. It had been years since I'd been in this house, but there was a sense of familiarity to it. When my dad and Marty were partners, our families would have each other over for dinner once a year. And my parents used to come here for parties without Rachel and me many times. Most people were dressed as if just returning from church, many of them holding plates of food or drinks. If I didn't know better, I would have thought we'd stumbled into a first communion or confirmation party. Nobody paid us much attention as Allison and I snaked our way through the room.

The next room we came to was the kitchen. This group of people, crammed into the smaller space, looked identical to the one we just passed through. The countertops were filled with bottles of wine, liquor, and beer. This was the bar area and, therefore, a popular gathering place. I grabbed a couple of Bud Lights, handed one to Allison, and we excused ourselves as we squeezed through the crowd into the next room.

The dining room was also jammed with people. The room was huge, just as I remembered it, and memories of past meals came flooding back. Helaine Stover had been quite the hostess back in the day. My mother used to speak of the Stovers' dining room with envy, somehow trying to get us to believe that she'd host more events if only she had a bigger space. The truth was, as I recalled, my mother always stressed out when the hosting duties fell on her.

Today, the dining table was overloaded with food; some of it obviously catered, and the rest was a mix of homemade items that guests had brought. I noticed two college-aged kids – one male, one female – dressed in identical white shirts, black vests, and pants, walking around the room picking up stray plates and cups. Marty Junior or his mother had hired some help. Smart idea on a day like today. I found myself amazed at how someone could put together a function like this in less than forty-eight hours.

As Allison and I made our way past the food table, I noticed Bobby Taylor holding a green beer bottle. He was in a dark blue suit that didn't quite fit him like the one I'd seen him in two days ago. He also looked tired, not the sharp guy I'd seen at The Tippler on Friday. I went up to him and touched him on the elbow.

'Bobby,' I said. 'This is my girlfriend, Allison Rogers.'

Allison offered her hand, and Bobby gave us both an uncomfortable look. It took me about five seconds to realize why. I felt like an idiot when it came to me.

'I'm Billy,' he said. He looked around the room. 'Bobby's around here talking to some people if that's who you were hoping to see.' He said that as if he were used to the idea of people realizing he was the 'Other Brother.'

'No,' I said, trying to hide my mistake. 'I'm Raymond Donne. My dad used to work with Marty.'

He thought about that. 'Oh, yeah. I remember him. He was nice.'

I had the feeling he was going to say more. When he didn't, I spoke again. 'I saw Bobby the other night at the benefit. He said you've been doing pretty well for yourself since . . . these past ten years.'

He nodded and shrugged. 'I guess.' Now he looked at Allison and said, 'I'm Billy. Nice to meet you.'

Allison hesitated now to take his offered hand. When she did, she gave him a quick handshake. 'Same here,' she said, but not like she meant it. She slipped her hand back into mine very quickly. She was nervous. I could count on one hand the number of times I'd seen her this uncomfortable.

'It's good you could make it,' I said, unable to think of anything else and looking for an exit line. 'I'm sure Helaine and Marty appreciate it.'

That seemed to confuse him for a bit, and then he said, 'Oh. Martin *Junior*.' I watched as he processed that. 'Yeah, I thought I should . . . pay my respects.'

He said that last part as though he'd rehearsed it. His natural slowness and, I had to imagine, the ten years he'd spent in prison, made this an awkward occasion for him. Now that I thought of it, I was surprised he had chosen to come. He must have known that a good number of the guests would know who he was. I can't imagine most people would welcome a convicted sex offender at a function like this. I could tell by the way Allison was holding my hand that she fell into that group. So she surprised me by what she did next.

'Billy,' she said, pulling another card out of her pocket while still holding on to my hand. 'I'm a reporter and would love to hear your story of how you put your life back together after serving your sentence.' She got over her nervousness quickly.

Billy looked at the card like he was going to be quizzed on it. For some reason, he turned it over and looked at the other side. When he turned it back to the front, he said, 'I don't know, Ms Rogers. The newspapers said a lot of bad stuff about me a while ago. I don't think I want to go through that again.'

'You have a different story this time, Billy. Twenty years ago it was about what you had done. *Why* you went to jail. The story I want to write is what your life is like *now*. How you've become a productive, successful member of society.'

He half-smiled. 'You sound like my old social worker.'

To me, she was starting to sound a bit cold. Ten minutes ago, she was making the same offer to the brother of the victim. I was sure when we talked about this later, Allison would explain to me how she had to remain objective when telling a story, and she'd be right. I just didn't get how she could do it so effortlessly. Or at that time.

'Allison,' I said. 'Maybe you shouldn't put Billy on the spot right now.' *Didn't we just have this conversation?* I wasn't sure she was picking up on his developmental delays, but I couldn't come right out and say that in front of him. 'How about you give him some time to think about it?'

'Oh, yeah,' she said, as much for me as for Billy. 'Of course. Why don't you take a few days to think about it, Billy, and give me a call?'

He looked at the card again and nodded. 'OK,' he said. 'I really should talk to my social worker about it. And maybe my brother. He's kinda my boss now, and I usually have to run things past him. Big things like this, I mean.'

'I understand completely,' Allison said.

'Thanks.'

'We're going to go mingle now, Billy,' I said. 'My sister and mother are around here some-where, I think. And we haven't seen Mrs Stover yet.'

166

Billy shook our hands again. 'It was nice to meet you,' he said.

Allison and I nodded and turned to go deeper into the dining room. I could feel Allison's grip on my hand tighten again. There was some aggression behind it this time.

'Don't do that, Raymond.'

'Do what?'

'You shut me down back there,' she said. 'Like I don't know when to stop.'

'Did you pick up,' I said, lowering my voice, 'that he's a little delayed, Ally? He's always been that way, and the past twenty years haven't helped.'

'At least he's been able to move on with his life, Ray. Unlike Melissa.'

'Is that why you were pushing him?' I let go of her hand. 'I thought you just couldn't resist the story, but now . . .'

'Now what?' she asked.

'What story do you want to write? The one where two people involved in a horrible event end up two decades later, or the one where the perpetrator makes out better than his victim?'

'Be careful, Ray,' she said just above a whisper. 'You're either questioning my objectivity or my integrity, and I don't think you want to go to either of those places.'

'You're right, I don't.' I took a pull from my beer. 'Just no more today, OK? We're here to support the Stovers. Not for you to get a story.'

She held my glance for a few seconds then gave the room a quick look.

'How about we just agree to disagree?'

167

'How about we just agree that I'm right?'

The look she gave me told me everything she thought about that idea.

'Why don't you go see if you can find Rachel and your mother,' she said. 'I need to find a bathroom.'

I watched as she made her way back through the dining room. Part of me wanted to go after her, and the other part knew it was better if we both had a little time to cool off. Maybe she knew I was right. Or maybe we were back where we were six months ago. Neither one of us wanted that, and this was not the time and place to figure that out.

I took another sip of beer and noticed a familiar face across the room. It took me a few seconds to place it. Joshua Stern, Hector's mentor from the store. I made my way over to him. When I was about five feet away, I realized he was standing next to a junior version of himself. They both wore dark suits and yarmulkes.

'Mr Donne,' he said as I approached. He put his hand on the kid's shoulder. 'This is my son, Daniel. Daniel, this is Mr Donne. Hector's teacher.'

We shook hands all around. The son seemed about the same age as Hector. A shame, I thought, that because of the cultural divide they'd probably never get the chance to be friends.

'It was nice of you to come all the way out to the Island, Mr Stern,' I said. 'It's a long drive from your home.' Just as long as mine, I remembered, but I had a driver.

'We were at the store today,' he explained. 'I

168

left my manager in charge. Daniel works with me on Sundays to learn the business. The way I did from my father.'

From where I stood, Daniel didn't seem all that thrilled about the idea of learning the business like his father had or, for that matter, attending a shiva on Long Island for a person he had probably barely known. Nice to see that teenagers are teenagers no matter what their background. I'm sure if he had his way, he'd be back in Williamsburg playing with his friends on one of the first warm weekend days after a long winter.

'I'm actually not Hector's teacher,' I said to Daniel. 'I'm his dean.'

Daniel looked at me with bored, brown eyes and said, 'Are you the boss?'

I laughed. 'Just the dean. When things go wrong at the school, I deal with the kids and try to fix the situation before it gets worse.'

'Does Hector get in trouble a lot?' His eyes lit up a little at that thought. 'Is that how he got stuck working with my grandfather and father?'

'Daniel,' his father said. 'We do not ask questions like that. It is rude to be nosy.'

'It's OK, Mr Stern. No, Daniel. Hector's a pretty good kid. Mr Stover and I just thought he'd benefit from another perspective in his neighborhood. Your dad and your grandfather were nice enough to agree.'

If Daniel liked that answer, or even believed it, he gave no sign. He did give off the signal that he was done with this conversation. Fine with me. I didn't come all the way out here to

169

try and charm a teenage boy. I had all week for that if I wanted.

'Nice to see you again, Mr Stern,' I said. 'I have to go find my family.'

'Yes,' he said. 'And perhaps I will see you at the store sometime. We have an educator's discount.'

'That's good to know.' I looked at his kid. 'Good-bye, Daniel.'

He looked at me with blank eyes and said, 'Goodbye, Mr Donne.'

His father gave him a look of disapproval and said, 'Shake his hand, Daniel. Mr Donne deserves your respect. He's an adult and a teacher.'

Daniel reluctantly stuck out his hand like he was testing the temperature of a shower. There was something we had in common: we both hated forced handshakes. The grip he gave me wouldn't have crumpled a piece of paper. As I suspected, the boy was not charmed. I shook the father's hand and waved as I stepped farther into the dining area.

I went for another beer to replace the almost-empty one I was holding when someone grabbed my elbow.

'You're not sneaking out are you, Raymond?' my sister asked.

'No,' I said. 'But the thought crossed my mind.'

She looked around. 'Where's Allison?' She was holding a fresh beer of her own.

'Looking for a bathroom, the last I saw her.' I looked at her beer.

'There's a cooler on the back deck.'

'Then let's go to the back deck.'

170

'Problems with the girlfriend?'

How do women know this shit?

'I'll tell you about it when I have a new beer.'

I placed my empty down on the dining table and headed toward the sliding glass door that led outside. I opened the cooler, grabbed another Bud Light and took a long draw.

'So,' Rachel said. 'You and Allison. What's up?'

I told her about Allison giving her business card to both Chris Miller and Billy Taylor. How she was acting more like a reporter than my girlfriend. How she had turned this shiva into a story opportunity. Rachel didn't seem surprised.

'It's who she is, Ray. It's what she does.'

'Does it have to be all the time? Marty's been dead less than forty-eight hours.'

Rachel gave me that look she'd been giving me ever since she got the idea in her head that I should have already asked Allison to marry me. It's the look that tells me I'm just too thick to see something so obvious.

'What do you want me to say, Ray?' she asked. 'That you're right and she's wrong and how dare she act that way?'

I thought about that and said, 'Yeah. That's exactly what I want you to say.'

'OK. You're right, she's wrong, and how dare she act that way?' She took a sip of beer. 'Feel better now?'

'Don't be flip about this, Rache. We went through the same thing last year. It almost ended our relationship.'

'From what you told me,' she said, 'that was a little different than this.'

171

'How so?'

'You told me – and so did she, by the way – that last year's thing was because you knew stuff you couldn't tell her, and the two of you had to work that out. Although, again, at the risk of sounding like Uncle Ray, why you get involved in shit you can't tell your reporter girlfriend continues to astound those of us who love you.'

I let that last part slide. 'And this is different how?'

'She's trying to find out things on her own,' she said. 'Maybe she really thinks there's a good story here. I gotta tell ya – and not just because I usually side with her – I agree. There are lots of people out there who would want to read about Melissa Miller and where she is now. Same for Billy Taylor, especially because his brother's famous.'

If a sip of beer could be taken in anger, I just did it. 'So I'm wrong?'

She smiled and shook her head. *My silly older brother.*

'You do that all the time, Ray. Someone has to be wrong when you and Allison argue. Maybe there's a middle ground. Maybe that's what's keeping you from throwing all your chips in and asking her to marry you. For a guy who sees gray where others see only black and white, you're kinda monochromatic on this relationship thing.'

I looked up at the maple tree branch hanging over the deck. In a few weeks it was going to start budding. I remembered my dad and Marty

172

hanging out back here under the tree during the summer. Sometimes Uncle Ray would join them, and I would sit off to the side, listening to their war stories. Uncle Ray always won, of course.

Suburban bliss.

'I thought we were here to pay our respects to Marty and his family,' I said. 'Not go over what's keeping me from proposing to Allison.'

'Consider it a bonus, Ray.' She touched me on the arm. 'Just go back inside and say you're sorry. It works for Dennis.'

'He's your fiancé and saves his backbone for the NYPD.'

'Still, he's a smart guy.' She took another sip of beer. 'Have you seen Marty or Helaine yet, by the way?'

'No, I've been too busy watching Allison work.'

Rachel shook her head. 'Drop it, Ray. Mom's upstairs with Helaine, I think. Redoing her makeup and hair. Marty might be over in the driveway with his golfing buddies. Why don't you take a look?'

'Trying to get rid of me?'

'I'm doing you a favor, big brother. I'll run into Allison before you do and soften her up.' Before I could argue, she said, 'You're welcome,' and went back inside.

I headed around the side of the house to the driveway. Just as Rachel had said, there was Marty with the two guys I'd seen when we got dropped off. Smart idea: grab some beers, head outside, get away from the constant hum of the mourners. Marty noticed me as I approached.

'There he is,' he said, making 'is' sound closer to 'ish.' He came over, put his arm around me, and led me toward his friends. 'Boys, this is Raymond Donne, my dad's former law partner's kid. We used to hang out together back in the day.'

That wasn't quite the way I remembered it. We were at a lot of the same parties, of course, but to say we hung out would be stretching it. But now was not the time to correct him. I stuck my hand out. 'Nice to meet you guys. Golf buddies or business associates?'

'Both,' the taller of the two said. 'You a lawyer, too?'

'Worse,' Marty said. 'He's a public school-teacher. And . . . he used to be a cop.'

The two friends looked at me as if Marty had just told them I studied the mating habits of sea urchins.

'I know,' I said, spreading out my arms. 'I'm a slave to the almighty dollar.'

All three laughed as they sipped their cheap American beers while wearing their expensive foreign suits. They probably weren't used to rubbing elbows with the likes of me, unless they represented one of us.

'That's good,' the shorter one said. 'Marty said you were on the news a while ago. Something to do with a dead kid. You found the killer or something?'

'The dead kid,' I said, 'was one of my students.' I let that sink in. 'And I didn't really *find* the killer. The cops were largely responsible for that.' That was a lie, but I didn't feel like telling the

174

story of Douglas Lee's murder and the capture of his killer to these guys. 'In fact, my sister's marrying the detective who solved it.'

'Well, Raymond here helped,' Marty said. 'He's a good guy. His uncle's the Chief of Detectives in the NYPD.'

'And you left the job?' the taller one said. 'Sounds like you had your future laid out for you.'

'You make that sound like a good thing,' I said.

That stumped him. 'Well, yeah. Isn't it?'

'Not for me it wasn't.'

We were quiet for a bit and then the three of them started laughing. I didn't know what was so funny until the shorter one said, 'You're single, aren't you?'

Christ.

'What's that got to do with it?'

'Single guys don't think about the future like us married guys with kids.' He suddenly looked a little less jovial. 'Sometimes that's all we think about.'

'My kid's not even three yet,' the taller guy said. 'And already we're worried about what schools we can afford and should we move to a better neighborhood.'

'Everything becomes about your kid, Ray,' Marty added. 'Everything.'

I took a sip of beer as we all contemplated that. Suddenly, I was the happiest guy on the driveway.

'Marty,' I said after a while, 'I feel like an idiot. I haven't even asked if your wife and boy are here. I'd like to meet them.'

'They came and left,' Marty said. 'Jeffrey's

175

barely two. He couldn't last, and Marsha was exhausted so I let them go home.'

I remembered that his wife hadn't come to the benefit the other night either. The child was the excuse then, also. I found myself wondering for some reason if Marty had any idea of his father's affair with Maria Robles. Could that have been what they were arguing about at the benefit? That'd be a real good question for the detective in charge to ask if I hadn't already promised to keep my mouth shut about the matter.

'Your day will come, Raymond,' the taller guy said. 'We saw the young lady you got dropped off with. You'd be a fool to let that one get away.'

I smiled and held my beer up in a toasting gesture. 'You've been talking to my mother, haven't you?'

That got another round of laughs as we clinked our bottles, and I figured it was as good a time as any to excuse myself. We shook hands all around – I never did get those two guys' names – and Marty told me he would be right behind me. Somehow, I doubted that. The driveway was much more fun than inside.

Back inside, I noticed Helaine Stover. She was surrounded by three ladies, none of them my mother. She wore a simple black dress and a pearl necklace. Her friends were dressed the same. Shiva-wear, I guessed. I maneuvered my way around a group of other guests and made it over to the widow. She saw me before I could speak.

'Oh, Raymond,' she said, stepping through two

176

of her friends. 'Thank you so much for coming all the way out here.'

We hugged for about ten seconds. 'Of course,' I said as we broke the embrace. 'I am so sorry about Marty, Helaine. How are you doing?' The dumb question we all ask at times like these.

She looked at me and forced a small smile. 'I'm . . . I'm still in shock, I guess. I can't believe it. The last two days seem like a bad dream. Our rabbi told us this morning that's to be expected when someone . . . .' She was fighting back tears. 'When we lose someone so suddenly. In such a way. I always feared it would be Marty's heart what with the hours he kept and all the stress. This,' she was losing the battle against the tears. 'This is literally unbelievable.'

She wrapped her arms around me again and cried. Her friends all looked at me and gave me sympathetic smiles and nods. Unable to come up with any words of comfort, I just patted Helaine gently on the back. When she got herself back under control, she said, 'I'm going to ruin my makeup again, Raymond. Your mother was so kind to help me touch up before.'

'Maybe you should go sit in the living room, Helaine. Get off your feet for a bit. Maybe have some water. Let people come to you.'

She nodded. 'That's a good idea. Marty has me taking some of his anxiety pills. I feel a little . . . what's the word? Buzzed?'

I thought about Marty slurring his words in the driveway. Maybe buzzed was the way to get through this early part of the mourning process.

177

The problem is, once the buzz wears off, your loved one is still gone.

'Buzzed is OK,' I said, taking Helaine by the elbow. 'Where is my mother, by the way?' I started walking her toward the living room.

'She was talking to some friends from our bridge club in the kitchen,' Helaine said. 'Although, to be honest, we don't play much bridge these days. It's more of an excuse to get together and have lunch.'

'And a glass of wine, I bet,' I said.

She laughed a little buzzed laugh. 'Maybe one or two.'

I got her to the big chair in the corner of the living room that was currently being used by an elderly gentleman nursing what looked like a club soda. When he saw us, he got up and offered the seat to Helaine.

'Thank you, Arthur,' she said and used the armrest to help herself down. 'And thank you, Raymond. Where's that lovely girlfriend of yours? She did come?'

'She's around somewhere,' I said. 'I'll find her and bring her over.'

'That would be lovely.'

Some other guests had started to gather around the chair to pay their respects. One brought her a glass of water. I was getting crowded out so I took that as my cue to walk away from the Widow Stover. It was time to find Allison and my mother. Maybe I could hear a few more of my faults before heading back to Brooklyn.

Sixteen

Who I found first was my Uncle Ray standing by the front door. He was in his dress uniform, the one normally reserved for official ceremonies, cop funerals, and press conferences. He looked impressive and he knew it. There was already a crowd gathering around him, no doubt hungry for the latest info on Marty's murder. He'd be his usual tight-lipped self but give out just enough details to make his audience feel they got their money's worth.

There was no drink in his hand, so I figured he had arrived less than a minute ago. He noticed me from across the room and waved me over. Instead of marching to his orders like usual, I gave him a drinking gesture by making a C with my hand, bringing it up to my mouth, and tipping it a few times. He returned that with a smile and a thumbs-up, so I went back to the kitchen – oddly, my mother was nowhere to be seen – to get him a Diet Coke and whiskey. I hoped they had Jack Daniel's. They did. I made one for myself, too. The beers just weren't cutting it.

When I returned to the living room, Uncle Ray was shaking a few hands and slapping a few backs. The man knew how to work a room no matter what the occasion. I stepped over and held out his drink. He grabbed the drink

179

and brought it to his nose as if he were a wine taster. He smiled and said, 'How'd you know?'

'A wild guess,' I said and touched my glass to his.

'Everybody,' he said to the two men and three women still listening to him, 'this is my nephew, Raymond. Nephew Raymond, this is everybody.'

'Nice to meet you all,' I said.

The two men shook my hand and introduced themselves as old friends and business acquaintances of Marty and my father. I was told what good men Marty and my dad were, and I thanked them for saying so. I was about to introduce myself to the women, when Uncle Ray spoke again.

'Now, if you'll excuse us,' he said, 'I need to speak with my nephew privately.'

He put his hand on my shoulder and ushered me toward the front door. When we got outside, I asked, 'Where's Aunt Reeny?'

'She decided to stay home,' he said. 'Said she had a headache and a cold, but the truth is she hates these things.'

'What do you need to talk to me about?'

'I don't,' he said. 'I just needed some air.'

'You were in there for all of three minutes.'

He ignored that. If my uncle said he needed air, he needed air. He took a few deep breaths and then a long sip of his drink. It didn't happen often, but I could tell something was bothering him. I could wait five hours and maybe he'd tell me after too many Jack and Cokes, or I could just come out and ask. I chose the latter.

'What's bugging you, Uncle Ray?'

'I think Marty was cheating on Helaine.'

That didn't take long. I took a sip of my own drink before speaking.

'Why do you think that?' I asked, pretending the idea was unthinkable.

'I read the statement she gave to the detectives Friday night,' he said. 'She said he'd been working longer hours, a lot of them in Brooklyn. Some nights he didn't get home 'til four in the morning. She didn't like him driving on the LIE at that hour. The nights he didn't come home, she said he told her he stayed at a hotel.'

'She didn't believe him?'

'Of course she believed him, Ray. This is Helaine Stover we're talking about. Her husband was Williamsburg, Brooklyn's, *Man of the Year*, for God's sake. He's been a good husband and father for forty years. He was a pillar of the goddamned community.' He took another sip of his drink. There was maybe one left. 'It's me who doesn't fucking believe him.'

'Because you're a cop and you don't buy into the late-night story.'

'Because I'm a cop who's had enough conversations with guys who've been stepping out on their wives to know when a guy's been stepping out on his wife.' He turned to me. 'Did you talk to Marty at all Friday night?'

'Yeah,' I said. 'But he didn't mention cheating on Helaine.'

'Don't be an ass, Raymond. You didn't notice anything different about him? The new suit, the new haircut? How he seemed like he couldn't wait to get out of there?'

181

'It was a benefit in his honor. He was excited and wanted to look good.'

'Did you notice the weight loss?'

'I hadn't seen him in a while, so, no, I didn't.'

'There's three reasons guys Marty's age lose weight,' he said, and then clicked them off on his thumb, forefinger, and middle finger. 'They've got cancer, their cardiologist told them to drop a few, or they've got something going on the side.' He looked at his three fingers. 'Helaine said nothing about Marty's health.'

'Maybe it has to do with him working too much,' I said. 'Maybe he was too busy or too tired to eat.'

He looked at me like I was slow, and repeated himself. 'There's *three* reasons guys Marty's age lose weight.' He held out the three fingers as a visual aid in case I still didn't get it. 'We also – and don't repeat this to anyone – believe he had a phone his wife didn't know about.'

'Why do you think that?'

'Where do you keep your cell?' he asked.

'In my front pocket.'

'Like most guys, right. We found Marty's phone in his front pocket. It was the same one I have in my contacts list.'

'So?'

He finished his drink. 'So, he was also wearing one of those cell phone holders people clip on to their belts.' He paused for effect. 'And guess what?'

'It was empty,' I said.

'Bingo. When the detectives asked Helaine for Marty's cell number, she only gave the one. He had an extra she didn't know about.'

'Which means he was cheating on her?'

'Marty was about as low-tech – and cheap – as you could get in this day and age, Raymond. I saw the report from the break-in at his office. If he'd had a decent alarm system, the cops woulda been there before the burglar left. Why's a guy like that need a second phone?'

'Did you ask Helaine about it?'

'And open up that bag of shit? Not unless I have to.' He gave that some thought. 'I'm ninety-nine percent sure he had something going on the side. I'm not bringing it up to his wife or kid until I'm a hundred percent sure.' He swirled the ice in his glass around. 'Of course, there's the possibility that one, or both, of them already knew. If that's the case . . .'

'It provides motive,' I said.

'One of the oldest in the book, Boyo.'

'But you don't really think Marty Junior or Helaine would be capable of killing Marty, do you?' I remembered the two of them leaving the party early Friday.

'I've seen stranger things, Raymond. And not just on TV.'

It was at that point I knew I should tell him about Maria Robles and Marty, but I just couldn't bring myself to do it. But I did make a deal with myself that if the detectives needed to know that Marty was cheating on Helaine, I'd somehow – more than likely through an anonymous tip – let them know with whom. Until then, I was keeping my promise and staying shut. Like my uncle said: Why open that bag of shit unless absolutely necessary.

'The detectives check his records to see if Marty had another phone?' I asked.

'They did and came up with zilch. They're thinking now maybe he just kept buying those pay-as-you-go-jobs.' He must have seen the smirk I was trying to hide. 'What is it, Raymond?'

'The thought of Marty Stover with a burner,' I said.

'Yeah. It'd be funny if he weren't so dead.' He looked at his cup and tossed his ice cubes on to the front lawn. 'I'm gonna get another and pay my respects. You good?'

'For now,' I said. 'And thanks.'

'For what?'

'For sharing the info about Marty with me. I appreciate it.'

'I knew you'd be curious. I also knew you'd keep your mouth shut.'

'Right on both counts.'

'Where's your better half, by the way?'

'Inside,' I said. 'We had a little disagreement.'

'Happens to the best of us. Go find her, say you're sorry, and that'll be that.'

'You're the second person to give me that advice today.'

'Must be as wise as me, then.'

He disappeared inside as I took another sip of my drink. OK, maybe it was time to go back in and track down my girlfriend. I wasn't sure about apologizing, but I was getting tired. I'd put in my time and wanted to go home.

Allison was easy enough to find. I spied her as she was coming out of the kitchen with what I assumed was a fresh beer in her hands. She noticed

184

me soon enough, and we met in the middle of the living room.

'I just finished talking to your mother,' she said.

'I keep missing her.'

'According to her, she's been quite the social butterfly today. And not just today. I didn't know she played bridge.'

I smiled, remembering what Helaine had told me. 'Every week,' I said.

Making small talk with Allison was awkward. I wasn't sure if we were still arguing or if we were good. Maybe Rachel and Uncle Ray were right: I should just apologize and get it over with like a good boyfriend. I was composing an apology in my head when she beat me to it. Kind of.

'I thought about what you said,' she said. 'And maybe I did come on a little strong with Chris and Billy. This is not the place for that, and I couldn't help myself.'

I noticed the absence of a real apology in what she had just said, but I kept that thought to myself. Like a good boyfriend. Instead, I kissed her on the cheek and said, 'Thank you. So, we're good?'

'We're good.' She tapped her bottle against my cup. 'Let's go say good-bye to your mother.'

Thirty minutes later we had spoken with my mom, finished another drink each, met about another half dozen different people who had known my father, and decided it was as good a time as any to make our exit. I had school tomorrow, and this past weekend seemed to have been ten days long. We said our good-byes, Officer CJ Gray drove us to the LIRR train station – he would have taken us all the way home if we'd let him – and Allison and I went our separate ways at the Woodside stop, where I jumped on the subway to Brooklyn and she stayed on the train to Manhattan.

I have to admit it would've been nice to spend the night with her, but we probably needed a break from each other. At least I did. I wondered what married people did at moments like these.

Seventeen

After the weekend I'd just had, going back to work almost felt like a day off, especially after the district office called and said the suspension hearing had to be rescheduled for another day. The feeling lasted until five minutes past nine, when the phone in my office rang.

'Raymond Donne.' I took a sip of my second cup of coffee.

'Mr Donne,' a female voice said. 'It's Susan. Down in the nurse's office?'

Susan McClarty was our new school nurse, and I had the feeling that working at a middle school was not exactly what she'd had in mind as she worked her way through nursing school. Although, in actuality, nothing prepares you for middle school. Even the five years I'd had as a New York City cop.

'Yes, Nurse McClarty. What's up?'

'I have a young man down here,' she said. 'Thomas Avila?'

'Tommy,' I said. 'Don't tell me he's got a headache again. Or is it a stomach ache this time?' Tommy had a bad habit of getting sick in school, especially on test days. His number of absences was also creeping up to the danger point; anything past eighteen and students run the risk of being held back. We'd had his parents in a few times, but nothing was getting through to the kid.

'It's a bit more serious than that, I'm afraid, Mr Donne.' She took a breath. When she spoke again, her voice was shaky. 'I was hoping you could come down.'

'I'm on my way.'

I got to her office in less than a minute. It was next to the main office and just two flights of stairs below mine. She met me at the door.

'Thank you,' she said. 'It seems Tommy had a bit of an accident on the way to school this morning.'

'What kind of accident?' I asked, worried he'd pissed his pants.

She lowered her voice as a pair of girls walked by.

'He says he was . . . attacked when he got off the bus.'

'The stop in front of the school?'

'No. He said he got off a few blocks away. He wanted to get breakfast.'

Great. Not only was the kid running late for school but he felt he had time to hit the deli for a quick bite. I looked through the window of her door. I didn't see him. 'Did he say who attacked him?' I took a step closer to the door. She moved in front of me.

'I want him to tell you, but I want you to be prepared.'

Nurse McClarty didn't know me too well. I thought of telling her I was not too easily shocked, but I chose to let her have her moment.

'Thank you,' I said. 'Now I need to see him, if you don't mind.'

She stepped aside and I went into her office.

'He's in the room on the right,' she said, her voice still quiet and shaken. She followed me but kept her distance.

I found Tommy sitting down on the chair closest to the sink. He was doubled over, hugging his jacket, and had his chin buried in his chest. His breathing was labored enough for me to hear it from across the room. Maybe that's why my day had seemed to start so smoothly; all the drama was in the nurse's office.

'Tommy,' I said. 'It's Mr Donne.' I pulled over another chair and sat next to him. 'Tommy, what happened?' I put my hand on his back and could feel his heart beating through his ribs and spine like it wanted to bust out.

'Tommy,' I said. 'Try to calm down, OK. Just breathe.'

I waited as he got his breathing somewhat under control and then he lifted his head. His eyes were full of tears, and his face looked as if he'd just run a few miles. I didn't think he was ready to speak until the words came out.

'Some guys,' he said between breaths. 'They jumped me when I got off the bus. They took my bookbag. One of them had a knife.'

Shit. I turned to Nurse McClarty. 'Call nine-one-one,' I said. After she'd left, I realized we also needed to call his parents. His dad worked about ten minutes away in an auto parts ware-house by the Queens border. 'Do you have your dad's number?' I asked.

He reached into his pocket, pulled out his cell, and handed it to me.

'It's under "Dad,"' he said.

189

I found the number, pressed it, and the call went right to voice mail. I left a message that made it quite clear he needed to call me as soon as possible, but not enough to scare the crap out of him. I then found his mother's number – under 'Mom' – and did the same. The nurse came back into the room and said, 'They're on their way.'

Tommy sat up straight. 'The cops?' he said.

'Yes, the cops,' I repeated. 'You were attacked and robbed, Tommy. We have to call the cops.' I looked at Nurse McClarty. 'Was he injured?'

'Show Mr Donne your shirt, Tommy,' she said.

Tommy stood up slowly as if nervous about making a class presentation. He put his jacket on the chair and first showed me his T-shirt, which had a tear in it that ran across the width of his midsection. He then lifted the T-shirt and showed me a red line on his skin a few inches long that looked like someone had drawn half the letter V above his belly button.

'The guy with the knife did this,' he explained.

I looked at the scratch – something didn't seem right about it – and motioned for him to pull his shirt down. 'How'd you get away from them?' I asked.

'I just tore ass, Mr Donne. Soon as the guy with the knife swiped at me, they all started laughing and I ran as fast as I could right here.'

'Did you tell school safety?' He had to have passed their desk to get here.

'No. I was so scared and I thought I was bleeding, so I came right to the nurse.'

'I washed the wound,' Nurse McClarty said behind me. 'It wasn't deep enough for stitches,

190

but I do want to put a bandage on it after the police look at it. He's going to need a new shirt, too,' she added for some reason. 'He's very lucky.'

That's when it hit me what was wrong. The rip on the shirt was cutting straight across his midsection. The scratch on his stomach was slanted. Was he wearing his jacket when attacked? And why would some guys – one of whom had a knife – take his bookbag but not his cell phone? Tommy was in trouble all right, but I was starting to feel it was not the kind he was trying to sell me.

His cell phone rang. The caller ID said 'Dad.'

'Mr Avila,' I said.

'What's wrong, Mr Donne? Is Tommy OK?'

'He's fine,' I said. I stood up and walked out of the room. 'He says he was attacked when he got off the bus.'

'Attacked? How can you say he's fine if he was attacked?'

'How soon can you get here?'

'I'm on my way now. I'm working deliveries today and I've got the truck. I'll be there in five minutes.'

'He's OK now. Drive carefully, Mr Avila. I'll explain it when you get here.'

He ended the call.

'Your dad's on his way, Tommy,' I said. 'He should get here about the same time as the police. Is there anything else you want to add to what you've already told me?'

He looked at me warily. 'Like what?'

'I don't know. Anything else you remember

191

about these guys. The cops are going to want to know what they were wearing, how many there were, which direction they were headed.'

That last question was designed to confirm my suspicions, which Tommy did as soon as he spoke again.

'There were three of them and they went the other way, Mr D. I don't know what they were wearing. Jeans and hoodies, I guess.'

It wasn't the number of attackers or what they were wearing that concerned me. What didn't match was how could a kid who 'tore ass' away from his attackers know which direction they went? I also wasn't sure how he made his way past the school safety officers at the front desk, but I'd talk to them later.

My walkie-talkie spoke as I stood up. 'Mr Donne, what's your twenty?'

'I'm in the nurse's office.'

'I've got two youth officers here at the front desk.'

'I'm on my way.' I turned back to Tommy. 'Stay here.'

'Should I give him a new shirt, Mr Donne?' Nurse McClarty asked. 'I have some in the back for . . . situations like this.'

'No,' I said, putting on my serious cop voice for Tommy. 'The shirt's evidence. The police are going to want to see it exactly where it is.'

I left the room without waiting for a response from either of them. I walked over to the school safety desk and stuck my hand out to the youth officers, both of whom I recognized from previous incidents in and around school.

'Officer Martinez,' I said. 'Officer Johnson. Thanks for getting here so quickly.'

Officer Yvette Martinez was about ten years younger than I was and looked as if she had given up a career in modeling to work with troubled youth in Williamsburg. Officer Johnson – I never did get his first name the few times we'd crossed paths – looked as if he was just about ready to put in his papers and move on to greener pastures. I didn't waste any time telling them Tommy's story and my take on it.

'This the kind of kid that would make up something like this?' Martinez asked.

'I wouldn't have thought so until this morning, but his story's a bit shaky, don't you think?'

That's when Johnson said, 'Why don't you let us determine that, Mr Donne.'

'That's why we called you,' I said, choosing to ignore the reminder of whose job description this fell under. 'Follow me.'

We turned at exactly the time Tommy's father came barreling through the front doors. He ran right up to the three of us and said, 'Where's Tommy? Where's my kid?'

I put my hand on his shoulder. 'He's in the nurse's office, Mr Avila. We were just going in to talk to him.'

He looked at the three of us. 'I'm going with you.'

I turned back to Martinez and Johnson. 'Officers?'

'OK with me,' Martinez said. 'Hank?'

Hank shrugged. 'Let's go talk to the kid,' he said.

When we got to the nurse's office, Mr Avila ran straight to Tommy and put his arms around him carefully. He held him for almost half a minute. The room was silent except for Tommy crying. The silence was finally broken by Officer Johnson.

'We need to talk to your son, Mr Avila,' he said.

Avila looked at the two cops and then back at his son. 'You feel OK enough to talk, Tommy?'

Tommy shrugged and said, 'I guess. I already told Mr Donne what happened.'

'We need to hear it from you, Tommy,' Officer Martinez said. 'We have to fill out an official report and try to get these guys before they do it again to some other kid.'

Tommy considered that for a bit. Through his tears, he said, 'OK. Can my dad be here?'

'Of course,' Martinez said.

Tommy then went on to tell the exact same story he'd told me a few minutes ago: three kids in hoodies, one with a knife, the stolen bookbag, and how he got away. Officer Martinez wrote it all down in her pad. When Tommy was done, she said, 'Can you show us where he cut you?'

Tommy showed us the cut shirt and then reluctantly lifted it to expose the small wound above his belly button. Martinez took a few steps closer to get a better look at the injury. She was inches away as she studied it. When she was done, she nodded and told Tommy he could lower his shirt.

'Why don't we all talk outside while Nurse . . .'

'McClarty,' Nurse McClarty said.

'While Nurse McClarty puts a bandage on the cut.'

194

We all followed Officer Martinez out of the office. When we got to the hallway, Martinez took the lead.

'I think you're right, Mr Donne,' she said.

'About what?' Mr Avila asked like he'd walked in five minutes late to a movie.

Martinez looked at me, urging me to speak now.

'We think Tommy's wound is self-inflicted, Mr Avila,' I said.

His face went blank, and then he gave me a look as if I'd just told him the two police officers next to me were from Mars.

'Self-inflicted?' he repeated. 'You think he did this to himself? That's crazy.'

I told him how the wound didn't match the cut on the shirt, Tommy's cell phone wasn't taken, and somehow he knew which direction his attackers had gone while he was running toward the school. He thought about that for a few seconds.

'But why?' he said. 'Why would he do something like this?'

'I know it sounds far-fetched,' I said. 'But Tommy's been showing signs of school phobia lately: leaving school sick, a lot of absences. Didn't you tell me the last time we spoke what a struggle it is almost every day to get Tommy to school?'

'Yeah,' he said. 'I just figured that's 'cause he's a middle school kid. I hated school too when I was his age. Now you're saying he made this whole thing up? I can't wrap my mind around that, Mr Donne.'

'Do me a favor,' I said to the cops and Tommy's father. 'Let Dad and me have a talk with Tommy. See if his story changes.'

The two youth officers looked at each other and Martinez said, 'OK with me.'

'Thanks.'

I led Mr Avila back into the nurse's office where Nurse McClarty was putting a gauze pad and some tape over Tommy's wound.

'All done,' she told her patient. When she saw us, she said, 'Will you be taking him home now, Mr Avila?'

'We want to talk to him again first,' I said. 'You mind if we have the room for a few minutes?'

'Sure,' she said.

After she left, Tommy's dad crouched down to eye-level with his son. This was not going to be an easy conversation for either one of them.

'Tommy,' Avila began, 'Mr Donne thinks there's something you're not telling us.' He put his hand on the kid's shoulder. 'That there's more to your story.'

'Like what?' Tommy said. 'I told you what happened.'

Mr Avila went silent again and looked to me for help.

'We're confused,' I said, 'about where your wound came from.'

He looked at me. 'I told you. The guy with the knife swung it at me.'

'Yeah, that's what you told me. It's just that the cut on your shirt doesn't match the cut on your stomach.'

'Whatta you mean?'

'The shirt is cut straight across and it's pretty long. Your wound is short, it barely broke the skin, and goes up and down on a slant.' I let that sink in for a few beats. 'Do you see how that would confuse us, Tommy?'

He stared at me and started breathing heavy again. He looked at his dad and said, 'What are you saying?'

Dad took a deep swallow. 'Did you do this to yourself, Tommy?' he asked.

Tommy gave us a shocked look and stood up. 'Why would I do that?' he asked.

Avila looked at me, then back to his boy. 'Mr Donne told me that he thinks you maybe have some sort of . . . school phobia.'

'What's that?'

'It's when you're scared to go to school.'

'Why would I be scared to go to school?'

'I don't know,' his father said. 'But you have to admit, you've been sick a lot this year, and a few days a week you try to talk your mom and me into letting you stay home.'

'Yeah, but . . .' He stopped there, not knowing where to go with the thought. I've learned it's best to stay silent in situations like this. The kid knew what I thought. He was either going to confirm it or stick to his story.

'What if,' he began again after taking a deep breath, 'what if I did make it up? What kind of trouble would I be in?'

Mr Avila's face fell. To his credit, he recovered quickly and said, 'We just want to know the truth, Tommy. You can always tell me the truth.'

197

Tommy looked at me. 'Would I get in trouble with the school and the cops?'

'We all want what's best for you,' I said. 'If you made up the story, my only concern is why. As far as the cops go, I think you'll be OK. They're here to help.'

He nodded as he considered that. I found myself hoping he had enough trust in me to believe me and to be straight with us. This would be a tough situation to be in for anyone, but for a twelve-year-old? *Shit.*

'I cut myself,' he mumbled. 'First the T-shirt, then my stomach. Then I threw my bookbag into a garbage can.'

Mr Avila slipped his hands into his pockets as the words came out of his son. He looked down at the floor and said, 'Why, Tommy? Why would you do something like this? You scared the crap out of me.'

'I don't know, Dad. I guess it's like Mr D said. I don't like coming to school. I thought maybe if something bad happened, you'd find me a new school. Or maybe I could get homeschooled like those kids I saw on TV.'

Mr Avila shook his head. 'Oh, Tommy. How am I going to explain this to your mother?' He looked at me and said, 'What happens now?'

'Now,' I said. 'I think you and Tommy need to speak with the school counselor, Ms Stiles.' Elaine Stiles would surely recommend outside counseling, but there was no need for Tommy to hear that from me. 'I'll talk to the youth officers and explain what happened.'

Mr Avila offered me his hand. 'Thank you,' he said.

'You're welcome. Let me call Ms Stiles and make sure she's available.' To Tommy, I said, 'It's going to be OK.'

He didn't look like he believed me. I wasn't exactly sure I believed myself.

After the cops and the Avilas left, I remembered I needed to check on Hector Robles. His weekend hadn't been much better than mine. I found him in the gym, running around with the rest of his class, so I decided not to bother him, as he seemed fine for the moment.

Mc? I needed another cup of coffee and decided to get some fresh air and hit the Spanish restaurant a few doors down. I was barely off school grounds when I heard someone call my name. I turned to see Bobby Taylor. Or was it Billy Taylor? By the confident way he'd called me, the sureness of his steps, and the way his suit fit, I gathered it was the former.

'Bobby,' I said, not even trying to hide my surprise. 'What's up?'

He ignored my outstretched hand and said, 'I'll tell you what's up.' He stepped closer to me, making the difference in our sizes more apparent. He held a business card up to my face. It was Allison's. 'Your girlfriend ambushed Billy at Marty's house yesterday and got him to agree to an interview.'

'First of all,' I said, 'Allison didn't "ambush" your brother. We ran into him, and she *asked* him about telling his story. I agree with you: it was the wrong time and place, and I spoke to her about it.' I took a breath. 'Secondly, he didn't agree to anything. He said he needed to talk to you first. I guess he did.'

'Damn straight he did. He's done his time, and for the past ten years he's gotten his life going in the right direction. Why would I want him to risk fucking that up?'

There was something in Bobby Taylor's tone that told me he was more concerned about how this would reflect on him than on his brother. After all, Billy worked for Bobby now, and any conversation about how he'd gotten his life back together would have to include his new job. Bobby obviously wouldn't want his brother's past to hurt his company's image. I didn't say that to Bobby, though.

'So you advised Billy not to talk to Allison, I guess?'

'I *advised* him of shit. I *told* him not to talk to any reporters.' I think he realized he was getting a little too hot and, like any great athlete, he took a moment to cool himself down. A half minute later he spoke again. I took that time to step back a foot or so. He was a little too close for comfort. He now lowered his voice. 'You know Billy's a bit slow, Raymond. I assume your girlfriend knows the same?'

I nodded. 'She does.'

'Then why would she ask him to do something like this? The least she coulda done was consult with me first, you know. I'm still looking out for the guy.'

'I told her that,' I said. 'But he is a grown

200

man, Bobby. You said so yourself: he runs the repairs operations of your business.'

'That's because that's what he's good at,' he said. 'Talking to reporters? Hell, talking to anyone he doesn't know well is hard on him.'

I had picked up on that the day before but decided to try a compromise. 'What if you're there when she speaks with him?'

He shook his head and gave me a look like he was trying to figure out how many bites it would take to eat my face. Through gritted teeth, he said, 'I don't want him talking to her under any conditions, Ray. Is that clear?'

'It's clear to me,' I said. 'Did you call Allison?'

'I was hoping you would do that,' he said. 'I didn't want to get too heated with her.' His tone got a little lighter. 'Of course, I could also go over her head at the paper. But I don't think she'd want that, do you?'

Ah, pulling out the celebrity card. It also occurred to me that he probably spent a lot of ad dollars at Allison's paper. Must be nice being Bobby Taylor.

'I'll tell her we spoke,' I said.

'You can also tell her to leave Billy alone.'

'She's my girlfriend, Bobby. Not my daughter.'

'Tell her to stay away from Billy.'

'And if she won't?'

He took back the few feet I'd put between us. He looked down on me, and I thought I could feel his breath on my forehead. 'Then we'll have to talk again, Ray.'

'And what,' I said. 'You'll beat me up, Bobby?'

201

He stared at me, shook his head, and then laughed.

'Twenty years ago, I already would have, man,' he said. 'Now I got lawyers for shit like that. Make sure your girlfriend knows that.' He accented that by waving Allison's card in front of my face.

He turned to walk away, but I wasn't done yet.

'Hey,' I said. He turned around. 'How'd you know where I worked?'

'I called Bridges to Success,' he said. 'I'm on the board, remember.'

Right. He was leaving me with one more reminder that he was Bobby Taylor and I was a schoolteacher. I went off to go get my coffee.

Eighteen

I was outside the building drinking my coffee and still trying to calm down after Bobby Taylor's surprise visit when the front doors opened and out came Hector Robles and his father. Hector gave me a wave and his father gave me a look that said he was trying to place my face. I decided to make it easy for him.

'Raymond Donne,' I said as I stepped over to the two of them. 'We met on Saturday when I swung by your apartment to check on Hector.'

'Oh, right,' he said and shook my hand. His was the handshake of a guy who hadn't spent too much time behind a desk. 'Thanks for that, by the way. I'm not sure I got a chance to say that the other day. I was in a bit of a hurry.'

'Your wife explained it all. How's the work coming?'

'Slower than I'd like, but I wanna get it right. My dad was a carpenter and he taught me one of the most important rules about woodworking.'

'Measure twice,' I said. 'And cut once?'

He smiled. 'Your dad teach you that?'

'My dad and my uncle. Neither one was a carpenter, but they loved their little woodworking projects. They each helped the other build back-yard decks and a tree house for my sister and me. I got about as far as birdhouses.'

'Don't tell me you're a Jersey boy?' he asked.

I pretended to cringe. 'Long Island. We used to make fun of Jersey.'

'I grew up in Brooklyn,' he said. 'We made funna both of you.'

I laughed. 'What's up?' I asked. 'You feeling OK, Hector?'

'Yeah,' he said. 'I just got an orthodontist appointment. They're gonna fit me for braces.'

'*Maybe*,' Mr Robles said. 'First we gotta see how much they're gonna run us, then we'll see if they're gonna fit you or not.'

'They're not covered by insurance?' I asked.

'Not my wife's. And I've been outta work for a while, so . . .'

I remembered my conversation on the driveway yesterday with Marty Junior and his friends. Someone had said at one point it all becomes about the kids. I guessed this was one of those times.

'I'm thinking,' Hector's father said, 'that maybe I can make a deal or something. Maybe this orthodontist needs some carpentry done, and we can come to some kinda arrangement.'

'Woodwork for dental work,' I said. 'Pretty good idea.'

'If he goes for it, yeah.' He pulled out his phone and checked the time. 'We gotta run, Mr Donne. It was nice meeting you again.'

'Same here.' We shook hands again. 'You coming back later, Hector, or will we see you tomorrow?'

'Tomorrow,' he said without hesitating. 'Dad's gonna take me to lunch after the doctor's appointment.' Hector had a big smile on his face. He did need braces, I realized. But the way his eyes lit up when he smiled? No need to fix that.

'Sounds like a good deal. See you tomorrow then.'

I watched as they headed down the steps and off to their errand. Father and son, doing something as simple as going to the doctor's, and yet it wasn't all that simple. The guy's kid needed braces, and he wasn't sure he was going to be able to afford to get them. I don't remember growing up with issues like that. In his own way, I guess my dad made it look easy. But he never took me to lunch instead of back to school.

When I got back to my office, I called Allison. She was out in the field trying to find out from a private contracting firm why construction on a city-owned building was already six months behind and a million dollars over budget. She told me she could give me five minutes before her next interview.

'I just had a visit from Bobby Taylor,' I told her.

'Cool. Looks like you rate. Is he working with other kids from your school?'

'No, and I don't think that's gonna happen anytime soon.' I gave her the blow-by-blow description of our conversation.

'Ah, geez,' she said. 'Another minor celebrity with lawyers. You don't know how many times I have to deal with them. They all think they should have their own reality shows.'

'I think most of them do. But he seemed

pretty serious about protecting himself and his brother. And I got the strong feeling it was in that order.'

'His brother's a grown man and can make his own decisions.'

'You got the first part right. I'm not so sure about the second.'

'Well,' Allison said, 'that's why the paper has our own lawyers. It's not going to matter anyway if Bobby controls Billy's life the way you say he does.'

'That's the impression I got, Ally.'

'Maybe I'll luck out with Melissa and her brother.'

'If you can't get the perp, get the vic.'

'Are you trying to sound like a cop or can you just not help yourself?'

'Let's not have that conversation, OK? I'm still at work.'

'Me, too,' she said.

The silence that followed was typical of the kind that had preceded most of our recent arguments. The outcome depended on who spoke next and what they said. I went for it.

'Wanna have dinner tonight? Your 'hood this time.'

'Yeah,' she said. 'Let me call you. I got a few more interviews to do with some of the city's Building Authority people. I never know how long it's gonna take when I know the interviewee does not want to be interviewed.'

I almost told her my story about Tommy Avila but figured I'd be better off sitting on it for dinnertime talk.

206

'I'll talk to you later, then,' I said.

'Yes, you will.'

She ended the call without saying good-bye again. Whatever. At the moment the class period was changing and I liked to be out there and visible when the hallways were filled with kids. 'Proximity Control' we called it in the business. Just being a visible presence prevented half the things that could go badly. Maybe Allison had a point; I couldn't help thinking like a cop sometimes.

I was halfway through a turkey and Swiss sandwich when my cell phone rang. I was going to ignore it, but it was Edgar. I wondered if he'd gone to work or if he'd actually taken the doctor's advice from the other night and gotten some rest. That was my first question. His answer surprised me.

'Yeah,' he said. 'I still got a little headache and some nausea, but my vision's good. I've been flicking back and forth between the cable and Marty Stover's files.'

'You find anything good?'

'There's a Columbo marathon on.'

'I meant in Marty's files, Edgar.'

'Oh.' He thought about that for a bit. 'Nothing somebody would want badly enough to break into his place or mug me for, if that's what you mean.'

'That's what I meant.'

'I know you don't like coincidences, Ray,' he said. We've had that conversation many times. 'But maybe Marty's office break-in and me getting mugged have nothing to do with each other.'

'Maybe,' I said, not convinced of that yet. Then another thought hit me. 'Do the files you have go back as far as the Billy Taylor case?' I knew it was wrong that Edgar had downloaded those files, but since it was already done, what the hell?

'Give me a sec.' I could hear the sound of him working the keys on the other end. I almost felt guilty asking him to do me a favor. Almost. He had my answer in a flash.

'Yep,' he said. 'Looks like these files go back a few years before your . . .'

'Before my dad died?'

'Yeah. Sorry.'

'It's OK, Edgar. Do me a favor and make a separate folder for the Taylor files. You can do that, right?'

'And have it printed out in five minutes.'

'I don't need you to do that, Edgar, but thanks.' Then another thought struck me. 'Is it possible for you to make a copy of the Taylor file and send it to my school email?'

'Are you testing me, Ray? My head's not that bad.'

I laughed. 'Never. Sorry. When you get to it, I'd really appreciate it.'

'Consider it on its way, Ray.' He paused. 'Hey, that rhymes.'

'You're a real poet, Edgar.'

'Call me when you get it. I don't trust the Department of Ed system. It's a pretty big file so give it a few minutes before you open it. Good-bye, Ray.'

See? Even Edgar knew to say good-bye when ending a phone call.

Five minutes later, I checked my email and there was the file I wanted. I called Edgar, said thanks, and told him I'd check on him later. Then I set about to print out the file. I knew it was technically against the rules to use school equipment for personal reasons but I rationalized that with all the lunches I'd missed and overtime I'd put in since becoming a dean, the New York City Department of Education owed me a little something. I also set the printer on double-sided, saving paper on what turned out to be thirty pages. It was a big file. When the printing was done, I used a large paperclip – more school property – to bind the pages together and put the whole thing in my bookbag. I'd read it at home later.

The rest of the day passed by uneventfully and I was home on my couch with a beer and Marty's file on the Taylor case by four-thirty. I learned nothing new except the fact that big-time cases can make for boring case files. I went on the Internet and found old news articles about the case. All four major papers had covered the case extensively. Each article I read seemed to match up with what Marty had memorialized on his computer. Not that I expected anything different.

I shut down my laptop, put the case file back in its envelope, and shut my eyes. If nothing else, I could get in a quick nap before meeting up with Ally on the Lower East Side. Any teacher who tells you they don't crave afternoon naps, has either more energy than I do or is lying. I set my phone's alarm to not let me snooze past six-fifteen.

The excitement never ends.

Nineteen

'You get all the interviews you needed?'

'I got three of them,' Allison said. 'One guy was on another job across town so I missed him. I'll try tomorrow.'

'You learn anything useful?'

She laughed. 'Depends on your definition of the word. I asked all three why the job was already a million over budget and taking much longer than expected, and all three gave me different answers.' She took a sip of her vodka and tonic. 'I love it when I let these guys – although one was a woman – just talk. They practically write the piece for me.'

I let that sink in as I took a sip of my beer. We were sitting at 2A – a cool little bar on the Lower East Side at the corner of Second Street and Avenue A, hence the name – and I was enjoying a Sixpoint Crisp. They didn't have any Brooklyn Brewery beers, but Sixpoint was in Brooklyn and a damned good brewery itself. One must make sacrifices when one has to.

I told Allison about my day, highlighted by the story of Tommy Avila and the lengths he went through to avoid school. She listened carefully and shook her head.

'School phobia?' she said. 'That poor kid. How do you deal with that?'

'Therapy, for starters,' I said. 'We've got a

211

great school counselor – you've met Elaine – but he's going to have get some outside help, too. Not just him but the whole family. I also have to figure out if there's anything happening at the school that exacerbates the problem.'

She smiled. 'I like how you don't put it all on the family. It really does take a village, huh?'

I've always hated philosophies that could fit on a bumper sticker, not that I was against using them when dealing with kids – and parents – with short attention spans.

'Something like that. I've never known him to be bullied or get into any kind of trouble. Not more than most of my other kids anyway.'

'Speaking of your kids . . .'

'Uh-oh,' I said and took another sip from my can of beer. 'I feel another story idea coming on.'

'You'll like this one, Ray. I promise.'

I leaned back as an ambulance sped up First Avenue filling the bar with red and white lights. 'G'head,' I said. 'Hit me.'

'It's about Marty Stover,' she said. 'More about Bridges to Success really, but his murder got me thinking.'

'I'm listening.'

'Since his murder is news, why not capitalize – OK, wrong word.' She caught herself. *Nice.* 'Why not take advantage of the situation and do a feature on his charity?'

'Sounds good so far. How does it involve me?'

'You got that kid involved. What's his name? Herbert?'

'Hector,' I said.

'Hector, right. I was thinking I could do a piece

212

on the charity and feature one kid who's been helped by it. And since you've got this student who you hooked up with the charity, I could interview him and shadow him during one of the days he's doing what he does with Bridges.'

I considered that. 'You'd have to get his family's permission first.' I thought of Maria Robles and her affair with Marty. 'His mom may not want any attention on her kid. Or her family.' I lowered my voice. 'People who've had affairs with murder victims are particularly wary of reporters. I'm sure you understand.'

She smiled again and placed her hand on my thigh. *Uh-oh.* 'That's where you'd come in, Ray.' She stroked my leg with her thumb. 'You could vouch for me. Tell the mom I'm only interested in her kid and the work he does.'

I looked down at her hand on my leg. 'You know,' I said, 'this leg thing doesn't work *all* the time.'

She continued stroking my thigh and said, 'Just most of the time.' The smile she gave me made me realize this was going to be one of those times.

'When would you want to talk to Hector?' I asked.

'The sooner the better,' she said. 'When does he work for the family?'

This is Monday, I thought. 'Tomorrow. He does Tuesdays at the art shop and Saturdays with the old man.' I told her about Hector's dual role with the Stern family.

'Oh, man,' she said. 'If I can get some quotes from the elder Stern, that would add some great

213

color to the piece. Didn't you tell me his family left Germany right before that shit got bad?'

'That shit' was the Holocaust, Ally.

'Let's not get too far ahead of ourselves. We – you – still need Hector's parents' permission to talk to him,' I reminded her. 'And, yes, from what I was told, Mr Stern's father read the writing on the wall and took his family to France and then here. He started the business around nineteen forty, and after he died, his son took over. Now it's run by his grandson.'

'My God, Ray. I hate to sound like a broken record, but this is another great story. The fact that I can tie it in with Marty's murder makes it a sure sell to my editor. This could even be a two- or three-part piece.'

I felt another snarky comment coming, something along the lines of how she was getting a little too excited about turning other people's tragedies – in this case, murder and the Holocaust – into stories she could pitch to her bosses. I stifled it, and instead said, 'Great. Then let's put tonight's dinner on your paper's expense tab.'

'You're becoming quite the source, tough guy.'

'Not the role I was hoping to play in this relationship, Ally.'

Her stroking turned to a playful slap. 'I'm teasing you, Ray. Let's not turn this into another argument.'

'I just don't want to have to watch everything I say thinking it might become fodder for one of your stories.'

'Then,' she said, back to stroking, 'stop leading such an interesting life.'

214

Right.

'Let's get two more of these,' she said, pointing to our almost empty drinks. 'And then see where the evening takes us.'

'Sounds like a plan,' I said.

The evening took us through a few more drinks and then dinner at a terrific Ukrainian restaurant around the corner from 2A. We shared a plate of beef stroganoff and another of goulash as Ally told me about the most recent spate of layoffs at her paper. This was a nationwide trend for over a decade now as more and more people were getting their news online, cancelling their subscriptions, and passing up the corner newsstand. A big part of that news was how businesses in all sectors across the country were cutting staff or moving overseas. Not for the first time in recent years, I marveled at the concept that we schoolteachers had more job security than most of the rest of the working class. I'm not the most pro-union guy out there, but it was economic times like these that made me glad I was part of one. Even when I was a cop I had my union's protection. How so many politicians who claim to be pro-police and pro-middle class could publicly speak out against unions and still gain popularity was something I'd never understand. Unions *made* the middle class in the fifties and sixties. People in this country were so willing to vote against their own best interests because some rich guy – usually white – in a suit and a nice haircut told them what they wanted to hear. This made me

215

think of the Stern family and how Hitler had convinced a large number of Germans that the Jews were responsible for their country's ills.

'Where'd you go there, Raymond?' Ally asked. 'I seem to have lost you for a while. Am I boring you?'

'Just the opposite. I think your story about the Sterns is a great idea, even if Hector's folks say no to his participation.'

'Are you trying to flatter yourself into coming home with me?'

'No,' I said. 'But is that how to do it?'

'It's a good start.'

I looked at the clock on the restaurant's wall. It was almost ten and I had to be at work the next day.

'Then let's pay up and head to your place.'

Allison reached into her bag and pulled out her wallet. 'It's nice to know I'm not the only one in this relationship with good ideas.'

Twenty

There are few things more smile-inducing than heading off to work after a night of good food and great sex. I'm sure more than a few of my fellow commuters on the L train were wondering what the bemused smile on my face was all about. Maybe they just thought I was really enjoying my cup of coffee.

When I got to the school, I checked my email and phone for any messages. There were none. After I got the kids inside and made sure the halls were cleared for first period, I checked to see if Tommy Avila had made it to school. He hadn't. I went back to my office and called his house. I got the answering machine and left a brief message saying I hoped to see Tommy sometime during the day. I also tried both parents' cell phones and left similar messages. Maybe they decided to keep him home after what had happened yesterday, which may have seemed like a good idea but did play into what the kid wanted. I decided to put off judgment for another time.

My next phone call was to Hector's house. His mother picked up.

'Is everything OK?' she asked.

'Yeah,' I said and then explained that I knew a reporter – who just happened to be my girl-friend – who wanted to include Hector in a story on Marty Stover's charity.

'I'm not so sure that's a good idea,' she said. 'Considering my relationship with Marty, I mean.'

I was prepared for that. 'Allison just wants to meet Hector at the Sterns' shop. See what he does and what he's learning. There will be nothing about you or the rest of the family in her story.' I went on to tell her that Allison also wanted to interview the elder Stern about his family history.

'So there'll be nothing about me or my husband and daughter?'

'Just Hector,' I said. 'It's all about Bridges to Success. I'm sure Allison will mention that Hector lives with his parents and sister nearby, but that's it.'

I waited a while as she considered that. After about ten seconds, she said, 'I guess that'll be OK then. Marty deserves it.'

I told her I agreed completely. She was reassured that I would be accompanying Hector and would be there during the interview. We agreed to speak again after the interview and then we both went on with our days.

Tuesday afternoon was warmer still, so Hector and I decided against taking the bus and walked from school to the Sterns' shop. Allison was outside on her cell phone when she noticed us approaching. She ended her call, gave me a chaste kiss on the cheek, and stuck out her hand to my student.

'You must be Hector,' she said. 'Man, they're making eighth graders bigger than when I was in middle school. Handsomer, too.'

Hector obliged her with a shy laugh. 'Nice to meet you, Ms Rogers.'

'Thank you for agreeing to talk to me, Hector. It's a shame, what happened to Mr Stover. I'm sure he'd be glad to know something good has come out of it.'

I gave Allison a look that said, *Ease up on the bullshit,* even though it was similar to the way I'd sold Hector's mom on the interview.

'He was a nice man,' Hector said. 'Bridges is a good program.'

Allison reached into her oversized handbag she used while working and took out her pad and pencil. I knew somewhere in that bag was also the camera she took with her when the paper didn't send her out with a photographer. She wrote something down in her pad and said, 'How long have you been with Bridges to Success?'

'A little over a year,' he said after some thought. 'Right after last Christmas.'

'And why did you decide to join?'

'Mr Donne thought it'd be a good idea,' he said. 'But also, I wanted to learn about how to run a business. I kinda thought it would be interesting to learn about another culture. I mean, these people – the Orthodox and Hassidic Jewish people – are my neighbors, and I knew so little about them.'

That last part could have been taken directly from the charity's literature, but it was nice hearing the words come from Hector. Allison ate it up and wrote it down. The conversation went back and forth like that for another few minutes. Then Allison said, 'Why don't you take me

219

inside? Show me what you do and introduce me to the Sterns.'

Hector opened the door for us and we entered what looked like a hardware store, except all the tools were smaller and designed to create art. Like any independent shop in the city, the aisles were tight and packed with as much merchandise as could fit. I could see toward the back of the store where the place seemed to open up a bit. Feeling a touch claustrophobic, that's where I wanted to be, so I headed in that direction as Hector pointed out and explained things to Allison.

When I got to the back, it became clear that this was where the framing and other services were provided. There was a big white counter with a cash register on one end and a small communications center on the other. In between, about five feet behind the counter and with his back to me, stood Joshua Stern doing something with a large machine. I said hello.

He turned around. 'Hello, Mr Donne. Is it four o'clock already?' He wiped his right hand on his apron, reached over the counter, and shook my hand. He looked over my shoulder. 'Your lady friend, the reporter. She is here?'

'Hector's showing her the nuts and bolts,' I said. 'Or should I say the brushes and paints.' I chuckled at my own little joke. Stern didn't.

'Good, good,' he said, brushing himself off some more and straightening his apron, which I now noticed had his store logo printed on the front. One of his print jobs, I figured. 'Did she bring a photographer?'

220

'No,' I said. 'She tends to take her own pictures, and then her editor decides if the story needs any art.' I realized who I was talking to and added, 'The newspapers call photographs art.'

'Of course.'

He seemed disappointed that there was no guarantee of any pictures to accompany the story. It occurred to me that he'd been looking at this from the point of view of a small business owner. He couldn't buy the kind of publicity this piece was going to bring him. *Good for him*. If Ally and her paper are getting something, and Bridges is getting something, why shouldn't Sterns' Art Supply get some free advertising out of it?

'Is your son here today?' I asked.

'He is downstairs. Usually on Tuesday he is at home doing his studies and schoolwork, but with the reporter here today, I wanted the extra help. Just in case. Besides, we are thinking of expanding, and the basement has been neglected for years.'

'You know,' I said, leaning over the counter. 'A picture with the two boys – from two different Williamsburg communities – would be hard for any editor to resist.'

He gave me a confused look that quickly turned into a smile. 'I will go get Daniel now, Mr Donne.' He was about to turn when he stopped and said, 'Thank you.'

I gave him a silent nod and a smile just before he went off to fetch his son.

'And here,' I heard Hector say from behind me, 'is where Mr Stern does the framing and

221

the big print jobs. I'm starting to learn how to make posters and enlarge photos, but most of the time I work with the computer or show customers where they can find supplies. I want to learn framing next.'

Allison wrote most of that down in her pad. 'Has your time here made you think about going into the art supply business?'

'Not really,' Hector said. 'But I'm learning that there's a lot more to running a business than I thought. There's ordering, inventory, keeping up on what the competition is doing. Mr Stern is always on the phone with suppliers, trying to get the same deals the big guys get. It's hard to keep up when the other guys can offer big discounts because they can buy so much more.'

'How does he stay in business?' I asked, more out of curiosity than trying to help Ally with her story. And Stern had just told me he was considering expanding.

'He likes to say he provides a more personal service than the chains. And there's a lot of artists in Williamsburg who like the idea of doing business with an independent instead of a nationwide store.'

'You have been listening,' Joshua Stern said as he came out from behind the counter with his son, Daniel, who had the same look he'd had at the shiva two days before. He was making it clear to everyone around that he'd rather not be here. 'Ms Rogers,' the father said. 'This is my son, Daniel.'

'Nice to meet you, Daniel.'

222

Daniel said the same thing back but with less enthusiasm.

Mr Stern said, 'Daniel. Why don't you and Hector show Ms Rogers around a little more?' He paused. 'Perhaps a picture of the two of you in front of the store?'

'That's a great idea, Mr Stern,' Allison said. 'And like I told you over the phone, I'd like to talk to your father. Get a little more history from someone who's lived it.'

'Of course. Daniel, when you are done showing Ms Rogers around – and she has taken your picture – bring her upstairs to see your grandfather.' He turned to Hector. 'I will call up to him so he is not surprised by your bringing a guest.' To Allison he said, 'I told him you might wish to speak with him, but he forgets sometimes.'

'I understand,' Allison said. 'Boys. Lead the way.'

The three of them walked toward the entrance to the store. I hoped Allison got a good shot of the two teenagers in front of the shop sign.

'That Daniel,' Mr Stern said. 'I sometimes worry about him, Mr Donne.'

'How so?'

'He seems so disinterested in the business. It will be his someday, and he seems not to care about learning how it works. Hector shows more interest than my own son.'

'He's a teenager, Mr Stern,' I said. 'They're not designed to please their parents. I'm sure he'll come around.'

Joshua Stern gave me a forced smile. 'I hope you are right, but with all the distractions kids

223

have these days, I find him to be . . . not like I was at his age.'

'He seems like a bright young man. Have you considered that maybe he won't take over the family business?'

He nodded. 'I have, and that saddens me, but I'm starting to realize it may be beyond my control. That is hard to accept when I knew my future when I was his age.'

'Different times,' I said. 'And he's still only a teenager. You never know what changes the next few years will bring.'

'That is true. I have also been told that maybe my daughter will take over.'

The idea seemed so foreign to him, I just repeated, 'Different times.'

We stood there for a while, considering the possibilities in silence. Then he said, 'If you will excuse me, I have to let my father know that Daniel is bringing Hector and Ms Rogers to see him.'

'Of course,' I said. 'I'll find something to keep myself busy.'

I knew that something was going to be the small restaurant that sold beer a few doors down. I texted Ally to let her know where I'd be when she was done with the boys and the elder Mr Stern. She might also want to talk more with Joshua Stern as well, so I had no idea how long she'd be.

When I got to the restaurant, I ordered a Dominican beer from the Hispanic woman who seemed to be server, cook, and hostess all rolled

224

into one. I told her I wouldn't be eating for at least an hour, and even that was up to my girlfriend.

'*Si,*' she said. '*Su novia. Siempre la novia.*'

Always the girlfriend. I smiled and took out the Taylor file Edgar had sent me from my bookbag. At least I'd have a beer and plenty of reading to do as I waited. I was hoping I'd be able to make sense out of Marty's decades-old notes.

I started with a copy of the police complaint. It was pretty easy to follow as I'd written quite a few myself during the years I'd been a cop. A little over twenty years ago, on June twentieth, Melissa Miller called nine-one-one early in the morning to report that she had been sexually assaulted the night before at a private party. Apparently, she had not yet informed any of her family members what had happened.

When asked if she knew her attacker, she said it was one of the Taylor boys, William. The report went on to say that Melissa was later accompanied by her brother – the detective had convinced her to contact a relative or friend – to Nassau County Medical Center where a rape kit was performed. It was determined that she had sustained wounds to her vaginal area as well as her left thigh, consistent with her accusation of sexual assault. There was no semen found, which indicated that the assailant wore a condom. She also had a wound to her right cheek and a contusion on the back of her head. The blood test revealed a high blood alcohol content.

It sounded – at least to me – as if she'd been

hit in the face, knocked down, and then assaulted. Her statement concluded with her regaining consciousness hours later – she wasn't sure how much time had passed since the attack – and then walking home. She said when she got home, she felt embarrassed about what had happened. She knew she'd been drinking pretty heavily and felt that no one would believe her story.

The cops interviewed all the other guests who were at the party that night, including the Taylor twins. Everybody agreed that they were all drinking heavily and had little recollection of what had transpired once they had returned from the beach and gone to the house. They admitted to a lot of 'making out' and 'feeling up' each other, both in couples and in groups. Not one of the kids could verify Melissa's story of being assaulted, but one girl did remember Melissa saying at one point that 'it would be cool to hook up' with the star baseball player.

As for the Taylor boys, they both admitted to kissing and hugging all the girls and that Melissa was a willing participant in these pairings. They both said that maybe she felt bad about what she had done and then made up the story about being assaulted. None of the guests – including the Taylors – could account for how Melissa had sustained her injuries. One of the other boys suggested that maybe she had fallen and hit her head while drunk. As for the vaginal injuries, they were a mystery to all interviewed.

In separate interviews two days later with another detective, the Taylor boys continued to profess their ignorance. Again, they both admitted that they had kissed and 'felt up' Melissa but that she was 'into it,' and denied any knowledge of her wounds or assaulting her. In fact, the cops now had a statement from Bobby's girlfriend that she and Bobby had left the party early. She had started to sober up and was angry that Bobby was 'fooling around' with the other girls.

On the third day after Melissa's accusation, the detectives assigned to the case called the Taylor home and requested a third interview. It was at this point that the Taylor parents hired a lawyer – Marty Stover. Transcripts showed that the subsequent interviews took place at Marty and my father's office, and that my father was present. Each brother's account of the night of the party was consistent with the other's. To me, after reading the statements three times – and ordering a second beer – they seemed a little too consistent, as if they'd been rehearsed with the help of their lawyer. Bobby's statement was somewhat more polished than Billy's, and the detectives pushed Billy hard enough to make Marty stop the interview.

Along with the interviews, Marty had made copious notes about his own conversations with the kids at the party. According to what I read, some of the kids admitted that Billy Taylor had paid particular attention to Melissa. Marty had made a note that he felt an arrest was imminent.

It never got to that point because, before an arrest could be made, Billy Taylor came to Marty, accompanied by his parents, and admitted he had assaulted Melissa. The alcohol and pot had made it 'very hard' for him to remember exactly what had happened that night. What he was sure of was that his brother had left the party with his girlfriend.

With Marty, his parents, and his brother Bobby, Billy Taylor turned himself in to the detective-in-charge and confessed to the sexual assault of Melissa Miller. In exchange for a reduced sentence, Billy pleaded no contest, thus ensuring that none of the parties involved would have to endure a trial that would have had strong media attention. Billy was sentenced to fifteen years, with the possibility of parole after ten.

The rest, as some would say, is history. Billy did his time in prison. Bobby went on to make millions in professional baseball and then turned his celebrity status into an extremely successful post-pitching career. Now both Taylor brothers were living their lives, and it was all Melissa Miller could do to leave the house for an occasional movie, trip to the beach, and dinner with her brother.

Life's like that sometimes.

'You studying for the bar exam?'

I looked up to see my girlfriend standing above me. 'The only bar exam I could pass,' I said, raising my beer, 'would involve some of these.'

She managed a forced laugh. 'What are all those papers?'

'Melissa Miller's case against Billy Taylor,' I said. 'And, before you ask, no, you may not have access to these.' I touched the pile of pages. 'These were procured through less-than-legal

228

means. Fruit from the poisonous tree, as my
uncle would say.'

'Edgar?' she asked and then caught herself.
'Never mind. I don't want to know. I would,
however, like one of those beers.'

I signaled for the woman to bring two more
beers over, and packed the file away in my
bookbag. Allison had a look on her face I hadn't
seen before. Something was bugging her and it
wasn't me.

'How was your visit with the Sterns and
Hector?' I asked.

'Good, good,' she said. She gave the small
restaurant a quick look-around. 'Does this place
have a restroom?'

'In the back, yeah. You want to eat here, by
the way? The food's good.'

'Right now,' she said, 'I'd like you to join me
in the restroom.'

Not one to be easily shocked, all I could say
was, 'Excuse me? Is this your way of thanking
me for setting today up?'

'Don't be an ass, Ray. I need to show you
something.'

'Something you can't show me here?'

She gave me the *duh* look. 'Just come with
me, OK?'

The woman came over with our beers. '*Su
novia?*' she asked.

'Yes,' I said. '*Mi novia.* We'll be right back.'

If the woman questioned why Allison and I
were both heading to the restroom at the same
time, she kept it to herself. I'm sure running a
restaurant in this part of Williamsburg she'd see

229

a lot of strange stuff. This probably didn't even register.

When we got to the restroom, Allison shut the door and made sure it was locked. She made me a little nervous as I waited for her to explain.

'How well do you know the Sterns?' she asked.

'Not well. I met Joshua and his son a few times, including today, briefly. Why?'

'What do you know about Joshua's father? The one that Hector works with on Saturdays.'

'Never met the man,' I said. 'What's going on here, Ally? You're obviously upset about something.'

She took a deep breath. 'Well, I just met him,' she said.

'And . . .?'

'He's a . . . fascinating man.' She paused. 'I'm definitely coming back for more stuff on him. He's a bit shaky on the present, but he's got an amazing story about his family and getting out of Germany.'

'So what's bothering you so much?'

'He gave me something,' she said.

I remembered my visit to the Sterns' house. 'Let me guess. A painting?'

She looked at me as if I'd just performed a mindreading trick. 'How could you possibly know that?'

'His son told me he does that from time to time. Just last week, he gave a picture his son had painted to his home health attendant. Is that the same one he gave you?'

'Not quite,' she said and then reached into her bag. She pulled out a small, framed painting

230

and handed it to me. It was about the size of a composition notebook and framed simply, like the one I'd seen the other day painted by Joshua Stern.

'Why didn't you say you couldn't accept it?'

'He insisted. When I tried to give it back, he got all upset and his breathing started getting all labored. He showed me where his oxygen tank was, and he took a few hits from it.'

'Yeah,' I said. 'I heard he gets upset if you refuse. That's why the aide gave the painting back to Joshua. If you're so upset, let's just do that.'

'I am not *upset*, Ray,' she said. 'I'm kind of shocked.'

I looked at the painting I was holding. 'Why?'

'Look at the name on the painting.'

I found it in the lower right corner. It was hard to make out, but when I did I could see what had Ally shocked.

'This guy's pretty famous.'

She smirked. 'Is Mariano Rivera pretty famous?'

Allison had this habit of, whenever she felt I was not understanding something, to put it in baseball terms for me. It usually worked.

'So how valuable is this?'

'If it's real,' she said. 'My god, Ray, it's a *Paul Klee*.'

'You gotta give this back, Ally. You can't be running around the city with something like this.'

'I'm not planning on *running around the city with* it, Ray. I am planning on showing it to an art expert I know to see if it's the real deal.'

'And what if it is?'

'Then, based on what you've told me about the Stern family history and what the elder Mr Stern just told me – and gave me – that family may be sitting on millions of dollars' worth of art.'

I took that in. 'You got all that from this one piece that may or may not be real?'

'You know me better than that,' she said. 'I'm just considering all possibilities here. Isn't that what cops do?'

That was another thing Ally did when I wasn't quite there yet: put things in terms of police thinking.

'Where's this art dealer?' I asked. 'And when can he meet us?'

'Us?'

I returned that question with silence.

'He's downtown,' she finally said. 'On Sullivan. I just got off the phone with him. He was about to close up until I told him what I had. He said he could meet me at six at his gallery, after he finishes up with a client.'

'OK. So we finish our beers and go see your guy. Then what?'

'Let's see what we find out.' She took a deep breath. 'This could be big, Ray. I mean really big.'

'Pulitzer big?' I asked.

'Remember the part about *not* being an ass?' she said. 'Keep it up.'

'I'll do my best.'

'Allison, my dear, you are absolutely amazing.'

The three of us were sitting around Charles

Mantle's computer in his gallery on Sullivan Street. Allison had told me on the subway from Brooklyn that she had met Mantle a few years back when she was writing an article on how the upswing in the economy was affecting the art-collecting world. It turned out Mantle – who, I am glad to report, did not call his shop 'Mantle Pieces' – was well informed about art looted by the Nazis and art that had been taken out of Europe before the Nazis could get their hands on it. The piece that Mr Stern had given Allison just might fit into the latter category.

'I don't see or hear from you for years,' Mantle said, stroking his black goatce. 'And then when I do, you bring me this extraordinarily mysterious piece.'

'But is it real?' she asked.

Mantle looked back at his computer to a picture of the artwork – *Landscape with Rising Moon,* according to the text. It had taken him all of five minutes to find it listed on a few sites dealing with looted or missing art from Nazi Germany.

'Allison,' he said, in an accent that sounded part New England and part British, 'I know *I* am your expert, but I cannot determine the answer to that question until I have consulted with *my* expert.' He leaned in closer to his computer screen and then looked at the picture in the frame we had brought him. 'However, from what you have told me, the timeline does seem to fit. This particular piece went missing circa nineteen thirty-seven. It is listed as "confiscated" by the Nazis, but that's vague at best. And . . . .'

233

We waited for him to finish the sentence. When he didn't, Allison said, 'And what, Charles?'

He looked at us both. 'With all due respect to Mr Klee,' he said, 'this is a relatively minor piece of work. In my opinion, it is not one worthy of forgery.'

'So it's probably genuine?' she asked.

'Don't go putting words in my mouth, dear. I am just saying that if one *were* to fake a Klee, there are far more worthy candidates than this one. But, if it is indeed the genuine item, it is quite valuable. It is a Klee, after all.' He looked at it again. 'And where did you say you found it?'

'We didn't,' I said. 'We'd prefer to keep that confidential at the moment.'

Mantle studied me for ten seconds and said, 'I like this one, Allison. He's got that rough-around-the-edges feel I find quite alluring.'

Somehow, his appraisal made me feel more like a piece of artwork than a person. I didn't know whether to feel flattered or objectified, so I let it go.

'When can your expert take a look at it?' Allison asked.

'Not until tomorrow,' Mantle said. 'I called him shortly after you called me about what you thought you had, and he's driving back from a long weekend upstate. He was quite excited about the prospect and promised to meet me here in the morning. Which tomorrow will be earlier than I usually open.' He ran his index finger lovingly around the frame. 'In the meantime, have you two decided what to do with the piece?'

'We were hoping you could help us with that,' Allison said.

'I can, indeed. I have a safe in the back of the shop. It will be quite secure I can assure you. It's where I store all my . . . extraordinary inventory.'

'That works for me,' Allison said. 'Raymond?'

'As long as we get a receipt,' I said.

It took Mantle a few seconds, but he laughed. 'Oh, I do like you, Raymond. Yes, indeed. I like you very much.'

Once again, I was being appraised.

'You know,' Mantle went on. 'If this piece is the real thing, it may have been part of the *Entartete Kunst.*'

Allison smiled. 'Charles,' she said, 'my German is limited to ordering bratwurst with sauerkraut and a Beck's.'

'Sorry,' he said. 'Sometimes I can't help but show off a teensy bit. In nineteen thirty-seven, Hitler and his Nazi cronies put on an art exhibition called *Entartete Kunst:* "The Degenerate Art Exhibition." It featured works by Mr Klee as well as Kandinsky and Kokoschka. He also made sure to include some German artists like Beckmann and Nolde.'

'For what purpose?'

'You know Hitler was a failed artist before becoming . . . a politician, right?'

'Yeah,' she said. 'I've seen some of his stuff online. Pretty bad art.'

'Well, poor, untalented Adolf preferred realism to modernism. He liked a good natural landscape or building. He equated abstract and

235

expressionistic art to the moral decay of society and promised they'd never find their way again to the German people. He spun it as one more way to keep Germany pure, but most historians feel it was his way of getting revenge for his own lack of success. The Nazis told those who came to the show – and it toured all over Germany – the work was done by Jews and Bolsheviks.'

'Klee wasn't a Jew,' Allison said.

'Most of the artists weren't,' Mantle explained. 'But if Hitler could sell his fellow countrymen on the lack of morals in their art, it would support his view that Jews were evil. This' – he held up the picture that may or may not have been painted by Klee – 'is one of the paintings rumored to have been publicly burned by the Nazis. A symbolic cleansing, if you will. The works that were displayed were done so poorly. They were hung askew, surrounded by graffiti; it was all designed to put a negative spin on the art and the artist.'

'Did the Germans buy into it?'

'Some did, the ones who wanted to believe whatever came out of their *Fuhrer*'s mouth. Others knew it was probably the last time they'd get to see the pieces in the exhibition so they went. Millions of people saw the show. Say what you want about the man, but Hitler knew how to attract a crowd. If he were to curate and promote such a show today, he'd make millions.'

'You sound like you almost admire him,' I said.

'Oh, no, Raymond. Not him. Just his showman-ship.'

'And he made the trains run on time.'

Mantle laughed for a few seconds longer than my little joke merited.

'Give me your card, Allison.' She obliged. 'I'll call you this evening after my friend calls me. But do be prepared to be here at eight in the morning.'

'I can do that,' Allison said.

'And you, Raymond?' he asked. 'Can I expect to see you here, as well?'

'I've got my day job, Charles. Sorry.'

'That's too bad. You two have a good evening then.' He looked at me again and said, in a tone dripping with sexual innuendo, 'Don't be up too late, now.'

Twenty-One

The suspension hearing that had been scheduled for Monday morning had been rescheduled for Wednesday morning. I knew this because it was the first thing my principal told me as I walked into school that day.

'I could have used a little heads up, Ron,' I said to my boss.

'They'll be here in an hour, Ray,' he said. 'That's your heads up.' Then he went back to his office to do what school leaders do.

Must be nice to be the principal. But, in all honesty, I wouldn't want that job no matter how much more it paid than mine. Too much paperwork, too much time with administrators who wouldn't know what a student looked like if one were chewing on their leg, and too many daily reminders of how 'data' was driving the field of education.

An hour later, I was sitting in my office with Carlos, his mother, and Elaine Stiles, the school counselor. A little less than two weeks ago, Carlos had made the mistake of bringing a small knife to school. He then made the bigger mistake of showing it off in the lunchroom. One of Carlos's friends, afraid of what trouble his buddy might get into, informed me of the knife, and Carlos was suspended.

If we – my principal, actually – wanted to, we

238

were well within our rights to request a safety transfer for Carlos to another school in our district. After discussing this with my boss, we decided that Carlos did not represent the kind of threat to the safety of our school as to merit finding him a new place to finish out the year. We also knew that if we did request a transfer, we were opening ourselves up to receiving a kid from another school who could very well represent a real safety issue. The devil you know.

'So,' I began, 'we're not going to waste any more time discussing that you found the knife on the way to school, or that it was your brother's and you're not sure how it got in your jacket, right?'

Carlos looked at me. Those were the two tales he had spun the day I found him to be in possession of the knife. He looked over to his mother, who shook her head slightly.

'No,' Carlos said, his eyes on his mom. 'It's mine.'

'Good,' I said. 'That saves us a lot of time. You want to tell us why you felt the need to bring a weapon to school, Carlos?'

He shrugged. 'I wanted to show off, I guess. One of my friends told you I had it, right. Somebody snitched?'

'Nobody *snitched*,' I said. 'Somebody – *a friend* – was looking out for you. They were worried you'd get yourself in trouble.'

'I did,' he said. 'I got suspended, didn't I?'

'Bigger trouble than that. Kids with blades sometimes end up using them.'

'He wouldn't have done that,' his mother said.

239

She looked tired, and I knew she had to go to work after this meeting; she was another parent at risk of pissing off her boss because her kid had done something. 'He's not that kind of boy.'

'Maybe not,' I said. 'But having a weapon on you can sometimes make you think you're more powerful than you are. It can lead to bad decision-making.' I turned to Elaine. 'That's why I asked the school counselor to be here.'

'You gonna make me go to counseling?' Carlos asked, not pleased with that possibility.

'We're not going to *make you* do anything, Carlos,' Elaine said. 'We'd like you to *choose* to go to counseling. The same way you *chose* to bring a knife to school.'

Truth be told, we *were* going to make him go to counseling. That was the deal I'd made with my boss. Carlos gets to stay at our school, but he sees Ms Stiles once a week for individual counseling and once for group. He was getting off easy, and Elaine convinced me to make it seem like it was his choice. Give him some sense of the power he was obviously looking for.

I explained to Carlos and his mother what the other option was. It didn't take Carlos long to make the right choice.

'OK,' Elaine said. 'I'll see you this afternoon during gym.'

'I can't go to gym?' Carlos said.

'We all have to make sacrifices,' I said. 'This is one of yours. You're going to like talking with Ms Stiles. She's very good at what she does.'

Mrs Negron nodded. Carlos was not happy. *Too bad.* I wrapped up the meeting, told Mrs

240

Negron we'd be in touch, and sent Carlos off to class. When it was all over, Elaine said, 'That was easier than I thought.'

'That,' I said, 'is why we get the big money.'

The last of the kids heading home had gone. Quite a few were still hanging around the play-ground – some of them actually playing – while the rest just talked and hung out, knowing that as soon as they got home that was it for the day. Most of my kids lived in neighborhoods where a lot of their parents wouldn't let them out after school. Hence, the longer they stayed 'at school' – even if that meant the playground – they could enjoy the company of their friends and avoid getting to their homework.

I was heading up the steps to the school when my cell phone rang. It was Allison so I stopped and answered.

'You didn't get enough of me yesterday?' I said.

'I think Charles didn't get enough of you, Ray. Again, it's a good thing I'm not the jealous type. I just got off the phone with him, and you were a major topic of our conversation.'

'What about the other topic of conversation?' I asked.

'His expert came by as promised,' she said. 'He studied the piece for over an hour and was quite impressed.'

'What exactly did he say?'

'He said, and I quote, "I see no reason to believe it is not the genuine item."'

'So,' I said. 'It's the real deal?'

241

'That's not exactly what he said, Ray. He needs more time to confer with his Klee expert, but at the moment, there's none of the obvious signs of it being a forgery.'

'Wow,' I said, almost to myself. I waved to a few teachers as they headed down the stairs. Josephine Levine had her usual large bag, which I knew was stuffed with lots of writing assignments that she'd be grading tonight. She gave me a big smile anyway. 'Did he say anything about what it might be worth?'

'He did.'

She made me wait. She enjoyed teasing me when the opportunity arose. Most of the time I enjoyed it. This was not one of those times.

'And . . .' I said.

'And . . . he said if it is a genuine Klee, it could be valued at over half a mil, maybe even pushing seven figures.'

'Holy fucking shit.'

'That's not the term he used, Ray. But it's close.'

And we were just walking around the city with it yesterday as if it were nothing more than some Chinese takeout. What the hell was Mr Stern doing with a painting that could possibly be worth over half a million dollars?

'And that was only one highlight of my day,' Allison said.

'Jesus, Ally. I thought my days were interesting. What else happened?'

'Billy Taylor called me an hour ago.'

'To tell you that his brother told him not to talk with you?'

'Quite the opposite,' she said. 'He said he *wants* to talk with me. Tomorrow.'

'Even though his brother forbade him?'

'It seemed to me that he wanted to talk to me *because* his brother forbade him. He seemed rather clear on that point.'

'How so?'

'He said he was tired of people telling him what to do and what not to do, and who to talk to and who not to talk to. He sounded like the way you describe your kids.'

I gave that some thought. 'Tomorrow, huh? That's pretty quick.' She'd just asked him about it three days ago at Marty's shiva.

'There's more,' she said.

'I'm listening.'

'He said he'll only talk to me if you're there.'

'Me?'

'That's what he said.'

'He say why he wants me there?'

'He did,' she said. 'He said your father was very nice to him.'

'My father wasn't even his lawyer,' I reminded her. 'Marty Stover was. Why doesn't he want Marty Junior there?'

'I asked him the exact same question.'

'And what'd he say?'

'It's more what he didn't say.' And she paused, another opportunity to tease. 'He made it seem like maybe Marty's father was not very nice to him, though.'

I took a few steps away from the shadows cast by my school building and stood in the sunlight. I let that last comment sink in before speaking.

243

'Wait a minute,' I said. 'Billy Taylor implied his own lawyer wasn't nice to him? Did you ask him what he meant by that?'

'No, Ray,' she said. 'It must have slipped my mind.'

'Sorry. What did he say?'

'He said he'd talk about it tomorrow. With you there.'

'Did he say when and where? I have to work tomorrow.'

'That's fine,' she said. 'He has to be at a dealership on the West Side at four o'clock. He wants us to meet him at a place called Clinton Cove. You know it?'

'No.'

'It's on the Hudson River, Fifty-Fifth and the highway. It's about a block away from the dealership. He said he likes to hang out there when he's got business over that way. Five o'clock work for you?'

'I'll make it work,' I said.

'I had a feeling you'd say that, tough guy. I do need a favor, though, Ray.'

Another one? I almost said. 'What's that?'

'I promise I won't use it for the story.'

'What's the favor, Ally?'

'I wanna read over the files from the Taylor case.' Before I could tell her why that was not going to happen, she said, 'I know. "Fruit from the poisonous tree," but I promise, I won't put anything from the file in my piece. I just want to make sure I can validate anything he tells me tomorrow. It was over twenty years ago, his memory is likely to have some gaps in it.'

'And you want to help fill them in?'

Silence. Then, 'I'm going to ignore the sarcasm, because I know how sensitive the file is, how you obtained it, and what a big favor I'm asking. And, no, I'm not going to put words in his mouth. And I'm not going to ask any leading questions. I just want to see how closely he remembers what he told the cops and his lawyer all those years ago.'

'The lawyer who may or may not have been very nice to him?'

'Yes.'

I closed my eyes and took in some sun as I considered her request. It felt good. It felt like spring. Opening Day was a few weeks away. I must have taken longer than I thought, because Ally said, 'Ray. You still there?'

'I'm here,' I said, opening my eyes, realizing I was just putting off the inevitable. 'I'll bring the file by your place tonight.'

'Thank you,' she said, the relief coming through loud and clear. She paused again for a few seconds, thinking or something else. 'You went over the file, right?'

'A little more than skimming, I guess, but I didn't study it.'

'Was your father mentioned at all?'

'Just that he was present during some of the interviews.'

'But he didn't ask any questions or interact with any of the interviewees?'

'Not that I could tell. Why?'

'That means whatever your father did or said to Billy Taylor that was "nice,"' she said, 'had to be off the record.'

245

She was right.

'I guess we can ask him tomorrow if he remembers that.'

'It's on my list,' she said. 'I'll see you tonight. Seven o'clock good?'

'I'll be there.'

As soon as I ended the call with Allison, my phone rang. It was Edgar. I hadn't spoken to him in what seemed like a while.

'How you feeling, Edgar?' I asked.

'I'm good, Ray. Went back to work today. Home gets boring.'

'I hear ya.'

'Anything new and exciting on your end?'

That didn't take long. I told him about my conversation with Allison and what her expert had told her.

'Cheese and crackers,' he said. 'I've got a friend who deals with helping families recover lost art from Nazi Germany.'

'Really?' I said.

'Well, she's *kind of* a friend. I did some work for her law firm a while ago.'

I was about to ask what kind of work, but I realized it had to do with computers and stuff I wouldn't understand. 'So,' I said, 'families hire her to recover art work?'

There was a pause on the other end. 'Well,' he began, 'not *her* exactly.'

'Then *who* exactly?'

'A guy she works with. He's been in the papers. Want me to call her for you?'

'I'm not sure, Edgar. Allison's got her own expert on this.'

246

'Yeah, but mine's a lawyer.'

Like that was a selling point.

'OK,' I said, as much to satisfy Edgar as myself. 'Thanks.'

'No problem, Ray. I'll reach out to her. Let's talk soon.'

'Absolutely,' I said. 'Glad you're feeling better. Let me know when you're up to dinner at The LineUp.'

'You buying?'

'Yeah.'

'I'll call ya soon.' Then he hung up.

Twenty-Two

The alarm went off the next morning at six-thirty as usual. My regular habit was to lie in bed for a few minutes, catch the sports and weather – *All news. All the time* – turn on the coffee maker, and hit the shower. After the weather guy said the temps were going to be in the low fifties under sunny skies, I did what any red-blooded American male who hadn't taken a day off all year would do, I called in sick. Actually, our wonderful secretary Mary picked up and said, 'You're calling in *well*, Mr Donne. Enjoy.' It was hard to slip one past Mary.

I thanked her, and rolled over for another half hour, then got up and started my morning. I took my coffee out on the balcony and watched as my neighbor's pigeons performed their own morning ritual: making circles above the buildings and then disappearing to who knew where. I raised my coffee cup to my neighbor who gave me a salute in return. With all the years we'd both lived here, we didn't know each other's name and I wasn't sure I'd ever seen him on ground level.

Back inside, I was about to jump in the shower when a thought occurred – reoccurred? – to me: I hadn't been to the gym in over a week. Muscles would be glad to see me. He wouldn't say as much, but it would be there in the way he

248

chastised me for not coming on a more regular basis. I decided the shower could wait.

As he often did, Muscles waited for me to start walking backwards on the treadmill before engaging me in conversation. One of these days he was going to distract me a little too much and I'd go flying.

'Shame about Marty,' he said. 'He was a good guy.'

I'd forgotten that Muscles was a corporate sponsor of Marty's charity. Although he would have made a great mentor, Muscles didn't think he had the time so he just wrote Marty a generous check every year.

'Yeah,' I said. 'I heard you donated a two-year membership for the benefit.'

'Least I could do. How about you? What's been keeping you away this time?'

I went through the usual litany of work, having a girlfriend, the whole past week heading out to the Island twice. He didn't look like he was buying any of it.

'You gotta be more consistent with coming here, Raymond,' he said. 'I keep telling you you've made good progress. Now you gotta keep it up. You're at the age now where all this work's gonna pay off when you're older. Don't you wanna run around with you grandkids?'

'I don't even have regular kids yet,' I reminded him.

'Yet,' he repeated and walked away to harass another client. I thought back to my morning coffee and how nice my non-conversation with my pigeon-loving neighbor had been. I did

249

another twenty minutes on the treadmill, worked on my core, and went through the regime Muscles had designed for me to keep my knees working. After the workout, I told myself, I was getting a cheeseburger.

I spotted Allison from across Twelfth Avenue; she was on her cell phone as usual, oblivious to the rest of the city. As I crossed the avenue, I saw she was standing next to a sign that stated cyclists must dismount at that point. Then I watched as a biker came within inches of knocking her down. Must have been a tourist who didn't read English, or an alien who didn't know what a guy on a bike with a red line going through him meant. Or, more likely, a New Yorker who felt that signs applied to other people, not him.

When I reached her, I said, 'That was close.'

She looked up from her cell. 'What was close?'

I shook my head. 'Never mind.' I kissed her on the cheek. 'Are we early?'

She looked at her cell again. 'Right on time,' she said. She turned around to face the river and we both noticed him at the same time. Billy Taylor was standing on a little pier that jutted out into the Hudson. He was reaching into a bag and throwing what looked like small pieces of bread into the water. We headed over to him.

'Isn't this the part where you tell me to do most of the listening?' I asked my reporter girlfriend.

'Preferably,' she said. 'Let's see how the conversation goes. He did request – insist – that you be here after all.'

250

'Right.'

'Oh,' she said. 'I almost forgot.' She reached into her bag and pulled out the file I'd given her last night. 'Thank you again.'

'You learn anything new?' I asked, putting the file in my bag.

'Nope. It was all pretty much what the papers ran with twenty years ago. I was able to access a lot of the coverage through my paper's archives and I even watched some of the TV news stories from back then. Marty Stover knew how to work the media.'

I recalled my father saying something along those lines. My dad, on the other hand, went his whole career – shortened as it was by his heart attack – never being mentioned in the news, print or TV. Just the way he liked it. Marty, the few times he'd had a case big enough for media attention, ate it all up. He even had special suits made just for those occasions, similar to the one he'd been wearing the night he was killed.

We were about ten feet away from Billy when Allison said, 'Mr Taylor?'

Billy Taylor turned to look at us, a piece of bread in his hand. It took him a little while to remember who we were. He absentmindedly tossed the bread into the river and said, 'Ms Rogers. Mr Donne.'

'Allison and Ray,' Ally said. 'Thank you for meeting with us.'

I looked down into the river and saw a group of about a dozen geese and a few ducks competing for the bread. The slight breeze coming off the water reminding me that, as nice as the weather had been the past week, April was still about two weeks away and we probably shouldn't pack away our sweaters and winter jackets just yet. Mother Nature had a habit of teasing New Yorkers with temperatures pushing sixty degrees in March only to throw a snowstorm at us in early April. She's funny that way.

'You're welcome,' Billy said. 'My brother doesn't know I'm here, by the way. I probably should have told him or at least contacted my lawyer, but . . .'

But his lawyer was probably still Marty Stover. And he was dead.

'We understand,' Ally said. 'Do you want to go somewhere warmer to talk? I know a good diner over on Eleventh.'

'No,' he said. 'I like it here. Guess I'll have to tell him before it makes the paper, though.' He looked down at his aquatic friends and dumped the rest of the bread into the water. He rolled up the bag and stuck it in his jacket pocket. Then he showed his empty hands to the ducks and geese as if they'd understand the gesture. 'Something my mom always told us. Don't waste what you can use. I keep the ends of the bread in the freezer so when I get to the water I can feed the ducks.' He pointed over to a sign that prohibited just that. 'I ignore those rules. I know why they got them. You don't want the birds to be dependent on humans for food, but I like feeding them, so . . . .' He gave his shoulders an exaggerated shrug. I guess once you've spent ten years in prison for sexual assault, ignoring the DON'T FEED THE WILDLIFE sign didn't seem like a big deal.

Allison reached into her bag and pulled out her mini-tape recorder. She showed it to Billy. 'Do you mind if I tape the interview?' she asked. 'I want to make sure I get everything right.'

Billy shook his head. 'I don't mind. I just don't know what you want me to say.'

'You can start,' Ally said, 'with what you did today. What's a normal day like for you now that you're . . .' She seemed to be at a loss for how to put that.

Billy helped her out. 'Out of prison? Working for my brother?'

'I wanted to say "a productive member of society," but I didn't want to sound like a cliché. But what's a normal day like for you? What did you do today, for example?'

He gave that some thought. 'I went into my office at the Great Neck dealership,' he said. 'That's where the office manager is, the one I work with for maintenance and repairs. I'm not too good with the paperwork end of things, so I – we – count on her a lot. Her name's Angela. Technically, she works for me, but I couldn't do half the job without her. Angela and me make sure the work we said was going to be done was really done. We make sure our billings and invoices are in order and stuff like that. That usually takes us right up to lunch. We got six dealerships you know.'

'I read that,' Ally said. 'Impressive.'

'Bobby doesn't do things halfway, Ms Rogers. In fact, he's thinking of buying two more dealerships out in Suffolk. Right now we got two in Nassau, two in Queens, and two right here on the West Side. These are my favorites, because they're by the river. Bobby's always thinking ahead. That's what made him such a good pitcher.'

'I thought it was his cut fastball,' I said, breaking the no-talking rule.

'Lotta guys had a cut fastball, Ray,' Billy said. 'It's knowing when to throw it that made him so good.'

'Weren't you his catcher when he pitched?' I asked. Allison gave me a look that said I'd forgotten the game rules here. I ignored it.

'Every game in high school. I also played second when he played short.'

I remembered that. The papers called them the 'Taylor Made Boys.'

'So, *you* had to know when to throw it, too, right? You called the pitches.'

He paused at that. 'We kinda called them together. Me, Bobby, and Coach. He shook me off a lot of times. But when he had that pitch working, sometimes that was all I called for. The cutter.'

I turned to Allison, who, I could tell, still wanted me to shut up. 'A cut fastball,' I said, 'breaks hard right before it crosses the plate. Bobby made a lot of good hitters look stupid, and that was his ticket to college.'

As soon as those words came out of my mouth, I wanted to take them back. I shouldn't have said anything that reminded Billy who went to college and who didn't.

'So it was a pretty good pitch, huh?' Allison asked Billy.

'Nasty,' he said, his voice clearly registering admiration. 'When it was breaking, it was nasty.'

'So what do you do *after* lunch?' Allison said, taking the conversation back to the present. 'Do you come into Manhattan a lot?'

Billy had a tough time transitioning from the past to the present, so it took him a while to answer.

'At least once a week,' he finally said. 'I try to split my time evenly between the dealerships. And Bobby likes me around the office most of the time.'

'Do you still get to work on the cars yourself?' she asked.

'Yeah.' He smiled. 'It's one of the perks of being the boss, I guess.' He paused again. 'That sounds weird when I say it out loud, but I *am* kinda a boss. If I wanna work on a car, I can do it. Just today over here, someone brought in a Maserati. There was nothing wrong with it, just a scheduled maintenance. The thing was a piece of art. And I got to touch it and help make it better. That's a pretty sweet thing to be able to do.'

Allison nodded at that. I watched her trying to phrase her next question.

'So,' she started. 'You've always been good with cars?'

'Yeah,' he said. 'Even back in high school. I took auto shop instead of art. Coach was also the shop teacher. I learned a lot from him.'

'How did you keep up with the changes in technology?' Ally asked. This was the tough part. 'I mean, when you were in high school it

255

was mostly hands-on stuff. And now it's mostly computerized. With you . . . being away for ten years . . .'

'You can say it, Ms Rogers,' he said. 'When I was in prison for ten years, I took some computer classes. That was another thing I was good at in school. They weren't like the computers we have now, but I kinda understood them. When I was in prison and Bobby got to The Show, he donated some money to the prison library for up-to-date computers.'

'The Show' is baseball lingo for the major leagues.

'So when you got out, you were prepared for the changes?'

'I had to take some more courses, but, yeah, I wasn't starting from zero.'

Allison spent the next five minutes or so asking more questions about his job, his social life, his relationships after getting out of prison. Billy seemed eager to answer all of them. Things were good for him now. Having had most of his twenties taken away from him, life pushing forty was remarkably normal. Then she shifted the conversation.

'I'd like to go back to the night of the assault,' she said.

Billy's face lost most of its emotion. It wasn't completely blank, but it was close. He looked like he knew the topic might come up but was hoping it would not.

'OK,' he said reluctantly.

'Can you tell me what happened that night?'

'You mean everything?'

'Whatever you remember. I know it was twenty years ago, but whatever you can remember would be helpful.'

He thought about that for half a minute and then let out a deep breath I didn't know he was holding in.

'It was a party,' he began. 'We were a few weeks away from graduation, the baseball season was over, and we were all going to college in a few months, so we decided to start the parties early. Bobby and me had scholarships, so we were really in the mood to party and hang out until September.'

'Do you remember who was at the party?'

He shook his head. 'Not everybody. A whole lot of us went to the beach. After that about ten or twelve of us went to the house. We probably shouldn't have drove, but we did.' He mentioned a bunch of names of the kids he remembered who were at the house that ended with, 'Me, Bobby, and Melissa Miller.'

'Was Melissa Miller part of your regular group of friends?'

'Not really. She was good friends with some of the cheerleaders we hung out with, so I guess she came along with them for the night.'

'What did you think of her?'

He gave that some thought. 'She was cute,' he said with a shrug. 'She kept hanging on Bobby, and that pissed off Bobby's girlfriend, Maura. Maura O'Neal.'

'What did Maura do?' Allison asked.

'She told Melissa to find her own guy.'

'Did she?'

'Find her own guy? I don't know. I was pretty drunk, and we were smoking pot, too. I'm not sure of too much after we started smoking.'

Allison gave that comment a few seconds, and then said, 'But you told the police – and your lawyer – that you remembered Bobby and his girlfriend leaving the party before everyone else.'

He shrugged again. 'I guess I did.'

'You remembered that but not too much else?'

I could tell by the way his face changed he didn't like that question. Whatever his intellectual limitations, he seemed to understand the purpose of that question.

'I think I remember that so good because Maura made a big deal of Melissa paying all that attention to Bobby and wanted to leave. Bobby told me they left 'cause when Maura got pissed, she wasn't in the mood anymore. If you know what I mean.'

Allison nodded. 'That makes sense,' she said. 'How long did Maura and Bobby go out with each other?'

'I don't think it was that long. I think they broke up before July Fourth. She and Bobby were going to different colleges anyway.' He took a quick pause. 'I didn't like her. I always had the feeling she was hanging with Bobby 'cause of who he was.'

'Knew he was going to be a star?'

'Yeah,' he said. 'But she did remind me that they left the party early.'

'She did?'

'Yeah. She said they tried to get me to come with them, but I was really drunk and stoned,

258

and I used to get angry when I drank and smoked at the same time. Nobody could tell me what to do when I got that way.'

'Is that what happened that night?' Allison asked. 'You got wasted and angry and assaulted Melissa Miller?'

'It musta been. Bobby was gone and Melissa said it was one of us, so it had to be me, right?' He closed his eyes and licked his lips. 'It took me a while for the memory to come back, and, when it did, it was fuzzy and scared the heck out of me. I mean, that I could do something like that. I liked Melissa. I'm not that kinda guy.'

With his eyes still closed, Allison and I looked at each other. Here we were with a guy who admitted to doing a horrible thing twenty years ago, and we both felt some sympathy for him. I had to admit it, Allison was right: this was a good story. How can you feel sorry for someone who sexually assaulted a girl about to graduate high school and start a new life for herself in college?

'So Maura and Bobby tried to get you to go with them, but you wouldn't.'

'Wished I did,' he said. 'Then we wouldn't be having this talk, right?'

'Right,' Allison said. 'And it took you all that time to remember that?'

'Yeah. Bobby reminded me, then Maura. Then Mr Stover said that if that's what happened, then I must've been the one to hurt Melissa.'

'Which you don't remember doing?'

'I remember some of it. I guess I was pretty out of it at that point, Ms Rogers. It's not an

259

excuse, I know, but I was as horny as the next teenager, and Melissa was coming on to me a bit after Bobby left.' He drifted again; then he came back. 'I guess maybe she figured if she couldn't have the star, she'd settle for the star's brother.'

'Were you and Melissa getting physical?'

He had mentioned that in his statement; she was 'hugging all up on' him and they kissed a little.

'Yeah,' he said. 'That's what I remember.'

'But it took you a while to remember that?' she repeated.

'Yeah. My family and Mr Stover helped me some.' He turned to me and said, 'I remember your dad telling me only to say things I absolutely remembered. I thought that was nice of him, considering.'

'Considering that everyone else was telling you what you remembered?' I asked.

He looked me in the eyes and nodded. 'That's a funny way of putting it, but, yeah. It was like I needed help, and I felt better when the memories came back.' He looked at Allison and said, 'You ever know you did something wrong, but you weren't sure what it was and then you know?'

Allison went along with it and said, 'I guess.'

'That's what it was like,' Billy said. 'I had this feeling it was me who did . . . you know, that stuff to Melissa. And when I was able to remember it, I felt better. Even though I knew it was a bad thing and I was going to be in a lot of trouble.'

'Did Marty Stover tell you how much trouble you'd be in?' Allison asked. We both knew the answer to that, because it was part of the interview Marty had conducted before Billy had given his official statement to the Nassau detective.

'Yeah. He said I'd probably end up getting fifteen to twenty years. I got out in ten because of good behavior. And because I confessed. Marty made a big deal out of me saving both families and the county from going through a trial. That's not why I confessed, though.'

'Why did you confess?'

'Because it was the right thing to do,' he said. *The right thing for whom?*

'And I don't do any of that stuff anymore.'

'What stuff?' Allison asked.

'Drinking and smoking. Maybe I have a glass of wine with dinner once in a while, but I don't get drunk anymore. It was part of my parole when I got out – staying away from booze and drugs – and it just kinda stuck, y'know?'

'Is that why you didn't go to Marty's benefit the other night?' I asked. 'Too much temptation?'

'That was part of it. The other part was that I don't think people like hanging around me too much. After what I did and all. I don't blame them. It was a long time ago, but what I did was pretty bad.'

'Don't you feel you've paid your debt to society?' Allison asked.

Billy shrugged. 'I did the time they gave mc, Ms Rogers. I don't know about paying any debts. I'm sure Melissa Miller wishes I never got out.'

I could tell by the look on Allison's face that she agreed with him, but she kept that opinion to herself.

'Are you seeing anybody now?' she asked. 'Romantically?'

He shook his head. 'No. I tried for a while, but as soon as someone realizes who I am and what I did, they lose interest. Wouldn't you?'

'I don't know.'

He didn't believe her. 'So let's say you and me were going out for a few weeks and then you find out that I'm a sex offender. You'd still keep seeing me?'

Allison paused. 'I'm not sure how to answer that, Billy.'

'With all due respect, Ms Rogers. You just did.'

After we said goodbye to Billy, Allison suggested we head over to the diner she knew on Eleventh. I had an even better idea: Alfie's on Tenth. A friend had taken me there a few months before and I was impressed with their great selection of craft beers and good food. Feeling gracious, Allison acquiesced and I got my way.

We settled into a table along the wall and ordered a couple of Kelso Pilsners. After the server left to get them, Allison said, 'So what did you think of Billy Taylor?'

'He was more with it than I thought he'd be,' I said. 'I mean, I only spoke to him for a little bit the other night, and you were doing most of the talking. He seems to have come a long way since the assault. At least from what little I can remember about what my dad told me. Honestly, I'm not sure what I expected today.'

'Me, neither. He seemed to remember everything that was in the file, though. He may have

262

forgotten a few facts, but that's to be expected after twenty years.'

'What did you think of his confession?' I asked as the server came over with our drinks. We told her we'd be having dinner, but we'd be a while before ordering. I took a sip of the pilsner. Score another one for the borough of Brooklyn.

'What do you mean, his confession?'

'He seemed to get a lot of help "remembering" what happened that night.'

'He was drunk, high, and intellectually challenged.'

'And those are the ones who are most easily led down a certain path of thinking.'

'You're saying you think he was told what to remember?'

'I'm saying it's a possibility.' We both took sips. 'Between his brother, his brother's girl-friend, and his own lawyer, who knows how much is *his* memory and how much is what he was told was his memory. I wish I had more notes to read than just what Marty wrote.' *Did I just say 'I'?*

'And there's no videotape of his statement, right?'

'They weren't doing them back then. All we have is Marty's notes.'

Allison considered that for a few seconds. 'Do you remember your dad saying anything about Billy's confession?'

I shook my head. 'He wasn't Billy's lawyer.'

'But he was there. Billy said he was nice to him.'

'That could mean he gave him a soda or a

263

snack or something. My father didn't talk about his own cases very much. I barely remember him talking about the Taylors. Just that it was pretty obvious Billy was a bit on the slow side.'

'You think your mom would remember anything?'

'I doubt it. It was too many years ago.'

She ran her fingers up and down her glass as she thought about that. I always found it sexy when she did that, but I took the time to steal a glance at the menu. The fried chicken sandwich sounded good.

'Marty kept the files from the case on his computer for all these years, right?'

'Obviously.'

'I know it's a long shot, but is there any chance your father kept records of his own? Maybe even duplicates of Marty's?'

'Of a case that wasn't his? That is a long shot.'

'But it's a possibility.'

'Well, yeah,' I said. 'It's also possible he kept his doodles from law school.'

Allison put her hand on my leg. *Here we go again*, I thought. I took it off. Gently.

'Just tell me what you want, Ally. Stop with the leg massages.'

If she was offended, she didn't show it. 'I want you to ask your mother if she still has your dad's old records and files around the house.'

'I can answer that,' I said. 'Yes. She keeps them down in the basement. She had everything put into boxes, including his old computer. She says she feels a responsibility as a limited partner in the firm to hold on to them. I think it's also a way of holding on to my father's memory. Every year I ask her to get rid of them, and every year she tells me she will.'

The server came back, and Allison and I ordered two more beers. I got the chicken sandwich and Ally went for the salad. She had a habit of ordering light food when drinking beer. Didn't make much sense to me.

'So call your mother for me,' she said. 'And ask if I can come over and go through your dad's old records.'

'What are you going to tell her you're looking for?'

'Your mom loves me.' She gave me a big smile. 'I'll tell her I'm looking for more background on the story about Billy Taylor and Melissa Miller. You didn't tell her that Edgar stole Marty's files did you?'

I laughed. 'That's good,' I said.

'Then she doesn't need to know what I know,' Ally said. 'I'll even offer to take her to lunch. We can talk about how wonderful her son is.'

'As long as that's all you talk about.'

'Is that a yes?'

I shrugged. 'What the hell? Yeah, it's a yes. When do you wanna go out there?'

She took out her phone and opened up her calendar. After pressing a few buttons, she said, 'Tomorrow works for me.'

'That's kinda quick notice, Ally. This is a woman who needs three days' notice to take a one-hour train ride to visit Rachel in Queens. She doesn't do spontaneous.'

'You can call her.'

I had to smile. I just had to. I reached into my pocket and pulled out my cell and handed it to Allison. 'Or you can call her.'

'Wouldn't it be easier if you—'

'But she loves you, Ally. Just offer to take her to lunch.' I stood up. 'Let me know what she says when I get back from the men's room.'

Twenty-Three

The following morning at school, after getting the kids out of the playground and off to homeroom, the first thing I did was check on my two Boys of the Week: Hector Robles and Tommy Avila. Both were absent. I called Hector's home first – no answer. I tried his mother's cell and she picked up after one ring.

'He's with his father,' she said to me. She also explained that she was out showing an apartment to prospective renters, but her expectations weren't that high. If she was thinking at all about my knowledge of her affair with Marty Stover, she did a good job of hiding it. 'I hope it's OK that we kept him home today. My husband had to run some errands, and he wanted to spend more time with Hector. I thought they could both use the time together. My husband's really getting into building this extra room, and it seems to be cheering him up. And Hector, after what happened to Marty . . .'

'I understand,' I said. 'Just make sure Hector's in on Monday. I don't want him getting used to four-day weekends.'

She laughed, it sounded like it was her first one in quite a while. 'Thank you, Mr Donne. I appreciate it.'

After I hung up, I found myself wondering how many box cutters Hector's father owned. I put that thought out of my head and called the Avila home. Mr Avila picked up.

'I'm sorry,' he said. 'I shoulda called you. We took your advice and made an appointment with a shrink – a psychologist. It took my wife a while to find one who took our insurance, but it turns out there's one by my work. She had an opening at ten this morning, so it didn't seem to make sense to send Tommy to school for an hour.'

'I hear ya,' I said. 'You'll let us know what the psychologist thinks?'

'Definitely. I went online last night and god damn if this school phobia isn't a real thing.' *Like I make shit up to suit my needs.* 'Never heard of it. When I was Tommy's age I had "Daddy phobia." I didn't wanna go to school, and Daddy didn't wanna hear it. That settled that, if you know what I mean.'

I did know what he meant, and I hoped that Mr Avila would prove to be more enlightened than his father. And my own, who sometimes used his hands when he couldn't find the right words.

'Why don't you or your wife bring Tommy in sometime Monday? We can sit down with our school counselor, Ms Stiles, and come up with a game plan for school.'

I waited about ten seconds for his response.

'Can we do that as early as possible?' he asked. 'My boss is letting me off this morning, and he's not exactly known for his generosity. I lost an hour of work the other day getting Tommy home. I don't wanna push my luck.'

'Let's make it at eight then,' I said. 'Before the rest of the kids get in.'

He waited a few beats as if checking his calendar. 'I guess that'll have to work, Mr Donne. Thanks.'

'I'll see you Monday.'

I went up to my office for another cup of coffee and then down to Elaine Stiles to let her know she now had plans for eight a.m. on Monday. Her door was open, and I found her in a familiar position: phone cradled between her shoulder and ear as she tapped away at her keyboard. She noticed me and waved me in. She was talking to someone about foster care, Children's Services, and a possible grant for the school. Busy, busy. About a minute later, she wrapped up her call, spun around in her chair, and gave me her full attention.

'Tommy Avila, right?' she asked.

'You're good, Elaine.' I told her about my phone call with the father and our plans to meet on Monday. 'Sorry about the early hour.'

'I'm here at eight anyway, Ray,' she said. 'We still have about ten eighth graders I'm trying to place into a decent high school.'

In New York City, all eighth graders get to apply to high school. Most of them get into their first, second, or third choices. For those who don't, there are counselors like Elaine who try to get them into a school that doesn't have a metal detector and does have a graduation rate of at least ninety percent. As if the counselors didn't have enough to do, like help a kid like Tommy Avila and his school phobia.

269

'You ever deal with a kid who's done some-thing like this before?' I asked. 'I mean, school phobias are one thing; staging a crime scene, injuring yourself, and coming up with an almost believable story is another.'

We had one kid a couple of years ago who started out by taking what his mother called a monthly 'mental health day.' Well, monthly soon turned into weekly, and it got to the point where the kid refused to come in at all. We tried every-thing we could at school – late arrival times, early dismissals, counseling – and nothing worked. Finally, I suggested to Mom that she call the cops. Not coming to school is, after all, against the law. It only took one home visit from the youth officers – and an explanation of all the bad stuff that would visit the family if the kid continued to stay home – to scare him enough to start coming to school. That was the hardest case I'd seen. Until Tommy Avila.

'Not this bad, no,' Elaine said. 'Most kids with school phobia are quite skilled at actually making themselves sick. They buy into it to the point where they can give themselves fevers, hives, and other real ailments. What Tommy did was above and beyond. It was good you caught on to it when you did.' She took a sip of her coffee. I did the same. 'What are you going to recom-mend at Monday's meeting?'

'That's funny,' I said. 'I was going to ask you the same thing. You're the school counselor, I'm just a dean.'

'But you know Tommy better than I do. What's a good first move?'

'Not giving him what he thinks he wants. There's no way I'm going to recommend a transfer to another school. That just pushes the problem on to a set of people who don't know him.'

Elaine smiled at me. 'It would also remove him from your Special Project list.'

'Yes, it would.'

I had shared that concept with Elaine last year. My Special Projects – when it came right down to it – were a group of kids who really interested me. The non-boring students, if you will. They had clear issues, were intelligent beyond what they showed at school, and were workable. Funny how Elaine knew Tommy Avila had made my list the day before.

'He says he doesn't like coming to *this* school,' I said. 'I think a good first step would be to make *this* school more to his liking.'

That was cause for thought. 'And just how do you hope to do that, Ray?'

'Let's change his class.'

'Go on,' she said.

'Who's our best teacher dealing with troubled kids?' I asked. 'Besides me.'

'Besides you?' she laughed. 'Josephine Levine.'

'Let's put him in her class.'

'That's a great idea, Ray, but she's special education. Tommy's a general ed kid.'

'We convince the parents to place him in the class "at risk."'

'At risk' meant we could provide the student with special education services without making it official. Kind of a trial run.

271

'You think they'd go for it?' Elaine asked. 'More importantly, do you think Tommy would? Going from gen ed to special ed is not something most kids would look at as a step up.'

'Jo's got a great group of kids this year,' I said. 'There're only ten in there.' She was legally allowed a maximum of twelve. 'The small group and the idea of not moving from class to class each period would probably help Tommy with his . . . anxiety. There are only three months left in the school year. If he doesn't like it, we put him back in the mainstream in the fall. We'll sell it as a trial run in a calmer environment.'

'I already see most of Jo's students for counseling. I can put him in one of those groups.'

'Then that's where we start.'

'And we cross our fingers.'

'Couldn't hurt.'

Right as I got back to my office, my cell phone rang. It was Allison.

'Miss me already?' I asked as I sat down behind my desk.

'Desperately,' she answered. 'Sometimes it's all I can do to keep my mind on my work. Which is why I'm calling, by the way.'

'What's up?'

'How does a trip out to Jones Beach sound, tough guy?'

'In late March? Cold. Why?'

'I just got a call from Chris Miller, Melissa's brother. She's agreed to talk to me off the record, then see if she wants to be interviewed for the story.'

'You're on a roll. Where do I come in?'

'Well,' she said, 'Chris's going to be there, too. I figured I might have a better chance of getting her alone if you come along and take Big Brother for a walk.'

'When is all this happening?'

'This afternoon. Your mother said I can come by before lunch and go through your dad's stuff. Chris said he and Melissa will be available after four. If you ditch work a little early, I can pick you up at the Freeport station at three forty-five. How's your afternoon looking?'

'Nothing scheduled. I guess I'm meeting you in Freeport. Did Chris say why Melissa wants to meet at the beach?'

'After I asked, he did,' Ally said. 'She's still trying to put things back together. After the attack, she wouldn't go near the beach. Nowadays it's one of her favorite things to do, just not during the summer months. This time of year the beach'll be pretty empty. I think it's going to be a big part of my story. It's been over twenty years and she's still working stuff like this out. And, at the risk of getting a lecture from you, it'll make a great photo op.'

'You're not thinking of putting her picture in the paper, are you?'

'Not her face, no. Give me *some* credit, Ray. I'm thinking a shot from behind as she's walking the boardwalk with her brother.'

'Sounds like you got it all planned out.'

'It's what I do, Ray. Don't you think things through before meeting with a kid in crisis, or do you just go in and wing it?'

273

I thought of Monday's meeting with Tommy and his folks. Ally had a point.

'I'll check the train schedule to Freeport and get back to you,' I said.

'Already did. The two-forty-five out of Penn gets you into Freeport just after three-thirty. I went on the LIRR website in hopes you'd say yes.'

I could almost feel her hand on my leg.

'I'll see you at three-thirty then. Where'd you get a car, by the way?'

'The paper still has some perks,' she said. 'Remind me to get a receipt for gas.' She paused for effect. 'And dinner later.'

'Dinner?'

'I don't expect you to work for free, Raymond.'

Maybe she *was* learning.

Twenty-Four

'So you told them I was coming, and they were both OK with it?'

'Not at first,' Allison said, as we pulled into one of the hundreds of empty spots in the Jones Beach parking lot. I counted five other cars in the entire place. 'Chris thought it'd be fine, but it took some convincing to get Melissa on board. I explained that anything she told me – after our initial talk – would be in private. Just the two of us.'

'She knows who my father was?'

'She said she remembered him being there when Billy gave his plea allocution in court. She has a vivid memory of Billy standing between the two lawyers as he admitted to what he had done. Your dad, she said, spent most of the time with his head down writing in his legal pad.'

'Sounds like my father,' I said. 'Shit, that reminds me. Did you find out anything at my mother's house?'

'Yeah,' she said. 'Your dad was a lot more organized than you.'

'Remind me to laugh at that later. Did he keep any notes on the case?'

'I got one legal pad from the case that was in the box marked for that year. It was barely half-filled. Your dad kept one or two pads for each case he was even marginally involved in. You're

275

going to have to decipher some of his handwriting for me. It reminds me of yours. Your mom also gave me his old desktop computer, which I think I'm gonna need Edgar's help accessing.'

'He's gonna love that.'

She pulled her phone out of her pocket and checked the time. The little bell went off telling us she'd just received a text.

'They're here,' she said. 'They're meeting us in front of the West Bathhouse.'

We got out of the car and I had to zip up my jacket. I wished I'd brought a hat as well, but it hadn't been this chilly in Brooklyn that morning when I left the apartment. I shoved my hands into my pockets and followed Ally.

'How do you know where you're going?' I asked.

'I Googled it before I left the city,' she said. 'You come here a lot as a kid?'

'Yeah. When we weren't playing baseball or some form thereof. We could get here by bus or ride our bikes along the parkway.'

'Nice. I never saw a real beach until I was sixteen and we went on a family trip to Florida.'

Ally had grown up in the Midwest, but I tried not to hold that against her.

'We should come here when it gets a little warmer,' I said. 'I'm not much of a swimmer, but I like it here.'

She held out her hand for me. 'Sounds like a date,' she said.

I recognized Chris Miller right away. He was the only man standing on the beachside of the bathhouse. Next to him was, I assumed, his sister. She was dressed as if ready for snow: winter jacket, ski cap, and gloves. Ally's pace slowed as we approached. We were about twenty feet away when she said, above the crashing of the waves, 'Hello. I'm Allison Rogers.'

As we got closer, I could better make out the details of Melissa Miller's face. If I didn't know better, I would have pegged her for a recent high school graduate. Her fair skin was rosy in the brisk sea air, and she wore her brown hair long and pulled back into a ponytail. Only her eyes gave her away. They were strikingly blue, but not so far behind them was a far away look. I wondered how difficult this visit to the beach was for her.

Chris stepped forward and shook our hands. 'Ms Rogers,' he said. 'Mr Donne. This is my sister, Melissa.'

Allison stuck her hand out. 'Hi, Melissa. It's Allison. And this is Raymond.'

Melissa shook Allison's hand. I wasn't sure if she'd want to shake mine, so I kept them where they were, but nodded. 'Hello,' I said.

'Thank you again,' Allison said, 'both of you, for agreeing to talk with me.'

'Just so long as we agree that's all this is for now,' Chris said. 'A talk. My sister and I will let you know if she'll go on the record.'

Part big brother, part lawyer. I liked this guy.

'I told her that, Chris,' Melissa said, speaking for the first time. Even her voice sounded young.

'I'm just making it clear, Melissa. I don't want any misunderstandings.'

277

She reached over and patted his arm, sensing that her brother needed some support, too. If they were all the other had in the world, they were in good company.

'So,' Allison said, 'as I explained to both of you over the phone, I believe that Melissa has a story to tell that will help other women in her situation. I told Chris the other day I have an old friend from high school who went through a sexual assault. She's still recovering but leading a productive life.'

A little bell went off in the back of my mind. I wasn't sure why, but it'd probably come to me later. My little bells are usually trying to tell me something.

'Are you interviewing her?' Melissa asked.

That question seemed to take Ally by surprise. She recovered quickly. 'No,' she said. 'I hadn't thought about that. I don't usually use friends in my pieces.'

'Just strangers?'

'I was hoping by the end of our . . . talk that we wouldn't be strangers anymore, Melissa. But I do need to keep my objectivity. Interviewing someone I have a previous relationship with would make that difficult.'

Melissa gave that some thought and said, 'That makes sense, I guess. What's the first thing you want to know, Allison?'

'Tell me about your day.'

The same question she had asked Billy Taylor.

'Today?' Melissa asked. 'Or any day?'

'Whichever you'd like.'

Melissa took a deep breath. 'Today I got up

278

at eight. That's my usual time. I made breakfast for Chris and me, and he was out of the house by nine. I took a shower, got dressed, and put on my work clothes.'

'Sweats, a T-shirt, and a pair of slippers,' her brother chided.

She gave his arm a playful slap.

'When you work from home,' Melissa said, 'you don't need to spend much on clothes. I went to my computer and finished an editing project I started yesterday. That took me all the way to lunch.'

'Who was your client?' Ally asked.

'A medical student from Stony Brook. He's really smart and is going to make a great doctor, but he can't write very well. Most of them can't, if you want the truth. And that's good for me, because that's where most of my money comes from: seriously smart people who can't write.'

'Your clients are mostly students?'

'And researchers, some lawyers. But lawyers write better than doctors. They have to, I guess. For them, it's mostly copyediting and layouts.' She must have read the look on my face, because she added, 'I know. Real exciting, right? But it helps with the bills.'

'I'm sorry,' I said. 'It's just that sometimes I have all the paperwork I can handle. I wish I had someone to help me with it.'

'What is it you do, Mr Donne?'

'It's Raymond, please. I'm a dean in a middle school. Williamsburg.'

She smiled. 'I wanted to be a teacher a while ago.' The far away look returned, and she cast

279

her eyes out over the ocean. 'Things changed, y'know?'

'Yeah,' I said, thinking back to the accident that led to my own career change. 'They do at that.'

She nodded and came back to the present. 'Anyway, after lunch, I made some calls, sent some emails, and called a few prospective clients. Referrals.'

'You must be very good at what you do,' Allison said.

'She's the best,' Chris chimed in.

'You have to say that. You're my brother.' She turned back to Allison. 'This can't be very interesting for your readers, Ms . . . Allison. My life's kind of boring.'

'Not at all, Melissa. You've made a life for yourself after something horrible. It's inspiring, and people will want to read about it.'

'I take other people's words and clean them up. How's that inspiring?'

'To come back from . . . what you went through and to become self-sufficient is the inspiring part. It's not *what* you do, it's that you *do it.*'

Melissa looked at her brother. 'I'm not all the way back,' she said. 'I'm not even sure that's possible. And I'm only as self-sufficient as I am because of my parents and Chris. I couldn't have done what I've done without them.'

'And that will be part of the story,' Allison said. 'There are a lot of victims out there who don't feel they can rely on their families. You can show those victims and their families that you're not a burden just because you need help.'

Melissa grabbed her brother's hand and they stood together silently for about half a minute. They both closed their eyes, and for a while there I thought they were going to pray. I hoped they wouldn't. Allison and I briefly exchanged confused, uncomfortable smiles. When Melissa Miller opened her eyes again, she spoke.

'OK,' she said. 'You can interview me.'

'Are you sure?' her brother asked.

'Yeah. I am. But just me and Allison, Chris.'

Chris looked as if he might contest that idea and then thought better of it. Maybe he realized his sister would be more open to telling her story without any males around. That's what I was here for, I remembered. To keep the brother busy.

Allison reached into her bag and brought out her tape recorder. She asked if Melissa minded, and just as Billy Taylor had done the day before, she said it was fine. Allison looked at me. 'Go for a walk with Chris?'

I wanted to go for a beer with Chris, but I guessed a walk would have to do.

'Pick a direction,' I said.

He looked at his sister, who gave him a silent 'OK' nod. Chris let out a deep breath, pointed east, and the two of us headed off away from the descending sun, my girlfriend, and his sister.

'She's in good hands,' I told Chris. 'Allison's one of the good ones.'

'I hope you're right. Melissa hasn't spoken to anyone about this in a lot of years. Including

281

me. Sometimes she'll go weeks where she's just fine, and then she'll wake up screaming from a nightmare.'

'About the attack?'

He shook his head. 'From what she does tell me,' he said, 'the dreams are not about the attack, but they are.'

'I'm not sure I follow.'

'She has this recurring one where she's being chased in the fog. There's a pair of headlights behind her and they keep getting closer. The dream usually ends with her being blinded by the lights and falling to the ground.'

I was quite familiar with those kinds of dreams. I still have nightmares about my accident, falling from the fire escape while watching a teen die, but they've been largely replaced these days by the ones where I'm sitting next to Ricky Torres in his taxi as he's killed by a sniper's bullet, the inside of the taxi exploding with gunfire. I wondered if anything would ever take the place of that one.

'That's one reason I was against this interview,' Chris said. 'I was afraid it would increase the frequency of the nightmares. Having to live through it all again.'

'It could do the opposite,' I said. 'Sometimes talking about a horrific event helps you deal with it better.'

He gave me a look. 'You've been to a therapist?'

'A couple.'

'They help?'

'One did. The other not so much. How about you?'

He nodded. 'Yeah. The whole family went after the case was settled. It didn't help much. My dad didn't – couldn't – talk about anything, and my mom just cried a lot. Pretty soon Melissa was going all by herself. She's on her fourth or fifth one now, but she goes every week.'

I watched as a seagull dove into the Atlantic and came back out with a fish. It must be nice living a life so simple.

'You never tried it again?' I asked.

'Nah. I got a job and Melissa to look after. Doesn't seem to be worth the time.'

'You gave up a lot for your sister, Chris.'

'Wouldn't you?'

'Absolutely. But I think she'd want me to have as full a life as possible.'

He stopped walking. 'What's that mean?'

Oops.

'I didn't mean anything, Chris. It's just that—'

'That I'm a grown man living in my parents' home with my sister? That the two of us are the only real relationships we have? Who's being interviewed here, Raymond? My sister or me?'

'Chris,' I said. 'I'm sorry. Sometimes I talk too much. It's just that I've been through some shit and had a lot of stuff to work out.'

'Your turn, Ray,' he said. 'Shit like what?'

I took a deep breath and told him about my accident almost ten years ago and getting shot at last year. How close I came to dead both times. He listened carefully and when I was done, he took some time to process what I'd said.

'You're right,' he finally said. 'You have been through some shit.'

'And come out the other side. Maybe not all the way, but enough to see the light. I wouldn't have met Allison if I hadn't.'

We walked for a while in silence. Chris looked over his shoulder. I did the same. We could see Allison and Melissa standing in the sunlight just in front of the bathhouse.

'How long have you and Ms Rogers been together?'

'A couple of years now. We met when one of my former students was killed.'

'Sorry,' he said. 'You two gonna get married?'

I couldn't get away from that question. Even out here, walking along the chilly Atlantic, shooting the shit with the brother of a sexual assault victim, it comes up.

'I'm not completely sure,' I said.

'What's stopping you?'

Now I really wanted a beer. I had pushed it with him, and now he was returning the favor. *Fair enough*, I thought, but I'd much rather have this talk in a bar.

'I don't know,' I said.

'You one of those guys who's afraid of commitment?'

'That's not it. At least, I don't think so.'

'Why buy the cow when you're getting the milk for free?'

I laughed. Maybe we could be friends, Chris and me. He was already displaying a knack for busting my balls, and we'd only met twice.

'I think I just need a little more time to wrap my mind around the idea,' I said. 'I'm kinda set

284

in my ways. I've been on my own for a long time. I put in a lot of hours at the school.'

'I've been with Missy – Melissa – for a long time,' he said in a tone that told me he wished he had my problems.

'Does that mean you're ready for a change?' I asked.

'Maybe,' he said. 'Even if it's just turning the house into two separate living areas. Whatta the real estate people call those? Mother/daughters?'

'Yeah. Maybe what you need is a sister/brother.'

He laughed. 'Would take some money to do that. I'm not sure we can afford it.'

I realized I wasn't sure what he did for a living. I asked.

'I work for the town. I maintain the pools during the summer and skating rinks during the winter. Doesn't pay so great, but it comes with some good benefits, decent overtime. And I have to remember not to talk politics when the bosses are around.'

For years out here you couldn't get a job with the town if you weren't registered as a Republican. I wasn't sure how much, if any, that had changed, but Chris was right: it was best to keep your political thoughts to yourself.

My cell phone rang. It was Allison.

'What's up?' I asked.

'I think that's it for today,' she said barely above a whisper. 'I don't want to push too hard and lose the whole interview.'

'That's sounds like a good idea. You want to interview Chris now? He's a pretty good guy.'

'You two bonding, Ray?'

285

'We've got a few things in common. You wanna talk to him or not?'

'I do,' she said. 'But I think Melissa's ready to go home. I'll set up another time to talk to them both. Can you head back now?'

'I'm on my way.'

When I put the phone back in my pocket, Chris said, 'That it for today?'

'Yeah. Allison thinks Melissa's had enough for now.'

'She lasted longer than I thought she would.'

We started walking back. The sun was getting lower in the sky and turning what few clouds there were over the Atlantic orange. Hard to believe this was the same sun I watched set behind the Manhattan skyline from my balcony.

Chris must have noticed me admiring the sky, because he said, 'That's something I hope I never get tired of. Makes the whole trip out here worth it.'

I found myself liking him a little bit more.

When we got back to the bathhouse, Melissa pulled her hands out of her pockets and threw her arms around her brother. I watched as Allison slipped her tape recorder into her bag and gave the two Millers a sympathetic look. When they broke their embrace, I thought for sure one of them – if not both – would be crying. I was wrong.

'Ms Rogers – Allison – was right, Chris,' Melissa said. 'It did help to talk about it. Even now.'

Chris gave his sister a big smile. 'Ray said pretty much the same thing.'

'So,' Allison said, 'I'll give you a call tomorrow and we can talk some more?'

'I'd like that,' Melissa said. She turned to me. 'Will you come again, Ray?'

'Maybe,' I said. 'I'll talk to Allison about that on the way back to the city.'

A few minutes later, the four of us were back in the parking lot – empty now except for our two cars – saying good-bye. Chris and I shook hands; Melissa and Allison hugged.

Damn, my girlfriend is good.

Back on the parkway, Allison thanked me again for coming out with her.

'Anything for a free dinner,' I said. And then that little bell went off in my head again. Except over the past few hours, it had crawled its way to the front of my brain. 'Back when we first got there,' I said. 'You told Melissa you had a high school friend who'd been through a similar sexual assault?'

Allison checked her rearview mirror and said, 'Yeah?'

'The other day outside Marty's, you told Chris it was a college friend.'

She squinted. 'I did?'

'You did.'

'I guess I misspoke then.'

'That doesn't sound like something you'd misspeak about, Ally.'

With her eyes a little too intent on the traffic

287

in front of us, she said, 'Is there a question in there, Raymond?'

'Yeah,' I said. 'Did you have a college friend who was sexually assaulted or was she a high school friend?'

Without missing a beat, she said, 'Both.'

'You had *two* friends who were sexually assaulted?'

'No.' Now there was a beat. 'I knew her both in high school and college.'

'Oh.'

We were silent for a half-mile or so, then, 'Did you think I was making that up, Ray? About my friend?'

I took a deep breath. This might end up being one of *those* conversations. I should've kept my mouth shut. 'I honestly didn't know what to think, Ally. You're always so detail-oriented, it's not like you to say one thing and then contradict yourself. Now I get it.'

'I'm so glad that you do.'

I probably should have left it at that. But, again, I couldn't help myself.

'I don't like when you use that tone with me,' I said. 'I had an honest question. Would you rather I kept it to myself?'

'If it was a question about my integrity? Yes, I would.'

'I wasn't – I wasn't questioning your integrity.'

'Then what would you call it?'

Good question.

'Sometimes cops,' I began, 'are not completely truthful when interviewing a suspect. I thought maybe—'

'You mean cops lie? I know that. I also know it's legal when they do it. So you thought maybe I'd lie to get Melissa to tell me her story?'

'I thought it was a possibility,' I said.

'It's a real possibility I'm going to tell you to fuck off right now.'

'I'd rather you didn't.'

'Fuck what you'd—'

Her cell phone went off, preventing her from finishing her sentence. She took it out of her pocket, checked the caller ID, and pressed another button. She put the phone on the dashboard and said, 'Hello, Walter. What's up?'

'You still out on the Island?' Walter was an assignment editor or something at Allison's paper. At the very least, I knew he outranked her.

'Yeah. Just about to get on the LIE. Why?'

'I need you to turn back around.'

'Why, Walter?'

'How far are you from the hospital?'

'Which one?'

A pause for a bit, then Walter said, 'Nassau Medical. NUMC.'

Allison looked at me. I said, 'Ten minutes.' Allison said, 'Why, Walter?'

'Billy Taylor's in the ICU over there,' he said. 'Car accident.'

'Jesus,' Ally said. 'What the hell happened?'

'If I knew that, Ally, I wouldn't be asking you to head over there, would I?'

Besides being an assignment editor, Walter could also be a bit of a dick.

'I'll call you when I know something, Walter.'

'I'd appreciate that.'

Allison pressed the phone, ending the call. Without looking at me, she said, 'You know the quickest way to get there from here?'

'Take the next exit,' I said.

'Thank you,' she said. But not like she really meant it.

Twenty-Five

I'm not sure if it still is, but at one time the Nassau County Medical Center was the tallest building on Long Island, meaning Nassau or Suffolk County. Geographically, the NYC boroughs of Brooklyn and Queens were on the Island, but when one said 'Long Island,' it only meant Nassau and Suffolk. Some time after I moved away, the hospital's name changed slightly: it was now called Nassau University Medical Center. And it was no one's first choice for emergency surgery.

I knew a Nassau County cop who'd fallen off his roof some years ago while taking down his Christmas lights. He was rushed to the medical center with a broken bone in his hand and breaks to his lower spine. The doctors took care of the hand first – and screwed it up. Before they could get a shot at the spine, the cop's commanding officer, whose sister happened to be one of the head nurses at the Hospital for Special Surgery in Manhattan, got him transferred. The docs at HSS undid the damage done to the hand, fixed the back, and put the cop on a long road to recovery. He was back on the job a year later, restricted duty, but working. He later went on to win the prestigious Teddy Roosevelt Award, which is given to cops who've come back after major accidents. From what I'd heard, these days he only puts a few lights in his windows for the holidays.

Allison and I pulled into the visitors' parking lot. We hadn't spoken to each other for the fifteen-minute drive, except for me telling her where and when to turn. We entered the hospital through the emergency room doors and found Friday afternoons quite a busy time at the hospital. Allison pushed her way to the front of the information desk line, ignoring the five people ahead of her.

'I'm looking for Billy Taylor,' she said. 'He was just admitted. A car accident.'

The woman behind the counter gave Allison a nasty look. Instead of telling her to go to the back of the line, she said, 'You're not the only one. You a lawyer or a reporter?'

'He's my cousin,' Allison said, not missing a beat.

That softened the woman's face, but just a little. Everybody on line was probably somebody's cousin or sibling or son or mother. The woman worked the keys on her desktop and waited a few seconds.

'He's still in surgery.' Before Allison could ask another question, the woman said, 'That's all the information I can give you right now, ma'am. Cousin or not.' She then looked over Allison's shoulder. 'Yes, sir. Step up, please.'

Allison came back to me and I said, 'I heard.'

'You gonna give me shit for lying to her?'

I had a lot of answers for that, but I kept them to myself. Let her figure out if she deserved shit for her behavior while working a story. I was pretty tired of the argument. Does telling a lie make you a liar? I don't know. Maybe we should ask the next politician we run into. Or the next car salesman. Or the next cop.

Before I could explore the moral consequences of truths and half-truths, I heard someone yelling from across the waiting room.

'This is your fault, you son of a bitch!'

I turned to see Bobby Taylor hustling his way over to Allison and me. I stepped in front of her instinctively before realizing, at his size, he could probably barrel through the both of us if he wanted. I was glad he was slowed down when an older man grabbed him by the elbow. They both stopped about three feet in front of me. Judging by the resemblance, I guessed the older man who intervened was his father.

'Bobby,' he said. 'Not here. Not now. We don't need this.'

Now I was pretty sure it was the father, since he wasn't arguing against the potential for violence, just the time and location of it. A very worried-looking woman made her way up to the two men and stood behind them in silence.

Bobby Taylor pointed his finger at me and puffed out his chest.

'I told you I didn't want that bitch reporter of yours talking to my brother,' he said, breathing heavily. Then he noticed Allison and said, 'I suppose that's you?'

'It is,' she said, stepping around me. 'How'd you know about the bitch part?' She sized Bobby up. 'But I certainly don't *belong* to Raymond. If you're going to yell at someone, it should be me.'

'My god,' Bobby said. 'You people are unbelievable. Billy was admitted less than two
hours ago and you're already here, chomping at
the bit. I guess this makes your fucking *story*
even better now, huh?'

The woman behind him rubbed his upper back.
'Robert,' she said softly. 'There is no need for
that type of language.'

As big as he was, Bobby Taylor looked just a
bit smaller when flanked by his parents. He took
a few moments to gather his composure. Mr
Taylor gave Allison and me a look that said he
might have been sorry he had stopped his son.

'You shouldn't be here,' he said to the two of
us. 'Do you people have no respect for the
injured? Or their families?'

Allison took a deep breath. 'With all due
respect, Mr and Mrs Taylor,' she said, leaving
out Bobby, 'Raymond and I were already out
here when my editor called. It may sound disre-
spectful to you – and I'm sorry for that – but
your son's accident is news. The fact that it's
me here and not one of my colleagues is pure
coincidence.'

'Your editor have the hospital on speed dial?'
Bobby asked.

'What usually happens in a case like this,'
Allison said, 'is that when a patient of importance
is admitted to a hospital, someone calls the paper.
It could have been an EMT, a police officer,
someone who works at the hospital who recognized Billy's name.'

'Another vulture,' Bobby said. 'I suppose
whoever called your paper's gonna get paid?

294

Maybe get a pair of free tickets to the next Billy Joel show?'

Allison turned to me and then to Bobby. 'Why did you say this was our fault? I was told Billy was in a car accident.'

Bobby laughed. 'Like I'm gonna talk to you. Serve you right if you read it along with all your readers in tomorrow's paper, bitch.'

'Robert,' his mother said. 'Come with me. Your father's right. Making a scene does nothing to help your brother.'

Bobby pointed at Allison now. '*She* did nothing to help my brother. She sold him a set of lies and he bought them and . . . now this.'

Mr Taylor patted his son's arm. 'Go over and sit with your mother, Bobby. I'll deal with these people.'

'Don't you tell them anything, Pop. And remember, I'm waiting to hear from Dr Strong so we can get Billy transferred out of this place.'

'Go,' he said. 'I'll be right there.'

Bobby made sure to give both Allison and me a stare before he allowed his mother to lead him toward the exit. Maybe they'd go outside for a walk. He certainly needed one.

'You are Ms Rogers,' Mr Taylor said.

'Yes. I interviewed Billy yesterday for a story I'm working on.'

'Robert told us all about it, as you can imagine. We were all upset when William told us he had agreed to speak with you. We – the family – had thought the whole incident was behind us. William told us about the story you're working on, and we want no part of it. We've had a bad history with . . . people in your profession.'

'I think that's the closest I've ever come to being called a whore, Mr Taylor.'

'Don't think the word didn't cross my mind.' He looked at me. 'And not just because you're a woman.'

Allison smiled. 'No, just because we get paid to screw with people.'

'That has been my family's experience, yes.'

'Mr Taylor, I'm not here to defend what I do for a living, neither to you nor your son. I'm here to do my job. I was with Billy yesterday to do my job. I was out here on the Island today doing my job.'

'Billy said you are going to interview the Miller girl, as well.'

'Yes. It's her story, too.'

'She's a little liar, that one. Ruined my son's life.'

'Your son confessed to sexually assaulting her.'

'I don't need you to tell me what my son said. I was there.'

'And you didn't believe your own son's story?'

'I didn't know—' He stopped. 'Robert was right. I shouldn't have told you anything. Just talking to you people makes me crazy.'

'I'm sorry you feel that way.'

'No you're not. You get people to say things, twist their words to suit your needs, and then put it out there for the whole world to see. You cash your checks and move on to the next headline.'

'Is that what you think I did to Billy, Mr Taylor?'

He stared at Allison for a few seconds then turned to see where his wife and son were. They were still by the exit door, arms around each other.

'I'm done talking to you, Ms Rogers. I'm sorry if my son or I said anything to offend you.' No he wasn't. He gestured with his head somewhere over our shoulders. 'Go get your story.' He paused before walking away and joining his family. 'I'm sure it'll be a good one. Sell lots of papers.'

When he was out of earshot, Allison turned to me.

'How could this possibly be my fault?' she asked. It wasn't like she was asking me; it was more like the question was addressed to the universe.

'Maybe they think Billy's accident was a result of him being upset about yesterday's interview.'

'Is that what *you* think?'

'I don't know what I think, Ally. I was there. He didn't seem too rattled by your questions. Certainly not upset enough to make this happen.'

A look approaching gratitude flashed across her face. Then it was gone. She reached into her pocket and pulled out her cell phone. 'I'm calling Walter back.'

'I thought he didn't know anything.'

'I bet he knows the press liaison for the hospital.'

'It's after six,' I said.

She gave me a look like I just didn't get it and walked away, leaving me standing there by

297

myself in the busy waiting area of the emergency room. Being alone, and given time to consider where I was, triggered enough memories to make me feel a little light-headed. All hospitals had the same smells and sounds and feel. None of them designed to put people at ease. I made my way to the first water fountain I found and took a few deep sips, followed by a few deep breaths. I was beginning to feel better but still felt shaken. Grown man that I was, I headed toward the exit. I ran into Allison still on her phone.

'She's got me on hold,' she told me. 'Where are you going?'

'Out.' And I went. I stood outside the sliding doors for about a minute then I stepped over to the first bench I could find and sat down. After regaining most of my composure, I remembered I was supposed to call Edgar – or he was supposed to call me – about his lawyer acquaintance. He picked up after two rings.

'Yo, Ray,' he said. 'What's the haps?'

'Someone's feeling much better,' I said.

'Just got to The LineUp, and I'm having my first beer away from home since my accident. Feels pretty darn good, I tell ya. Sorry I didn't call you sooner, but . . .'

'Don't go feeling too good, Edgar. Too much too soon and all that.'

'I hear ya, Ray. I'm having two and then heading home. I'm still kinda tired.'

'Good,' I said. 'Hey, did you get in touch with the lawyer you kinda worked with? The one who works with the guy who knows about Nazi-looted art?'

'Laura Feldman? Yeah.' He paused for what I imagined was a much-enjoyed sip of beer. 'I did. She said she can meet you outside her offices tomorrow morning.'

I didn't know I was going to meet with her.

'Tomorrow's Saturday,' I said.

'She's a lawyer, Ray. They don't look at weekends like us normal folks.'

'She say what time?'

'Nine o'clock. She's gonna be with her family for a bit, then her hubby's gotta take the kids off to lessons or the museum or something.' Another pause. 'You're gonna like the husband, Ray. Kenny knows even more about audio than I do.'

'I didn't think that was possible.'

'I know, right? He used to work at BB King's, now he's at Merkin Hall. He also has one of the coolest goatees.'

'That's good to know, Edgar. Can you text me the address?'

'As soon as we hang up, partner.'

He had a habit of calling me 'partner' when he knew he was helping me out. It didn't bother me because he was often helping me out.

'Thanks, Edgar. Maybe I'll see you tomorrow.'

'That'd be good, man. Have a good one.'

It was getting a bit chillier, the sky more dark than orange now, so I decided to go back inside and see how close Allison was to heading home. She must have been reading my mind because, as soon as I stood up from my bench, I saw her exiting the hospital. We met halfway.

'You're not going to believe this,' she said.

'Try me.'

'I just got off the phone with the hospital press relations person and it turns out we worked together years ago in the city.'

'Is that the unbelievable part?' I asked.

'No. She was able to tell me – but not on the record – that the EMTs who brought Billy Taylor in said he reeked of booze *and* there was the unmistakable odor of marijuana coming from his car when they pulled him out.'

'Alcohol and pot? A combination Billy said he's avoided for the past twenty years.' I gave that some thought. 'You think that's why the Taylors are blaming you?'

'What?' She was using her outside voice. 'That my interview pushed him off the wagon? That the big bad *bitch* reporter lady bullied their son into a liquor- and pot-fueled accident?'

'Hey, lighten up. I'm not saying I believe it. I'm asking you if you think *they* believe it. All of the Taylors seemed to be looking for someone to blame and that someone was you, Ally.'

That quieted her down for a bit. I couldn't recall Ally soul-searching before, but the pained look on her face made me think she was doing just that. When she didn't speak for almost two minutes, I decided it was time I did.

'Listen, Ally,' I said. 'You know I didn't want you to interview Billy.'

'You made that rather clear, yes.'

'But there's no way in the world this is your fault. People drink and smoke because they choose to, not because someone *made* them do it. Sometimes addicts just relapse. They don't need an excuse.'

That look of gratitude slowly came back to her face.

'Even someone who's . . . limited like Billy Taylor?'

'Even someone like Billy Taylor,' I agreed. 'You said it yourself: he's a grown man and capable of making his own decisions. That's what happened here. Nothing more and nothing less.' I reached out and touched her arm. 'You're just not that powerful.'

She gave me a small smile. 'You're not just saying this because you're feeling sorry for me? Or because you want to end our last argument?'

'Both of those are excellent reasons for saying what I said, but, no. I'm saying it because it's true. You're good here, Ally.'

'Thanks, Ray.' She threw her arms around me in a hug. After a ten-count, she said, 'Then you wouldn't mind driving back to the city?'

'You too tired to drive?'

'I gotta write up what I got on Billy Taylor. It's not gonna be much, but it'll make it to the paper's website and it might be the only thing we have for press tomorrow.'

I looked at her and shook my head. Her ability to rebound was remarkable. Instead of commenting on that, I said the second-kindest thing I could think of:

'Give me the keys.'

The first would have been 'I love you.'

Twenty-Six

We were driving for almost half an hour when Allison remembered she was in possession of my father's notes on the Taylor case. It was still early so we decided to head to my place and look over the legal pad.

'You know,' I said. 'I bet if we called Edgar he'd come over and see what he can get from my dad's computer.'

'That's a good idea,' she said. 'You think he's available?'

'We're talking Edgar here, Ally. He'll be available. I just spoke with him, actually.' I reached into my pocket, pulled out my cell, and handed it to Allison. 'He's in my contacts.'

'Of course he is.' She found his name, pressed the screen, then put him on speakerphone. A few seconds later we heard, 'Ray. What's up? You forget something?'

'It's Allison, Edgar. Ray's driving.'

'Hey, Edgar,' I said.

'Where are you two?' he asked.

'We're coming back from the Island,' Ally said, leaving out the reason why. 'We need your expertise.' She knew how to speak Edgar's language.

'At your service,' he said. 'What can I do you for?'

Allison explained how, in addition to some

antiquated disks, she had my father's old computer and that there might be some files on it that she'd need his help to access. Edgar asked what kind of computer it was, Allison told him, and Edgar said he was looking forward to it.

'So,' I said, in that loud voice I used when on speakerphone. 'You wanna meet at my place in an hour? We're gonna order in some takeout.'

'Polish?' he asked.

'If that's what you want.'

'Cool,' he said. 'But I think we need to meet at my place.'

'Why?'

I heard him let out a deep, frustrated breath. 'That's where all my equipment is,' he said. 'I don't wanna lug it all over to your place because I'm not sure what I'll need exactly. What kind of disks are we talking about?'

Allison and I looked at each other. I said, 'We're not sure. The floppy kind?'

'Exactly. I know I have the technology, I just need to see what you got.'

'We'll bring the food,' Allison said.

'I'll see you in an hour.' He hung up.

'That was easy,' Allison said.

'You had him at "I need your expertise." The Polish food just sealed the deal.'

The three of us were in Edgar's living room: Ally and I on the futon couch and Edgar on a separate chair sitting in front of my father's decades-old computer. The food we hadn't finished was sitting on a counter in Edgar's kitchen. Edgar lovingly petted the grayish-beige

303

of my father's old Macintosh Performa 6300 and said, 'It's like being in a museum or traveling back in time. I haven't touched one of these babies since my first years with Transit.'

'Can you do anything with it?' Ally asked.

'Not with this computer, nope. These old Apples were good for their time, but, this one, with all the moisture in your mom's basement, and all the time it spent down there, it's pretty worthless.'

'So what do we do?' I asked.

'I have some conversion and retrieval equipment that'll help me migrate the data from whatever was backed up on these' – he held up the floppy disks – 'to my laptop. This is not the first time I've been asked to do this. At least these were stored in plastic.'

I shook my head. 'You're amazing, Edgar.'

'Tell me that when I'm done, Ray.'

He left the room to get what he needed. Allison and I turned our attention back to my father's more basic technology: his legal pad. Its pages were crumpled at the edges, hard and brittle, and gave me the impression I was holding a piece of history. I carefully turned each of the pages. Out of the eighty pages available to my father, he had written on only about a dozen of them. Allison was right: my father's handwriting looked very much like my own. Part script/part print, often illegible. Was it genetic? What other traits did I inherit from my father?

I got goose bumps holding these pages my father had written. We didn't have family videos to look back on after he died, only photographs.

Somehow holding this work he'd done was like holding part of him. I'm not the sentimental 'Let's take a trip down Memory Lane' kind of guy, but these were my father's words, in his handwriting. Holding them was like holding a part of my father. They were important to him all those years ago and might prove to be important now.

'Ray?' Allison said. 'You still with me?'

'What?' I said. 'Oh, yeah. It's just . . .'

She put her hand on my leg. 'Take your time, tough guy. Let me know when you're ready.'

'I'm good.' I looked at the first page. 'This seems pretty straightforward. It's a list of people interviewed by Marty. We got all this from Marty's computer. It's all in the police report. These here,' I pointed to the three names with stars next to them, 'might be the ones my dad thought were most helpful?'

Allison looked at them and said, 'Helpful to whom?'

'His firm's client. Who do you think?'

'Keep reading.'

I turned to the next page. It had the date on top, and here my dad had written in something close to complete sentences, but mostly they were brief observations in bullet points. I could make out that someone with the initials SM was 'unclear about what happened' and would make . . . some kind of witness. It took me a few seconds to decipher the words 'unreliable and unhelpful.' Another interviewee – a TR – admitted to being high the evening of the incident and my father had made a note that

TR also seemed high during the interview. My dad had put a circle around the initials and drawn smoke lines around it. I was reminded of my dad's occasional bursts of humor.

The next page had the following day's date and started with the initials KW. KW had left the beach with the group, but only stayed at the house for a few hours. KW confirmed that everybody seemed to be touching everybody and felt what I first read as 'uncontroversial' about it, but then was able to translate that into 'uncomfortable' and KW claimed to have 'left before everyone else.'

Edgar came back into the room with some equipment and set it up at his worktable. He came in with a small piece of equipment, then connected some wires to it and his own desktop, which was already turned on.

'I should know something soon, guys,' he said. 'How you doing over there?'

'Not bad,' I said. 'But my father only used initials when referring to the kids Marty interviewed. Let me know if you come up with any full names, OK?'

'You got it.' He went to work, plugging the old disks into his equipment.

The notes on KW took up most of the page, so my father started the next page with the same date but another witness: BL. It took some time to figure out what my dad had written on this page, probably because the more he wrote, the sloppier he got. I had the same problem. What I originally read as 'James Birch' – a real name – I later figured out was 'Jones Beach.' 'Horse' became 'house,' 'bronze' was 'booze,' 'pat' was obviously 'pot,' and so on like this for a good ten minutes. In all, BL didn't seem to have much more to say than the other interviewees, but at the bottom of the page, my father had clearly written 'BT & BT' and circled it with an arrow pointing at the initials 'MM.'

Allison pointed at the circle and said, 'What do you make of that?'

'BT & BT?' I said. 'Bobby Taylor and Billy Taylor. I'm gonna guess and say that the arrow pointing to MM means they were both paying attention to Melissa Miller. We already knew that about the Taylor boys.'

Allison turned the legal pad toward herself to get a better view of it. She gently flipped through the remaining pages and sighed. 'It reads like this until the end. No offense, but your dad didn't seem too interested in this case.'

'He had his own cases to deal with,' I said. 'I know because that's nearly all he did when he got home from the office.' I looked over at Edgar, who was working his magic with my father's old disks. 'If Edgar's able to pull anything off those floppies, it'll more than likely be my dad's case stuff. Not the Taylor case.'

'Well,' Allison said, 'it's not like we had anything else planned for tonight.'

I could have argued that point but, once again, chose to keep my mouth shut. I flipped to the next page and found more of the same: initials, followed by more of my father's almost-illegible handwriting. I laughed.

'What's so funny?' Allison wanted to know.

'My mom used to tease my dad that his hand-writing made him more suitable to the medical profession than the law.'

'Keep reading,' she said. 'I need to stretch my legs and use the bathroom.'

When she had gone, Edgar whispered, 'Everything OK?'

'Yeah,' I said. 'She just had to get the blood flowing and pee.'

'I mean,' he was still whispering, 'is she mad at me or something?'

'She's a bit mad at me, Edgar. We had an argument earlier. You've done nothing but be helpful. Again.'

'That's what I thought. But sometimes I don't know. Especially with women.'

Welcome to the club.

'You're fine, Edgar.' I stood up myself and walked over to him. His setup was impressive. 'You having any luck yet?'

'I just put in a random disk. I'll know in a minute or two. That's the good part of this kind of work. If a disk is permanently corrupted, you usually know right away.'

'I wouldn't know anything if it weren't for you, man.'

He shrugged, looked at the blank screen, and said, 'Probably not.'

It was good to see his sense of humor coming back. My knees were starting to ache, so I did a couple of deep knee bends and some runner's stretches while holding on to Edgar's desk. I needed to get back to Muscles' again before he and my knees complained too much.

'Bingo!' Edgar said. 'Looks like this disk is still readable.'

I looked at his screen and saw the kind of computer image you only see in movies from twenty years ago: bright bluish-green letters and numbers, a lot of periods, and some flashing rectangles. All we needed was Matthew Broderick telling us he'd hacked into the Pentagon's computer system.

'Go through the bag with the disks,' Edgar said. 'See if you can find one with the dates you're looking for.'

There were about twenty disks, all of them labeled with white tape, and it took less than a minute to find the one with the year we wanted. I handed it to Edgar. He ejected the test disk out and inserted the new one. When the disk data appeared on the screen, Edgar pressed some keys. 'What's the name of the file we're looking for?'

'I'm guessing "Taylor" or something like that? If it's even there.'

'Let's find out.'

'You boys playing *War Games*?'

Allison had returned. She was a bit of a film buff herself.

'Edgar's looking for the file. He was able to do the conversion.'

She patted me on the back. 'I can see that. How about I take you boys out for some Pac-Man and Space Invaders if we luck out?'

'*Luck*,' Edgar said, 'has nothing to do with it. And, if we are successful, I'll take you up on your offer and you can take us to Barcade.'

309

He was referring to the bar over by the L train that not only specialized in vintage video games but also had a hell of a beer list. Something for the both of us.

With Allison and me looking over his shoulder, Edgar maneuvered around the new screen/old data, pressed some more buttons, and found the file we were looking for. It was marked 'Taylor.'

'Now let's see if it'll print,' he said as he pressed another key.

It did, but only came out to one page.

'Is that it?' I asked Edgar.

'That's all he wrote.' He giggled at his own little joke.

Edgar pulled the page out of the printer and handed it to me. Allison took it before I could read it. It might have been my father, but it was her story. I let it go.

She walked away and glanced at it for a few moments. She turned around and asked me, 'What was the name of Bobby Taylor's girl-friend who Billy said left with Bobby the night of the party?'

I gave that some thought. 'Maura,' I said when it came to me. 'Maura . . .'

'O'Neal,' she finished. 'Maura O'Neal.'

'Yeah. Why?'

She handed me the page and waited while I read it. I let out a breath when I came to the part she was referring to.

'What is it?' Edgar asked.

'The girl who left the party with Bobby,' I said. 'Essentially giving him an alibi? His *only* alibi.'

'Yeah?'

'Billy said she helped him remember the details of that night.'

'So.'

'So,' I said. 'It says here she and Bobby not only got into a fight before leaving the party, they got into one *after* they left, at her house.'

'I'm still not following you, Ray.'

'Maura told Marty and my dad that Bobby was so pissed he told her he was going back to the party.'

Edgar thought about that and said, 'Shit.'

'Yeah,' I agreed. 'Shit.'

For the next hour or so, the three of us worked our computers, trying to find out as much as possible about Maura O'Neal. At one point, Allison complimented Edgar on the amount of bandwidth it must take for us all to be on the Internet at the same time working at such speed. He shrugged.

'I'm sure,' I said, 'even some of his neighbors could be hitchhiking on his Wi-Fi right now.'

'Some people have stuff,' Edgar said. 'I have megabits.'

Allison checked all the newspaper sites and was able to come up with zilch on the Maura O'Neal we were looking for. In fact, she was never mentioned in any of the scores of print articles about the Taylor case that Allison had been able to find. I came up just as empty. I checked the White Pages, Yellow Pages, and the software Edgar had installed on to my laptop – legal, I allowed myself to believe – that allowed

311

me to search other databases. There were a lot of Maura O'Neals, but none matched the one we were looking for. Then Edgar said the magic words that told us he'd hit pay dirt: 'Cool beans!'

We both turned to him. 'What'd you find?' I asked.

'I found Maura Delaney,' he said.

'You sure it's her?' Allison asked.

Edgar started his 'duh' face but stopped. Instead, he patiently explained, 'I searched for their high school website. What I found was they had their twentieth reunion not that long ago and were kind enough to put their program on their events page.'

'And . . .'

'And one of the attendees was Maura (née O'Neal) Delaney. She lives in Seaford with her husband and two children.'

'Nicely done, Edgar,' I said. 'What else do we know about her?'

'She's been married for just over ten years,' he said. 'She's a member of the Chamber of Commerce, Independent Women's Business Association, and about a half dozen other organizations.'

Allison asked, 'What kind of business is she in?'

He clicked a few more keys. 'Says here she owns her own beauty salon, also in Seaford. Been in business for almost twenty years.'

'Not too long after the case was resolved,' I said, doing the simple math.

'Schooling?' Allison asked.

A few more strokes of the keys. 'Two-year

degree from Long Island School of Beauty and Fashion.'

I did a little more mental math. 'How does someone barely twenty years old get enough money to buy her own business?'

We all thought about that for a few seconds, and Allison offered, 'Maybe her family has money?'

Edgar moved his fingers across the keyboard again. 'Both parents are – were – schoolteachers, and she has four siblings.'

'A loan?' I asked.

'To a twenty-year-old kid just out of trade school?' Allison said. 'I doubt it.'

'Give me a few,' Edgar said. 'Let me see what else comes up.'

Allison and I went into the kitchen and straight to the leftovers. I grabbed a cold pierogi, dipped it in some warm sour cream, and she took the last piece of pork. Good thing neither one of us is a germophobe. It wasn't long before Edgar called us back into the living room.

'Either of you ever hear of Taylor Made Holdings?' he asked.

'Yeah,' Allison said. 'That's the company Bobby Taylor started. They own all the car dealerships, a few apartment buildings, and two sporting goods stores upstate.'

'Wanna guess what their first business dealing was?'

It took me a beat or two before saying, 'You're shitting me, Edgar.'

'I shit you not, Raymond.' He pointed at the text on his computer screen. 'They bought the building where Maura O'Neal Delaney started

313

her beauty salon. She owns not only the business – The MODern Look she now calls it – but also the building.'

'Son of a bitch,' my girlfriend said. 'They bought her off.'

I put my face closer to the screen, as if that would help clarify things.

'Is there any way to prove that, Edgar?' I asked. 'Can you find anything related to the transfer of ownership? Are there online records of real estate sales, small business startups, things like that?'

'Raymond,' Edgar said, like me talking to one of my kids, '*everything's* online. Just give me another minute or two.'

It literally took him three. Later than he'd promised, but there was a good reason for the sixty-second discrepancy.

'Bobby Taylor bought the building, all right,' he said, 'with the help of his parents taking out a second mortgage on their house.'

'Before he signed with the big leagues,' I said.

'Two years before,' Allison said, looking over Edgar's shoulder. 'His folks must have been pretty convinced he was going to make it.'

'Sure enough that they set up a company and weren't going to risk his ex-girlfriend screwing things up for him before he got into college.'

An unpleasant thought crossed my mind. It was a moment before I could verbalize it. Then I knew the answer just as the words were coming out of my mouth.

'Which law firm handled the transfer of deed ownership?'

He gave me the look I expected.

'My dad or Marty?' I asked.

He paused and squinted. That was Edgar's go-to face when having discovered something unpleasant. Again, I had my answer.

'Sorry, Ray,' he said.

'It's not your fault, Edgar. But it does help explain why my father kept such crappy notes on this case and almost nothing on his computer files.'

Allison put her hand on my shoulder and said, 'You said so yourself, Ray. It was Marty's case, not your dad's.'

I know I had said that, but it must have bothered my father to have been party – in any capacity – to what the three of us figured had happened. Second to the Church, the Rules of Law prevailed in the Donne household. The few times we had dinner as a whole family, my father would constantly figure out a way to work The Law into our mealtime conversations. To see it bent in such a horrible way must have eaten away at him. Hell, it was twenty years ago and it was giving me a pain in the gut right now.

'OK,' I said. 'Just so it's out there. It looks like the Taylor family bought Maura O'Neal's silence by giving her the money to start her own beauty shop. They also used my dad's firm to facilitate the deal.'

'But can we prove any of that?' Allison asked.

Do I want to?

'After twenty years,' I said. 'I highly doubt it. They have lawyers who could provide half a dozen viable reasons why the family did what it did. And there's few things cops dislike more than having to reopen a case that's been closed for two decades.' I paused for a few seconds. 'The real question,' I said, 'is can any of this be used in your stories in any way?' I looked at my reporter girlfriend.

'Oh,' she said. 'I don't think so, Ray. This is exactly the kind of stuff that gets newspapers tied up in court for years. I can't allege that the Taylors bought Maura's silence. I'd probably lose my job before I hit send.'

She was right, and I knew it. But maybe there was another way.

'You can't be sued for printing facts, can you?' I asked.

She laughed. 'We can be sued for anything, Ray. It'd be almost impossible to lose a suit if we only printed the facts, though. We have to be able to prove to a judge there was an absence of malice on our part.'

I thought about that. 'But some of this can be used to help someone, right?'

'I'm not following you, Ray.'

'Here's what I think we should do.'

'*We?*' Allison asked.

Twenty-Seven

I woke up alone the next day at my own apartment. Allison and I – was this happening a lot lately? – had decided to spend the night at our own places. It was the first Saturday morning in a long time I didn't find myself in a bed with Ally. I lay there for a few minutes considering how that felt. I didn't like it. As much as I didn't want to think about a long-term commitment right now, I liked having Allison in my life and didn't want to imagine that ending.

I grabbed a quick shower and shave, a coffee and bagel downstairs, and took the subway to Laura Feldman's office in Midtown Manhattan. When I got there, about ten minutes early, I noticed a family of four waiting outside. It had to be The Feldmans because the man did have one of the coolest goatees I'd ever seen.

'Laura?' I said as I approached.

She looked at me and then at her phone. 'Raymond?' she asked. 'You're nine minutes early!'

'You're doing me the favor. I wanted to make sure I wasn't late.'

She looked at her husband and said, 'How thoughtful of you.'

I stuck out my hand to the husband. 'Raymond Donne.'

'Kenny Feldman,' he said. 'So you're friends with Edgar, huh?'

317

'Yep. For quite a few years now.'

'He's an interesting fellow,' Kenny said.

'That's a pretty good word for him.'

'I love Edgar!' Laura said. 'He knows so much about so much. He's been a big help to our firm.'

'What exactly does he do for you guys?'

Before answering my question, she looked over at her son and daughter, who were keeping busy on their phones. 'Kids! Come over here and say hello to Mr Donne.'

Both children dutifully came over. The boy looked to be about thirteen, the girl a few years younger. She wore a pair of bright blue eyeglasses you'd expect to see on Elton John's daughter. They both somehow hid how excited they were to take their attention away from their phones and meet Mommy's new friend.

'Hey, guys,' I said. 'I'm Raymond.'

The boy gave me a quick wave and said, 'I'm Max.'

The girl, barely above a whisper, said, 'I'm Zaz. Do you play Frisbee?'

I laughed. 'I used to. Why, do you?'

'No, but my brother does, and he's really good.'

'Really. That's cool.'

'What's cool?' she asked.

'One: that he's good at Frisbee. Two: that you brag about your big brother.'

'I wasn't bragging about—'

'Yes, you were,' Max said. 'You were bragging about me.'

Laura looked at her phone again. 'OK, family. You should get going. I've got to speak with Raymond, and you guys gotta get to class.'

'I sing,' Zaz informed me. 'In a chorus.'

I turned to Max. 'She any good?'

'I guess,' Max said with a degree of reluctance.

'Now you're bragging about me,' Zaz countered.

'OK,' Kenny said. 'Let's let Mommy work.' He gave me his hand again. 'Nice to meet you, and give my regards to Edgar. Maybe we can all get together for a beer or two. We got some great places in Hell's Kitchen.'

'I've been to a few of them,' I said. 'I'll mention it to Edgar.'

'OK, OK,' Laura said. 'Off with you all!' She gave kisses all around and said quickly, 'Bye. See you later and I love you.'

They all said something similar back and headed off to other parts of the city. Laura turned back to me.

'So,' she said. 'I hate to do this, but I have to be up there,' she gestured with her head at the building behind her, 'a bit earlier than I had thought.'

'OK,' I said. 'I'll try and make this quick. Who's buying and selling art looted by the Nazis or smuggled out of Germany before the war?'

'Yeah. Edgar said that's what you wanted to know. First, I have to tell you my firm represents some of the wealthiest families in the world. I will not mention any names. But if I did, you'd know them.'

'I didn't expect you to.'

'Good. Edgar told me your girlfriend's a reporter and the last thing I need is—'

'I just want to know what kind of market there

is out there and how someone gets involved in the buying and selling of that particular art.'

'Also, my firm does not specialize in this, but we do have one guy who does pro bono work to reacquire Holocaust art and return it to its rightful owners.'

'I understand.'

'OK. The buying's easy,' she said. 'You need a lot of money. Either private or from an endowment to a museum. We've seen both.'

I considered that. 'So, let's say I'm a private individual with enough money to buy a painting that's been missing from the art world for almost eighty years. Why would I want to do that if I knew I could never show it off?'

'You might be a dick,' she said. 'There're more people out there than you'd like to think who have Picassos and Matisses and Chagalls hanging on their living room walls for the same reason dogs lick their you-know-whats.'

'Because they can.'

'Exactly. My firm has been affiliated with some of these families.' She coughed into her elbow. 'Then you get the auction houses and museums.'

'I thought they'd be the ones against this kind of thing.'

'You would think so, and most of the time you'd be right, according to my colleague. But there are professionals in the art world whose desire to own some of these pieces apparently trumps their respect for the law and rightful ownership.'

'What do they do with them if they can't display them?'

'Some do.' She paused. 'Edgar said you used to be a policeman.'

'Years ago.'

'You never ran into people who thought they were above the law?'

I laughed. 'I see what you mean.'

'And why are you so interested in this, if I may ask?'

I grinned. 'I can't mention any names,' I said. 'But if I did, you wouldn't know them.' Laura gave me a little chuckle. 'I know a family who seems to have somehow acquired some artwork that has been listed as missing or destroyed by the Nazis since the mid- to late-nineteen thirties.'

She let out a whistle. 'Any idea how they acquired the piece or pieces?'

'The family left Germany right before things got real bad for the Jews. They eventually made their way to Williamsburg and opened a business that's still running today. My guess is that they brought the art over with them and, as hard as it is to believe, forgot about it. My friend was given a piece that seems to be genuine by an elderly man whose father had moved the family to the states. The guy seems to have Alzheimer's so he had no idea what he was giving away.'

She thought about that and said, 'That doesn't surprise me all that much. I did a little research after Edgar called, and I found out that it's estimated there are sixty to a hundred thousand pieces of artwork missing from that time. I wouldn't be all that shocked if people sold them

321

at garage sales not knowing what they had.' She paused for a few seconds then said, 'Is your friend interested in selling the piece? Is that why you wanted to meet with me? If that's the case, I don't want you to say another—'

'No,' I said. 'Not at all. We're just interested in how someone would go about it. We're planning on giving the piece back to the old man's son. This is not the first time the old man's given away paintings. We need to tell the son what we know and find out if they're the rightful owners.'

'You think he may have given other valuable pieces away to people?'

'It's a real possibility.'

'Your friend,' Laura said, 'or the family should contact the State Department. Their New York office is at the United Nations.'

'They're the ones who handle this kind of thing?'

'They have in the past. The art was smuggled out of Germany, and that makes it an international matter. I can put you in touch with our pro bono lawyer. He's worked extensively with the State Department.'

'I'll keep that in mind,' I said. 'I've read that a lot of people who were able to get out of Germany before the war brought stuff to the states for safekeeping for other families. A lot of those families didn't survive the war.'

Laura put on her lawyer face as she considered that.

'Morally,' she said, 'if the family you're talking about is *not* the rightful owners, they should do all that they can to ensure that the art gets returned to the heirs of the rightful owners. There are lawsuits all the time with families trying to recover what their families lost because of the Nazis.'

'I'll talk to the guy. See what he says.'

Laura nodded and looked at her phone. 'I have to head in now,' she said. 'I hope I was able to help.'

'Very much so,' I said, shaking her hand.

She reached into her pocket and handed me a business card. 'If there's anything else I can help with, give me a call. No promises, but I'll see what I can do.'

'I appreciate that. Have a good meeting.'

She smirked. 'Right.'

I was almost to the subway when my phone rang. I looked at the caller ID. I didn't recognize the number, just that it was a 516 area code. Nassau County.

'Hello?' I said.

'Raymond?' A guy's voice, almost recognizable.

'Yeah, who's this?'

'It's Chris,' he said. 'Chris Miller. Melissa's brother.'

'Oh, hey, Chris. What's up?'

There was a slight pause on his end. Then, 'We need to talk.'

'Is Melissa OK?' I asked, hoping that yesterday's interview with Allison hadn't upset his sister too much.

'No, oh yeah, she's fine,' he said. 'It's about something else.'

I stopped just before heading down to the train

where I'd more than likely lose my signal. 'Go ahead,' I said.

'Not on the phone,' he said. 'Is your friend Edgar home?'

'I think so.' *Did I tell Chris about Edgar?* 'Why?'

'Let's meet at his place. Let's say in half an hour?'

'OK, Chris, but why—'

'Thanks, Raymond.'

He hung up before I could ask him how he knew where Edgar lived.

Then it came to me. *Shit.*

Twenty-Eight

Wanting to get to Edgar's as quickly as possible, I decided not to take the subway and hailed a cab. At first the driver told me he was not going to take me to Brooklyn – his shift was almost over and he didn't want to make the trip into another borough – then I explained the law to him, which he already knew, showed him my mini NYPD badge Uncle Ray had given me, and within a minute we were on our way to Edgar's. I'd called him before we crossed the East River to tell him I was on my way, so he was waiting for me outside his apartment when the cab dropped me off. The trip took about ten minutes. I added an extra ten to the cabbie's tip. If he was grateful, he did a good job of hiding it.

'What's up?' Edgar said.

'Chris Miller's on the way here,' I said.

It took him a bit to remember who that was.

'Why?' he said.

'I think he wants to confess.'

Just as those words came out of my mouth, a blue compact car pulled into the sole empty space in front of Edgar's place. Chris Miller got out and walked over to us. He had a gym bag slung over his shoulder. He shook my hand and then Edgar's.

'Chris Miller,' he said.

'Hello,' Edgar said. He thought about what to

say next, and all he could come up with was, 'What's up?'

Chris closed his eyes and took a deep breath. 'I owe you an apology,' he said. He opened his eyes again. 'A big one, I'm afraid.' He unzipped his gym bag and came out with Edgar's laptop bag. 'This is yours,' he said.

Edgar reached out and took it. He turned it around in his hands as if examining a rare, valuable book. I had to squash the powerful urge to punch Chris in the face. I had found myself liking the guy, a lot, but he'd hurt my friend. As my heartbeat increased and my body temperature rose, I stuck my hands in my pockets. Again, it took Edgar more time before he realized what this all meant.

'You?' he finally said. 'You were the one who mugged me?'

Chris cringed at the use of the word mugged. He nodded and then said, 'I'm sorry. I was desperate and couldn't think of anything else to do.'

'You broke into Marty Stover's office,' I added, keeping my tone as level as possible. 'Then you followed us back here.'

He nodded again. 'Like I said, I was desperate.' He looked down at his feet. 'If you guys wanna call the cops, I understand.' He looked up at us. 'But I'd like to explain myself first, if that's OK.'

I had a feeling I knew what he was about to say, but I told him to go ahead. Maybe the more he talked the less I'd feel like hitting him.

'Melissa's been having these dreams lately,' he began. 'They've been getting worse.' He swallowed

326

hard. 'I'm not going to go into too many details, but they involve her being held down and . . . and attacked. I think they started up again when she started seeing this new therapist.'

Oh, great. 'She's not seeing a regression therapist, is she?'

'No, no,' Chris said. 'Nothing like that. This one's real good. She lets Melissa do most of the talking and tell her story. I think Melissa called her a narrative therapist.' He took another breath. 'I think the dreams are coming because Melissa's story is getting clearer in her head.' He shrugged. 'I don't know how else to put it.'

I let that sit for a while before saying, 'And how does this lead to your breaking into Marty's office and then stealing Edgar's laptop?' *And hurting my friend?*

If anyone who'd just admitted to committing two felony crimes could look embarrassed, Chris Miller pulled it off. It took him a little time to gather his thoughts.

'I thought,' he said, 'that Marty Stover would have a file in his office on Melissa's case. I'd been by his office earlier that week to talk with him. He didn't want to discuss the case and practically threw me out.'

'That's how you knew about the old alarm system,' I said.

He nodded. 'When I broke in and went into the offices, all I saw was computers. The file cabinets were locked. Obviously, I hadn't thought it all the way through. I don't know what I was thinking. After a few minutes, I realized what I'd done was pretty stupid, so I panicked and left.'

'How did you know about us?' Edgar wanted to know. 'About me?'

'After I got out of there,' Chris said, 'I figured the cops would be showing up. Then I thought Marty's son would come, and I could ask him about my sister's case. So, I parked down the block and waited for him.'

'Instead you got us,' I said.

'You guys went in with the cops.' He turned to Edgar. 'I saw you with the laptop and . . . I don't know, I guess I thought if anyone had the file on Melissa's case, it'd be you.' His eyes filled up as he went on. 'I am really sorry that I hurt you. I just wanted to find out what I could. For my sister.'

In all the years I'd known Edgar, I'd never seen him hold a grudge. This time was no different. He offered his hand to Chris. 'It's OK. It wasn't that bad.'

Watching Edgar so graciously forgive the guy who had attacked him lowered my own body's electrical pulses. After a large truck lumbered by, I spoke next.

'Your thought process sucked, Chris,' I said. 'And so did your methods.'

'I know. I'm sorry.'

'But your instincts were pretty good.'

I proceeded to tell him what Edgar, Allison, and I suspected after going over the files, my dad's notes, and talking with Billy Taylor.

'So Bobby *was* involved?'

'That's what we think. What we can prove is another matter. And after all these years, I hate to say this, there's not much the cops can do.'

328

I watched as Chris Miller's face turned from apologetic to something approaching rage. The look someone gets when they realize that justice may not be in their future.

'So Bobby Taylor gets away with what he did?'

'Not exactly,' I said.

'What does that mean?' he asked. 'You just said—'

'I just said there's not much *the cops* can do.'

Twenty-Nine

With my Uncle Ray's permission – and his insisting I give him the Reader's Digest version of what Allison and I had planned, and his not objecting for once – Officer CJ Gray drove Allison and me out to Sea Cliff, Long Island. Marty Stover, Junior, met us outside the Taylor family home.

Billy and Bobby Taylor might have grown up in the same middle class Long Island as I had, but once Bobby signed with the majors, he'd bought his folks this place in Sea Cliff. Their home, like many on the block, was an old Victorian with a wrap-around porch situated on what must have been at least an acre of land made even more impressive by the light of the setting sun. It was a far cry from the homes on the block I had grown up on.

Marty, Allison, and I walked up the half dozen steps that led to the front porch of the Taylor house. We were a few feet from the doorbell when the door opened. It was Mr Taylor who met us and spoke through the screen.

'I was about to call you,' he said to Allison. 'And call this whole thing off.'

'That *is* your right, Mr Taylor,' Allison said. 'But then your side will not make it into my paper. I will write that you denied my repeated requests for an interview.'

'Repeated?' he said. 'You asked once and I reluctantly said yes.'

Allison didn't miss a beat. 'And now I'm asking again. That makes it repeated.' This part of the show was Allison's, and I couldn't help but be impressed.

We all stood a yard or so away from Mr Taylor, separated only by a screen door. I watched as he weighed his options. Truth be told, I didn't think he really had many at this point. That was proven when he opened the door, stepped aside, and said, 'Come in.'

The three of us stepped inside the Taylor home, which my mother would have described as gracious. At least the part I could see. Mr Taylor immediately steered us to the left into the living room where his wife was sitting on a love seat, her hands resting gently on her lap. Her face betrayed whatever calm she was trying to present to the world.

Marty, Allison, and I all said hello at the same time, almost as if we'd practiced it.

'Excuse me for not getting up,' she said. 'My sciatica is acting up again.'

'I'm sorry to hear that,' I said. Gesturing with my hand toward Marty, I said, 'You know Marty Stover, I'm sure.'

'We know *of* him,' Mr Taylor said. 'Not sure why you had to bring a lawyer along, though. Unless you're afraid of getting sued for defamation and slander.'

'That would be libel,' Allison corrected him. 'And that's not why he's here.'

'Whatever.' Pissed at our presence or not, Mr

331

Taylor remembered his manners. 'Have a seat, I guess,' he said, gesturing toward the over-sized couch that would easily fit the three of us. 'Bobby is not here yet.'

Of course not, I thought. Bobby Taylor made others wait for him. It was that kind of hubris we were counting on tonight. We all sat down.

Mrs Taylor made a motion as if about to get up. 'Can I get you all something? Some tea, maybe? Something cold? Hard to tell what to offer this time of year.'

When the other two didn't speak, I said. 'We're OK. Thank you.'

'You have a great home,' Allison said. 'I love all the landscaping.'

'Thank you,' Mrs Taylor said. She motioned with her head toward her husband. 'It's kind of a hobby with Warren. He never did feel comfortable having other people do his yard work. Although we do pay the boy two doors down to do the shoveling.'

'That's enough, Barbara,' her husband said. 'They didn't drive all the way out here to interview us for *House and Garden.*' He turned to Allison. 'I suppose you might as well start with the questions. The quicker we get started, the quicker we can get this over with. Bobby should be here any minute.'

As if on cue, the front door opened, and in walked the man himself. He took one glance at the three of us on the couch and looked as if his parents' home had been invaded by mice.

'I want you to know,' he said, his voice filling

the room, 'that I told my parents not to speak with you. I'm here to make sure they don't say too much.' He looked at the three of us for a while and, with his eyes on Marty, said, 'Sorry again about your dad.'

'Thank you,' Marty said. 'And thanks for the flowers. My mother loved them.'

Bobby nodded. 'I'll be right back. I'm getting a beer.'

A lot of people might have added, 'Can I get anybody anything?' But Bobby Taylor was not a lot of people. What he did say was directed at his parents.

'Don't say anything until I get back.'

None of us did as we waited for his return. When he came back, he had a green bottle of beer in his hand. I couldn't make out the label. He went over and sat in the biggest chair in the room. I had the feeling it was *the* chair reserved for his visits.

'So,' he said after taking a long sip from his bottle, 'what're you trying to get my parents to say?' His glare was focused on Allison.

'I'm not trying to get them to say anything,' she answered. 'I just want to ask a few questions about what the family went through and how they feel now.'

'You coulda just asked me,' he said.

'I want the parents' point of view, Bobby. You're more than welcome to add yours, as well. Quite honestly, I'd like that.'

'I don't give a shit what you'd like.'

'Robert,' his mother said.

He mumbled an unconvincing apology and

333

took another sip. When it was clear he was done talking, Allison began her interview. She started with the basic questions, stuff I probably could have answered for them. Questions about how they felt when Billy was originally accused, when he confessed, and when they realized he was going to spend the final part of his teens and most of his twenties in prison. They gave the expected answers.

'How often did you visit him when he was . . . incarcerated?' Allison asked.

'Every week,' his parents said in unison.

'It was very important for us to let him know that we still loved him,' Mr Taylor said. 'There was some pretty ugly stuff said about him – *in the press* – and he needed to know that he was still our son and we loved him. No matter what.'

Allison jotted that down in her pad. She went through some questions about his time in prison and how it changed him.

'He took every class they offered,' Mr Taylor said. 'At least the ones we felt he could handle academically. He was also in group and individual counseling, four times a week. We knew he needed to keep as busy as possible. We were also fortunate . . .' He looked at Marty for this part. 'Fortunate to get him into a minimum-security facility. Thanks to your father.'

Marty nodded as Allison wrote that down. I looked over at Bobby, who seemed to be listening to every word, making sure his parents didn't slip up. His eyes were darting from speaker to speaker as if filming a mental movie. It was this kind of awareness of what was going on around him, I knew, that had made him such a good ballplayer.

'And the past ten years,' Allison said, 'since his release. How have they been for you as a family?'

Both parents looked over at Bobby. Mrs Taylor said, 'Thanks to Robert, and the work William was able to do while he was away, he was able to start a new life almost immediately. He's a changed person. We feel blessed to have him back home.'

Allison asked a few more questions about the family's life now. The family's reliance on faith came up more than once, and if I heard the word blessed one more time, I was going to take out my New York Atheist's card. After maybe five more minutes, the interview reached a natural break. Natural, except for the fact that we had planned it exactly this way on the ride out here.

'Mrs Taylor,' Allison said, 'maybe I will take you up on that offer of tea. May I help you?'

Mrs Taylor looked at her husband. He took a few seconds to nod his approval. Again, the Taylors were nothing if not well mannered. He helped his wife off the couch, and she and Allison made their way to the kitchen.

After Mr Taylor sat back down, and when I was sure the ladies were well out of listening range, I clapped my hands together. 'Great. Now the boys get to chat a bit.'

Bobby leaned forward. 'What the fuck does that mean?'

I smiled. 'You have no idea how glad I am you asked that, Robert.'

For the first time since I'd met him, Bobby Taylor flinched. Maybe it was my using his given name. Maybe he felt the power in his parents' home shift a bit. Either way, he recovered quickly, and then stood up.

'I don't think I like your tone of voice, Raymond.' He closed the space between us with three steps and looked down at me. 'Maybe I'll have to rethink kicking your ass.'

I stayed where I was, next to Marty on the couch. I reached into my front pocket and pulled out my cell phone.

'Should I be scared now, Robert?' I asked, holding his gaze. 'Or should I just call the cop who's parked outside? The one who drove us here.'

He stared at me as he considered that. It didn't take long.

'You brought a lawyer and a cop with you?' he said. 'What the fuck?'

'Sit down,' I said. 'It's time to talk some business, and I'd like to be done with it before your mother comes back with our tea.'

He continued to stand there, his breathing getting heavier. The look he gave me was similar to the one a hungry man gives a pizza. After a while, his father spoke.

'Sit down, Robert. Let's hear what Mr Donne has to say.'

'What does he possibly have to say I'd be interested in?'

'Two words,' I said. And then I paused for effect. 'Maura O'Neal.'

The mention of her name took both Taylors by

336

surprise. The father showed it more than the son, but the look was there on the younger Robert's face as well.

Bases were loaded, and he'd just thrown three straight balls.

He walked backwards until he was seated again. I let out the breath I'd been holding as inconspicuously as I could.

'Let's not waste a lot of time going back and forth about Maura,' I said. 'Like I said, I'd like to have this part of the conversation done before your mom comes back.' I leaned forward. 'Long story, short: Maura's done rather well for herself since high school. Specifically, since she spoke with Marty Stover, Senior, about the events of the night Melissa Miller was attacked. She went through two years of school, and with your family's help, was able to start her own business at the age of twenty.'

'It was an investment,' Mr Taylor said, shifting his body on the couch. His response sounded like one he'd been rehearsing for two decades.

'That's exactly what it was,' I answered. 'But not really in Maura. More, I would say, in young Robert's future. And your family's.'

'You don't know what you're talking about,' Bobby said.

'Yeah,' I said. 'I do. Maura spoke to Marty Stover twice. The first time, she said that you and she had left the party early because you were paying too much attention to Melissa Miller. She was angry, and like the good, horny boyfriend you were, you left.'

'That's what happened.'

337

'Yeah . . . but then you went back to the party after an argument with her. That's what she said the *second time* she spoke with Marty.' I looked at the briefcase Marty had brought with him. 'We have the notes. Would you like to see them?'

The two Taylors looked at each other. The father spoke first.

'No,' he said. 'I see where you're going with this, Mr Donne. And there's nothing you or your reporter girlfriend can do about it. It was twenty years ago. Ask your lawyer friend here. There's something in the law called statute of limitations.'

'You're right,' I said. 'There's also something called freedom of the press.'

'Your girlfriend prints a word of that,' Bobby said, 'and my lawyers will be on her and her paper like fleas on a dog.'

I turned to Marty Junior. It was his turn now.

'That's probably true,' he said. 'There's absolutely no way Ms Rogers' paper could print that your father bought Maura O'Neal's silence twenty years ago.'

Bobby smiled, leaned back, and picked up his beer. He looked at me with victory in his eyes and said, 'See?'

'However,' Marty said. 'There's nothing to stop her paper from printing that Taylor Holdings' first piece of business – *two years* before you signed your first baseball contract – was to purchase the property Maura O'Neal used to start her beauty salon. They can also mention that Maura O'Neal was your girlfriend – your alibi – at the time of the attack and the main reason the police did not consider you a suspect.'

338

'That's libel,' Bobby said. 'I'll own that paper after the trial.'

Interesting how Bobby knew the difference between slander and libel.

'It's only libel if it's not true. Your lawyers could sue, of course, but they'd have to prove the presence of malice on behalf of the paper. But,' Marty picked up his case and put it on his lap, 'it's all true.'

'And it fits into a few sentences,' I added. 'Easy reading.'

The silence that filled the living room after those two words would have been painful had I not been on the side I was on. It was the Taylors' turn to talk, and neither one knew what to say. The only sound in the house was the clinking of teacups in the kitchen. Bobby Taylor, to give him credit, was as at least going to go down swinging.

'You still can't prove a thing,' he said.

'There's nothing *to* prove,' I said. 'Just printing the truth.'

'Who's gonna care? It's old news.'

'Not to your brother it isn't.'

Over on the couch, Mr Taylor let out an audible groan like someone who'd aggravated an old injury. Bobby looked over at his father with sympathy in his eyes.

'And,' I said, 'I'm willing to bet your mother has no idea about this either.'

Bobby stood again. 'Keep her out of this.'

'That's up to you, Robert.'

'Fuck you,' he said. 'Fuck the three of you. Coming into my parents' house with this shit.'

339

He pointed to the door he'd paid for with his Major League Baseball money. 'Get the fuck out of here!'

'We're not done yet,' I said.

'I think you are.'

He again took three steps and was a foot away from me. This time, I stood. I looked over at Mr Taylor and said, 'How does it feel, sir? Giving up one son to save the other. The more valuable son?'

'Fuck you!' Bobby repeated and pushed me hard enough to send me into the couch and almost into Marty. I was considering the merits of getting up again when Mr Taylor spoke.

'He confessed,' he said. 'William confessed.'

'Because he was told he was guilty,' I said. 'By the very people who should have been looking out for him. Instead, you figured out a way to quiet the only witness who, at the very least, could have provided an alternative to what the police were led to believe. However unpleasant that alternative was.' I scooted over away from Marty. 'Maybe you truly thought you were protecting the family. But don't for a second try to make me believe you didn't realize you were sacrificing your other son to do so.'

'Is that what you think I did, Mr Donne?'

'Convince me otherwise,' I said.

More silence. Then, 'Melissa Miller *said* it was William who attacked her,' Mr Taylor said. 'We just wanted to get the whole thing over with as soon as possible. If you want to call that protecting my family, then, yes, that's what I was doing.'

'And buying Maura O'Neal her own business?'

Mr Taylor shook his head. 'She was confused,' he said. 'We didn't need that.'

We looked at each other, both unconvinced by his words. I shook my head.

'With all due respect, Mr Taylor,' I said. 'Don't piss on my leg and tell me the game's rained out. We both – all of us in this room – know what you did.'

Bobby Taylor said, 'Don't speak to my father like that. In his home.'

I waved that away. 'The home you bought him, Robert.'

The sound from the kitchen got a little more active. Tea was about to be served.

'So what do you want, Raymond?' Bobby Taylor said. 'How much to keep this from making the newspaper?'

I smiled and shook my head. 'That's not like you, Robert, telegraphing a pitch like that. It's like I'm sitting dead red on a fastball, waiting for you to throw it.'

'So it's not about money?'

I laughed. 'Oh, no, it *is* about money. Just not for me.'

He waited and said, 'For who, then?'

I looked at Marty and he opened his briefcase. He took out the papers he had prepared after I called him a few hours ago. Boilerplate stuff, really.

'First,' he said, 'you're going to hire Melissa Miller as a consultant to your car dealerships. She will earn a salary of fifty thousand dollars a year.'

Marty took out the contract he had drawn up and placed it on the coffee table.

Bobby had difficulty processing that. When he had, he said, 'You're nuts. Why would she work for me?' He was looking at the contract, not me.

'We didn't say she was going to work for you, Robert. I wouldn't put her through that. I said you're going to hire her as a consultant. Call it quality control if you want. But she will never step foot in one of your dealerships or have anything directly to do with you except cash your checks.'

'That bitch put you up to this?' His face turned red. 'I shoulda known that.'

'She has no idea about this yet. She'll find out tomorrow.'

He got up and paced across the small space twice. When he was done, he took a seat next to his father on the couch.

'That's it?' he asked.

'Not quite,' I said.

Marty took out another contract. Actually it was one piece of paper.

'You,' I said, 'are going to make a generous donation to Bridges to Success.'

'How generous?'

'Half a million dollars generous,' I said and waited for the shock to pass. 'And, just so you know, that will also make the papers. But Allison will make sure it sounds like you wanted it kept anonymous. She'll have someone else write the piece and interview you and good will and all that shit.'

'Thank you,' he said, the sarcasm coming through loud and clear. 'Is that all?'

'One more thing,' I said and Marty took out one more piece of paper.

'Am I signing away my kids now?' Bobby asked. I ignored that.

'You will also be donating another five hundred thousand dollars to RAINN – the Rape, Abuse, Incest National Network. They do great work with victims of sexual abuse and their families, and you're going to be proud to be a part of their mission.'

Marty spread out all three pieces of paper, reached into his pocket, pulled out a pen and held it out to Bobby. 'Please sign on the designated lines,' Marty said. 'We'll take care of the actual checks on Monday. You can come to my office, or I can meet you at yours if that's more convenient for you.'

Now there were two faces in the room Bobby Taylor wanted to take a bite out of. To his credit, he waited, took a breath, and then signed all three documents. That's when his mother and Allison came back into the living room. His mother held an actual tea service tray like they have on those PBS shows from England. Allison held a tray of cookies and what looked like brownies.

Picking up on the awkward silence in her living room, Mrs Taylor said, 'Is everything OK in here?'

'We're fine,' Bobby said as Marty scooped up the papers to make room for our refreshments. He put them in his case and the case back on the floor. 'You really didn't have to go through all this trouble, Mom.'

'These people came all the way from the city, Robert,' she said. 'It's the least we can do to be hospitable.' She paused. 'Even if the reason for their visit is not as pleasant as we would all like.'

I found myself truly liking this woman and realizing how much it would devastate her if she ever found out what her husband, her son, and their lawyers had conspired to do twenty years ago. The fact that one of those lawyers was my father would be eating away at me for a long time.

The papers Marty Stover, Junior, had just placed in his briefcase would ease that somewhat.

The sins of the fathers somewhat undone by their sons.

At least that's what I told myself.

Thirty

Much to his mother's chagrin and embarrassment, Bobby Taylor didn't stay for the tea. Marty, Allison, and I spent another half hour with the Taylors making small talk. I don't believe Mr Taylor contributed a syllable. We said our good-byes and gathered in the early evening darkness next to Marty's car.

'I'll have all the paperwork drawn up and ready for Bobby to sign on Monday,' Marty said. 'Nice job in there, guys. I thought Bobby would put up more of a fight.'

'He wanted to,' I said. 'But then his mother, brother, and the rest of the world would never look at him the same way again. I think he did a quick risk analysis and chose the best possible outcome.'

'They say that's what the best pitchers do.'

'I've heard that.' I stuck out my hand. 'Thanks for helping out. It's nice to have had a lawyer on our side. We owe you one.'

'You're welcome,' he said. 'And you don't owe me a thing.'

'Let's talk on Monday. Make sure things went well on both our ends.'

'You got it.'

Marty got in his car. Allison and I walked over to my uncle's car where Officer Gray awaited our return. I realized too late we should have brought him some cookies from inside. Oh, well.

We got in the car and asked him to take us home.

'Whose?' he asked.

Before I could answer, Allison said, 'Mine. If that's OK.'

I could sense his smile from the front seat. 'Absolutely OK, ma'am.'

This whole having-a-driver thing was growing on me.

About halfway home, Allison's phone rang. She looked at it and her face lit up as she recognized the number.

'Hello, Charles,' she said. 'We were just talking about you.' Pause. 'Raymond and I.' A longer pause this time. 'That's amazing. Hold on.' She turned to me. 'Charles's expert confirmed the Klee is real. He wants us at his gallery tomorrow morning. Early.'

'How early?'

She asked. 'Eight,' she said to me, and I nodded. She told him we'd be there and ended the call.

'This is getting exciting,' Allison said.

'A bit too exciting for my taste.'

Allison dialed another number. I gave her a quizzical look. 'A lawyer I did an interview with a while back. He's been successfully reacquiring lost art and returning it to their rightful owners.'

So much for Laura Feldman's lawyer.

'What if the Sterns are the rightful owners?' I asked.

'Then they'll get it back.' She turned away.

346

'Hello, Arthur. Allison Rogers.' She paused. 'As a matter of fact you can.' She proceeded to tell him about the Klee. 'Not tonight, no, but I can be at your office tomorrow at nine.' Pause. 'Excellent. Thank you.' Back to me. 'We now have two appointments for tomorrow.'

Thirty-One

Sunday morning we had a quick and early breakfast. Allison lived close enough to Charles Mantle's gallery that we walked over. Spring was definitely in the air, and I couldn't wait to get the day's errands over with and spend the rest with my girlfriend. Mantle met us at the door and greeted us both with kisses on the cheeks. When on Sullivan Street. He then led us to the back of his gallery where the safe was located.

'Have you decided what you're going to do?' he asked as he punched in the combination to his high-tech safe.

'We're bringing it to a lawyer who has experience with this kind of situation,' Allison said. 'He's meeting us in half an hour at his office.'

'You got a lawyer to meet you on a Sunday morning? Nice.'

'When we called him last night and told him what we had, he wanted to meet right away. But we told him the Klee wouldn't be available until this morning.'

Mantle reached into the safe and pulled out the painting. 'Here you go. Please let me know how it all turns out.'

'Thanks for everything, Charles,' I said.

'Come back any time, Raymond,' he said. 'With or without Ms Rogers.'

I was trying to hail a cab on Houston Street while Allison was teasing me about Mantle's obvious affection for me. This was why I didn't see the guy in the ski mask come up behind Ally until it was too late. He grabbed Allison's bag, and she screamed. I turned and watched as he ran in the other direction. I took off after him.

I screamed, 'Hey, stop!' like that was going to work. There were a few other pedestrians on the sidewalk, and I screamed again. 'Stop that guy! He's a thief!'

People got out of his way, but my fruitless yelling somehow convinced the guy he needed to cross the busy street. This was not a smart idea as he had to slow down to let a bus go by, allowing me to shorten the distance between us.

'Stop!' I yelled again.

He turned and saw me getting closer. He darted into Houston Street without looking and never saw the cab that sideswiped him, spinning him around and knocking him to the ground. The cab pulled to a stop just as I reached the injured thief. Ally was right behind me.

'Call nine-one-one,' I said.

As a small crowd gathered around us, I looked down at the guy. He was still clutching Allison's bag. I took the bag from his hand and put it behind me. If this guy had gotten away with it, would he have known the value of what he had snatched? I put my hand under his head and removed his ski mask.

'Oh, my god,' someone said. 'It's just a kid.'

Not just any kid. It was Joshua Stern's kid, Daniel.

Holy shit.

In lieu of any other adult who knew Daniel, the EMT asked me if I'd ride with him to the hospital. The kid was in shock and mumbling incoherently, and they felt that a familiar face might help with the trip. Even mine. I was still in a bit of shock myself, but I agreed and told Ally to meet me at the hospital.

They strapped Daniel on to the gurney, and I sat in the seat by his head.

'Put your seat belt on, sir,' the EMT told me. 'We don't need two patients on this ride.' He climbed up inside and sat across from Daniel.

I buckled myself in as Daniel continued to mumble. Some of his ramblings sounded like they might have been in Hebrew. Maybe he was praying. The siren didn't make hearing him any easier. One thing I could make out was, 'I'm sorry, I'm sorry.'

I reached out and touched his shoulder. 'I know, Daniel. It's OK.'

'No,' he said. 'You don't . . . understand. I did it.'

'I was there, Daniel. I was the one who chased you.'

'No,' he said and then mumbled something that sounded like, 'It's all over.'

'It's not over, Daniel. The doctors'll take good care of you, then we—'

'No.' He took a big, labored breath and said slowly, 'Miss . . . the Stover.'

350

'Sir,' the EMT said. He had just taken Daniel's blood pressure. 'It's probably not a good idea to engage the patient in conversation at the moment. In addition to the hip injury, he more than likely has a concussion.' I think he was having second thoughts about me riding along with Daniel.

'Wait a second,' I said, leaning forward. The ambulance took a sharp left and the seat belt dug into my belly. 'What did you say, Daniel?'

'Sir, please. I'm advising you to—'

'Shut up for a second,' I blurted out. 'Sorry. Please, give me a minute here.' I said to Daniel again, 'What did you just say, Daniel?'

'I just . . . wanted the painting back.'

I turned to the EMT to explain. 'He . . . mugged my girlfriend for a painting. I chased him and he got hit by the cab.'

The EMT nodded and smiled. 'Fine,' he said. 'Now if we can just stay—'

'Not your girlfriend,' Daniel said. He took another big breath. 'Mr Stover.'

'What about Mr Stover?'

'He wouldn't . . . give it back.'

I took a few seconds to process that. Marty had a painting, too? *Oh, shit.*

'What did you do, Daniel?'

'I wanted . . . the . . . I'm cold.' Through chattering teeth, he said, 'The painting.'

The EMT reached over his head and pulled a blanket down. He draped it over Daniel as he gave me a look. I ignored him.

'Mr Stover had a painting?' I asked. 'Did your grandfather give it him?'

351

He shook his head slightly. 'Hector.'

'Your grandfather gave it to Hector, and Hector gave it to Mr Stover?'

'Yes.' *Yesh.*

'And you wanted it back.'

Another 'yesh.'

'So what did you do, Daniel?'

'Went to the . . . party.' *The benefit.* 'He wouldn't . . . give it back. So I . . .'

I leaned forward again. 'So you what, Daniel?'

'I got angry.' A pause for another breath. 'I had my box cutter from . . . the store . . . and I . . .'

'You stabbed Mr Stover.'

'I didn't mean to. I got angry.'

Kids with blades sometimes end up using them.

The ambulance came to an abrupt stop. 'We're here,' the EMT said.

That was one hell of a ride.

Thirty-Two

About twenty minutes later, Ally and I were sitting outside of the emergency room of Beth Israel Hospital. Daniel's parents hadn't arrived yet.

'What did he say?' Allison asked.

'This is all off the record, Ally,' I said. 'He's a minor, I'm not a law enforcement agent, and his parents or a lawyer were not present.'

'I know all that, Raymond. Just tell me what he said.'

'He told me he killed Marty Stover.'

'Holy shit,' she said. 'Because of the painting?'

'That's what he said. He knew Hector had given the painting to Marty, and Marty refused to return it.'

'How did he know Hector had the painting and that he gave it to Marty?'

'Hector told him one day when they were both working at the store. Hector had no clue what it was worth. He told Daniel he'd given it to Marty, hoping Marty would return it to the Sterns so he wouldn't hurt the old guy's feelings.'

'And Marty figured out it was valuable?'

I shrugged. 'He must have. Then the grandfather told Daniel. Daniel went to the benefit hoping to convince Marty to give it back to the family. When Marty refused, Daniel lost it. He pulled out the box cutter and stuck Marty in the leg.'

'What the hell was he doing with a box cutter?'

'He uses it for work,' I reminded her. 'He was actually in the city that afternoon making a small delivery for his dad.'

Allison shook her head. It looked like she was feeling sorry for both parties. 'Daniel knew what it was worth?'

'He must have had some idea. He's a smart kid. And with his family's business struggling the way it is, he figured this was a way out of their financial problems.'

'You got a lot of information during that ambulance ride.'

'What can I say? Kids talk to me. It's what I do.'

Allison gave that some thought and then shivered a bit.

'How did he know where I lived?'

'My guess is he followed us after we were at the shop the day his grandfather gave you the picture. His grandfather must have told him what he'd done while we were at the restaurant before we headed over to Mantle's gallery.'

'How did he know I'd have the painting with me today?'

'I don't think he did, not for sure. The kid was desperate. He was probably waiting outside your apartment every chance he got since his grandfather gave you the painting. It was just dumb luck that today was the day he saw you and got up the nerve to make his move.'

She let out a deep breath. 'So he might have been . . . stalking me?'

354

'In a sense, yeah.'

She shivered again. 'Why didn't he just come straight out with what he knew? If the paintings belong to his family, it all would've worked out.'

'I guess he didn't know if they rightfully belonged to the family or not. Daniel knows how to surf the net just as well as we do. He probably didn't want to take the chance that this would get tied up in the courts.'

'Jesus,' Ally said. 'He is a smart kid.'

Before I could respond, I saw Mr Stern rushing toward the ER desk. The woman at the computer looked like she was trying to calm him down as she found out what she could about his son. When she was done talking, he pulled out his cell phone and made a call. Then he turned and saw Allison and me. He came over. We both stood up as he approached us with a mix of concern and confusion on his face.

'Mr Donne,' he said. 'Ms Rogers. I don't understand. Why are you here? I received a call from the police that my son was in an accident. What was he doing on Houston Street? He told me he was going to a friend's this morning.'

'Maybe you better sit, Mr Stern,' I said.

'I *cannot* sit, Mr Donne. Not while my son – why are you here?'

I told him, starting with Daniel attacking Allison, then telling me he'd killed Marty Stover, and ending with the events of the past few days that had led us all to the hospital that morning. When I was done, he sat and put his face in his hands. He stayed like that for five minutes. Not

355

knowing what to do or say, Allison and I just stood there.

'I need to call our lawyer,' Joshua Stern said, breaking the silence. He stood and said, 'None of what you told me is to be in your paper, Ms Rogers. I know this must seem like a good story to you, but until we consult with our lawyer – and speak with the police, I guess – nothing my son said is to be written about. I hope you understand.'

'I do,' Allison said.

'Is this what you and Marty Stover argued about the week before his death?'

He appeared shocked I knew about that. He recovered quickly. 'No comment.'

Stern walked away to make his call.

How long had he known about his father's secret art collection?

When he was out of earshot, Allison said, 'I can't imagine what it's like.'

'Neither can I.'

'You've got so much to worry about, just being a parent. The normal stuff. Now he's got to figure out how to handle this.' She shook her head and repeated herself. 'I can't imagine.'

'Makes you wonder,' I said, 'what our parents' biggest worries were. Someone once described my father to me as a very fearful man.'

'Fearful of what?'

'Of what would become of Rachel and me.'

She took my hand and walked me out of the hospital into the sunshine.

'What do you think he'd say if he could see you now?' she asked.

356

'Honestly?' I said. 'I don't know. He'd be glad I had a steady job, but I think he always wanted me to follow in his footsteps.'

'And not Uncle Ray's?'

'*Definitely* not Uncle Ray's.'

She pulled me into a hug and whispered in my ear. 'I think he'd be pretty damned proud of you. And if he wasn't, too bad for him.'

'Thanks.'

The hug turned into a kiss. After a while, Allison said, 'It's a nice day. Wanna go to your place or mine?'

'Funny you should ask that,' I said, pulling her closer. 'There's something I've been meaning to talk to you about.'

Thanks to the usual (and some unusual) suspects:

The Computer School and Center School, The Feldman and Barrett families for their generous contributions to The Computer School – you're all great characters – Mike Kunin and Ramapo For Children – www.ramapo forchildren.org – and all the kids, parents, and educators I've worked with over the past thirty-plus years.

Mike Herron, Wayne Kral, Drew Orangeo, Rob Roznowski, Lisa Herbold, The Stokes, Kennedy, and Cohen families, The Tippler, 2A, Alfie's, Jasper's, and El Azteca for their support, encouragement, and steady flow of adult beverages.

Mariano Rivera, for inspiring the title of this book, and throwing the most beautiful fastball any pitcher has ever thrown year in and year out for nineteen seasons.

All the independent bookstores who've supported me and countless other writers. Go to www.indiebound.org and find the one closest to you.

All the public librarians who've bought my books, hosted me at events, and helped me spread the word. Contrary to popular belief, we authors love libraries and librarians. Hurray for Socialized Reading!

Many thanks to all at Severn House for providing Raymond with a place to stay – and to Margery Flax of Mystery Writers of America for making sure our paths crossed.

Eric Campbell of Down & Out Books for making it look so easy, and treating all of his writers with respect and dignity. And thanks for putting me between the covers with Charles Salzberg and Ross Klavan.

Former editor Matt Martz and my agents Erin Niumata and Maura Teitelbaum for getting me started in this biz, helping to make me a better writer, and teaching me when to say yes.

Jeannie Kerwin, you may have left this mortal coil, but I don't know anyone who will be forever more fondly living in the hearts of others or touched so many lives in a positive way than you. Thanks for showing the rest of us how it's supposed to be done.

All of you who've taken the time to write to me at my website – www.timomara.net – to praise, question, or chastise my work. I like the praise emails the best, but the other ones keep the ego in check, so thanks.

My mid-Missouri family, especially Les and Cynthia Bushmann (mother-in-law and proof-reader extraordinaire) and Maggie and Elise Williams. It's a joy and honor to have a second place to call home.

My mother Patricia O'Mara, who I know has read *all* my books, and told friends and strangers alike all about them. My siblings: Jack, Ann, Mike – *check the dedication, tough guy* – and Erin, and their families, whether they've actually read my books or not.

Finally, thanks to my wife, Kate Bushmann, you see the possibilities in everything and then turn them into realities. You astound me with your brilliance, resilience and remarkable taste. Eloise Bushmann O'Mara – I can't imagine any dad being prouder of his daughter than I am of you. You amaze me on a daily basis, make me laugh on occasion and help keep me grounded.